SHADEBORN

A BOOK OF UNDERREALM

GARRETT ROBINSON

SHADEBORN
Garrett Robinson

The author greatly appreciates you taking the time to read his work. Please leave a review wherever you bought the book or on Goodreads.com.

Interior Design: Legacy Books, Inc.
Publisher: Legacy Books, Inc.
Editors: Karen Conlin, Cassie Dean
Cover Artist: Sarayu Ruangvesh

1. Fantasy - Epic 2. Fantasy - Dark 3. Fantasy - New Adult

Second Edition

Published by Legacy Books

LEGACY

To my wife
Who gave me this idea

To my children
Who just make life better

To Johnny, Sean and Dave
Who told me to write

And to my Rebels
Don't forget why you left the woods

GET MORE

Legacy Books is home to the very best that fantasy has to offer.

Join our email alerts list, and we'll send word whenever we release a new book. You'll receive exclusive updates and see behind the scenes as we create them.

(You'll also learn the secrets that make great fantasy books, *great*.)

Interested? Visit this link:

Underrealm.net/Join

For maps of the locations in this book, visit:

Underrealm.net/maps

SHADEBORN

A BOOK OF UNDERREALM

GARRETT ROBINSON

ONE

LOREN SLOUCHED IN HER SEAT, SEARCHING AND FAILING to find any reason why this day should be better than the one before.

Her companions still lay upstairs in slumber. Even Albern had not yet risen, though the bowyer always woke before the coming of the sun. But Loren had been awake through the night, unable to close her eyes for fear of what she would see in her dreams. So a cup of wine had turned into two, and then a bottle, and some food just as the moons set, and now the sky outside crept towards the grey of dawn.

The innkeeper, Mag, stood behind the counter, polishing it with a damp rag, though to Loren's mind it shone bright already. Every so often the woman would gaze around the room, observing those within: the early wakers who had joined Loren for breakfast, or the nighttime arrivals who had come to the city of Northwood for purposes unknown—and, mayhap, best not asked after. Mag's gaze never sought Loren in particular, but neither did it shy away.

In the days since Loren and her friends had first arrived at the inn, that was what Loren appreciated the most. Whatever thoughts Mag kept to herself, outwardly she never treated Loren differently from any other customer. Loren could not say the same for the others, who mostly sought to avoid her gaze. Either that, or they tried to draw her into conversation, speaking soft words she was not yet ready to hear.

All of them except Chet, of course.

Mag noticed Loren's empty goblet, hers the keen eyes of a barkeep with experience. She sidled out from behind the thick oak counter and made her way across the room. Without a word she scooped up the goblet, as well as an empty bowl.

"Will you be wanting anything else, love?" The words held neither judgement nor too much concern. It was as though Loren were any other girl who happened to be visiting the inn. Yet in that plain tone, Loren thought she heard another kind of care.

"Another glass of wine would suit me well, except

that I feel my debt to you grows large," said Loren. "When will you let me cease to be a burden, and pay for my custom like the rest of your patrons?"

"Another time, mayhap. But not yet." Mag swept up the cup and dropped it in the bowl before returning to the bar. From the shelves she pulled a clean cup for Loren's wine, and then another, which she filled with ale. She brought them both to the table, and to Loren's surprise took the seat opposite.

Now at last she means to speak her mind, thought Loren. She should have expected it. Mag had seemed more understanding, less intrusive, than any of the others. But she must have felt the way they did all along, and chosen now to finally say something. Loren wondered idly why she had waited so long.

"I have heard what the others say to you, trying to urge you towards better spirits," said Mag. "You must know that they are wrong, and that this is not something you should try to hasten."

Loren blinked. "Those are not the words I thought to hear."

"I imagine not," said Mag, smiling gently and sipping her ale. "You thought I would lend my voice to theirs."

"They seem to think they know what is best for me, no matter whether I wish to hear it or not." Loren took a pull from her own cup, a deeper and longer drink than Mag's.

"Yet you will note that Albern has not joined them

in their insistence. Nor would I. He and I have seen many dark times together. Both of us have felt loss. Both of us have done deeds we wish we could undo, deeds that have haunted us every day since."

Loren saw a flash of a broken body draped in a red cloak. She saw an arrow protruding from a thigh, and a hateful man crawling through the dirt. She shivered and blinked hard, drinking again in desperation.

Mag's hand came gently to rest upon Loren's. "Only time can rid us of these wounds. You are fortunate to have that time. Take it—as much as you need. Let the pictures in your mind's eye fade away, one by one, until they trouble you no longer, neither while you sleep nor in your waking hours. It is not something you should try to hurry along, unless the healing stops on its own."

Loren picked at the cuff of her sleeve. Though it had been only a few days since they came to Northwood, she had seen no improvement in her mood, nor in the dark thoughts that plagued her day and night. "And what if it does? What did you and Albern do, when the darkness in your minds refused to leave you?"

"Only then are you close to the end. Embracing our grief plants the seed of healing, and once it is well-laid we must take it upon ourselves to foster the growth. If that crop lies untended, it twists within the earth. That is a sorry harvest, and one you have likely seen before: the drunkard who cannot think to spend his time anywhere but the tavern, his coin spent only on oblivion."

The wine soured in Loren's mouth. "You might as well say what you mean: *her* coin. Yet you will not take mine."

Mag's mouth twisted in a stern frown. "If I meant to rebuke you, I would do it without bandying words. I only mean to tell you that when the time comes for your next step, you must take it, or in truth you shall truly lose yourself. Action can help you along the road—any action, though deeds filled with purpose are best. Or sometimes, the comfort of another can be our medicine. That boy Chet, for example."

"He is trying. Often have we gone walking in the Birchwood, and under its eaves with him I find something closer to peace than I do with the others, with their soft words and careful glances."

Mag gave her a look that lasted a moment too long, and Loren blushed. Quickly she took another swallow of wine to hide it.

"You should eagerly embrace anything that helps," said Mag stoically, and Loren thought she heard the hint of a smile behind the words. "Remember: do not let the others push you sooner than you are ready. There will be time enough for their cares later. First you must tend to yourself."

Boots clumped heavily down the stairs at the back. Loren looked up to see Albern descending into the common room. He gave her a quick glance and a half-hearted smile. Mag rose quickly and went to the bar with him, there to take his order and fetch his breakfast. Loren sat in the quiet and thought upon the innkeeper's words.

She did not have long to enjoy her solitude. Soon Albern joined her at the table with his eggs and a rasher of bacon. He spoke no word to her, but he did not have Mag's skill at hiding his curious eyes. And soon Loren heard boots upon the stairs again, and looked up to see Xain glowering there.

The wizard's limbs had gone thin and bony, his cheeks so gaunt that from the outside she could see his teeth pressing against the flesh. His hair was thinning now. Loren knew that if she tugged on it, it would come out in clumps. He was like a specter of death, and the effect was not lost on the room's other inhabitants. Some had drunk too much to care, but others averted their eyes or stood to leave with quick, muttered excuses, though there was no one close enough to hear them.

Xain seemed not to notice, or mayhap he did not care. He stalked towards Loren and drew out the chair beside hers, slumping in his seat as his eyebrows drew still closer together. He leaned close, his voice a harsh whisper, though Loren was sure it carried to every corner of the quiet room.

"Tell me you have had enough at last of sulking, and are ready to take the road again."

"Xain," said Albern in a warning tone. His fingers tightened on the handle of his mug.

"And a good morrow to you, fair sir," said Loren. She tried to make the words light, but could not entirely keep an edge from them. "Break fast with us, I pray, and help yourself to some fine wine." She held her cup before him, wiggling it back and forth.

Xain failed to appreciate the humor. He snatched the cup from her to drain it in a single gulp. "I take it you do not mean to move on, then. Do you think we have an eternity to waste?"

"Have we spent an eternity here already, Albern?" said Loren, looking towards the bowyer with feigned wonder. "Sky above, I thought it had been a few days only."

"Your jests are stale, and grow more so each time the sun passes us," said Xain. "When will we speak, away from this room and its prying ears? Day after day passes, yet still you will not tell me that which you once thought so urgent."

She knew full well what the wizard meant. They had not yet decided where they must go next, and Loren had grave counsel for him, which might shed light upon their path. But that counsel had come from Jordel the Mystic, and he had died moments after uttering the words. Recalling them now was akin to recalling the man, and Loren could not think of him without her heart wanting to stop in grief. Nor had the past week made it any easier, for in Northwood she had learned a dark truth. A truth about herself, and about the cruel man she had shot in the thigh. The man she had once called Father, but whom—by her own hand—no one would speak to ever again.

"Soon," said Loren, her voice quieter than she meant it to be. "I promise you. Only give me a little more time. My grief still presses itself too close upon me."

Xain growled. His gaze darted about as though searching for another argument. Without thinking, he picked at his coat sleeve. A deep hunger gnawed at him, Loren knew, and his mind was not entirely his own. She was only grateful it was not like last time, when his thoughts had grown so dark that she had feared to be in the same room as him.

"Good morn," said a familiar voice, a warm and welcome sound. Chet appeared by Loren's side.

"Good morn," said Loren quickly. She rose from her chair before Xain could choose his next bitter words. But she had moved too fast, forgetting the many cups of wine that had passed her lips. She lurched and near-ly fell, and would have, had she not seized the edge of the table. She steadied herself quickly, cheeks flushing with embarrassment. "I thought to greet the sun from under the branches of the Birchwood. Would you join me?"

Chet looked worried. "Are you sure you need no rest? Did you find any sleep last night?"

"Who needs sleep when the world is waking? Come." Loren seized his arm and nearly dragged him from the table, taking each step carefully to see that she did not stumble. As they walked away together, she thought she saw Albern trying to hide a smile.

TWO

THE CRISP AIR OF MORNING DID MUCH TO CLEAR HER head, and she drank it in with a long breath. If she was honest with herself, it felt better to walk with Chet than to sit at her table and drink, but sometimes facing the wine was easier.

Dawn's thin grey light was just creeping into the sky from the east, and Northwood had begun to stir into wakefulness. She heard the sharp hiss of a smith's forge firing up, and the first tentative squalls of cocks greeting the day. But they met few faces upon the streets, and for that Loren was grateful. It let them walk to the northern gate with few curious eyes to see them. She no longer held much fear that her many enemies had followed her here, and yet the fewer people who saw them within Northwood, the better.

A single guard sat at a table by the open gate. She was well accustomed to seeing Chet and Loren take their walks, and gave them only a cursory glance before turning back to the game of moons that lay before her. Soon Loren and Chet found themselves among the trees of the forest they had once called home. A few steps farther still, and Northwood had vanished behind them, blocked from view by the trunks.

Now Loren felt herself truly relax, as though the last cobwebs had been swept from the edges of her mind. Here within the wood, her eyes saw things differently. Bent blades of grass told her of the passing of a deer, and when she heard a skittering within a bush, she knew it at once for the rustling of a vole. The forest was altogether different from the world of men, and she had greatly missed it since she left. It was all the more enjoyable because she knew Chet saw it just as she did. Sometimes they would speak as they walked. Other times, as now, they walked in silence and let their feet carry them where they would.

They found a narrow brook, making its eager way to join the Melnar to the south. In silent agreement, they turned to find a crossing upstream. Soon they came upon one: a place where the banks rose high above the surface of the water and drew together, close enough for a long jump to carry them across. Just as they reached the other side, the sun peeked its face above the branches of the eastern trees, and all the birds of the Birchwood burst into song together. Some hours later they came upon a clearing some thirty paces across, with a great boulder in the middle like a tombstone. There they sat, their backs against the rock, its cool surface chilling them after the eager pace of their walk.

Chief among the reasons Loren enjoyed their walks was that Chet seemed content with silence, or with speech, as Loren wished. He would converse with her eagerly, answering questions about what had happened in their village since she left. From him she had learned of her mother, who had vanished without a trace the same day Loren had. Loren had some half-remembered notion of family in one of the northern outland kingdoms, and assumed her mother had gone to find them. Too, Chet had told her that some time after his mother passed away, his father had begun to court Miss Aisley. Loren thought that a fine pairing, though Chet himself seemed unsure just what to think of it.

But when Loren wished for silence, silence was what Chet gave her. Now he simply looked with her into the trees, his hands toying with a stick he had snatched from the ground. Together they reveled in a quiet comfort. And without any pressure to speak, Loren found her tongue moved more freely of its own accord.

"In the city of Wellmont, I was caught trying to steal a man's purse," she began.

Chet glanced at her and smirked. "I thought you were a great thief. Is that a lie, for you to be so easily caught?"

"I was not *easily* caught," said Loren, shoving his shoulder. "I was betrayed by my own kindness. I saw the man beating his son and thought to relieve him of his coin—but then at the last moment, I thought the child might relish a life free from his father. That was a mistake. The moment I made the offer, he told his father of my words, and the father called the constables."

"A foolish boy," said Chet lightly. "He could have gone with you, and been pitched headlong into mortal danger. But at least you would not have beaten him."

"Mayhap," said Loren quietly. She had not meant to turn the conversation towards a father and his child, for that subject reminded her too closely of things she would rather not think of. "But in any case, the constables brought us to their quarters within the city. And there, to his shock as well as mine, I found Jordel inside. I will remember the surprise on his face —and the anger—forever."

Chet grew quiet, as he always did when her words turned to Jordel. Chet had never met the Mystic— something Loren desperately regretted. It seemed a crime that anyone should not have known the man, as great as he was, as quiet and heartfelt his praise, and as cold and terrible his wrath. She doubted she would meet his like ever again.

"What surprised me then, though it should not have, was how quickly Jordel guessed at what was going on. As soon as he heard that I had been caught stealing from the woodsman, his eyes grew sharp with suspicion. With barely a glance, he seemed to know the whole tale, and he was as merciless with the father as the father was with the son. And though his anger with me remained, it softened, and turned more to annoyance, as though he thought I was right to do as I did, though his duty meant he could not say so."

Her voice drew dangerously close to a tremble. One tear leaked from her eye, so she leaned her cheek on her fine black cloak where it draped over her arm, to soak up the drop and hide it.

Once more the clearing was silent, save for the morning birdsong.

She spoke again into the stillness, forcing her voice to remain steady. "Where did they find my father?"

Chet glanced at her from the corner of his eye, and then looked away again. "It is no tale for a day so beautiful."

"Likely it is too ugly for any day that may come to pass. Tell me, then, and let its darkness fade away once and for all."

"You have seen too much evil of late. I would not bring more upon you, not at least until you are ready.

When I tell you this tale, I wish to tell it only once, and in full, so that we need never speak of it again."

"Then tell it now," said Loren.

Chet sighed. Then he pushed himself from the rock and sidled over to sit in front of her, his eyes fixed on hers, though she turned her gaze away.

"His corpse was a league south of the village when we found it. He lay on his belly, his head turned to the side, eyes open and staring. There was no blood in his spittle, but it had frothed greatly and gathered around his lips."

Loren swallowed hard. She knew what would come next: the tale of his wound, the one that had slowly bled him out beneath the trees of the same forest in which they now sat. Chet watched her, gauging her reaction. She kept her face as still as she could.

"We could see at once that he had bled to death. Though the fletching had broken from the arrow, the shaft still stuck from his thigh. It had struck a vein, or nicked it as he crawled, and all his lifeblood had drained out. The trail of it stretched far away south, mayhap half a league more. When we followed it, we found at the end the signs of a struggle. Between him and, I guessed, you, but also a third person who we did not know. I hazarded another guess that it was the wizard the constables sought."

"You were right in that," said Loren, glad her voice had remained steady. "That was Xain. My father nearly strangled the life from him."

"He would have, if you had not stopped him," said Chet quietly. "And he might have killed you, too."

Loren remembered the fight as though it were happening again. She saw the spite that filled her father's eyes, the spittle that flew from his lips with each hateful word. And now she imagined him crawling north after the fight, the shaft protruding from his flesh, his life pouring into the dirt beneath him. She saw him shuddering and convulsing as he died at last, and wondered if he had spent his final words cursing her—his own flesh and blood, whom he had never given anything so wasteful as love.

"Likely my words cannot help you," said Chet. "But you should not blame yourself. You restrained your hand beyond all reason. You might have planted your arrow in his eye, or his heart. You did not. You tried to show mercy. And mayhap, if he had stayed where he was, he would not have died in the end."

But Loren knew better. She remembered when she would chop her father's logs for him, how he would come and threaten her so that she would work faster. And she remembered how he would take her into the woods and beat her, his thick and meaty fists leaving bruises beneath her clothing that would last for weeks. And she remembered going back to chopping his logs, and gripping the axe tightly in her hands, and picturing it lodged in his skull, or in his back.

Her breath came faster as her thoughts raced on. Images flashed through her mind's eye, the corpse, and the arrow, and the axe and the corpse and the spittle and the blood and the corpse and the corpse again. And then the corpse became Jordel's and she saw his twisted body upon the floor of the valley that lay between the arms of the Greatrocks.

She fought the urge to vomit and rolled to her hands and knees.

"Loren!" cried Chet.

He knelt by her side and placed a hand on her shoulder. Loren pushed him off, breathing faster until stars danced in her vision and her head spun. She tried lifting her gaze to look upon the sky, but she could see only blackness where there should have been blue. *Black and blue, like my bruises.*

She screamed and slammed a fist into the earth, and then struck again, and again. Her fist flew into the boulder, and she felt the skin of her knuckles break.

The pain gave her focus, and she clutched her hand to her chest. At last she could sit back without her gorge rising. Rage turned to hot, bitter tears that left their trails of grief upon her cheeks. Chet sat beside her with one arm around her shoulder, and his other hand cradling her mangled one.

"It was not your fault," he kept murmuring. "It was not your fault."

Soon she felt in control again. And as she had so often, she took her rage and her grief and hid them away, deep inside herself where no one else could see. At last she looked up at Chet and tried to smile. But she feared she only looked sick, for his look of concern deepened.

"I am all right," she said softly. "I am all right. Come. The children will have risen, and they are likely driving the others mad."

She rose shakily to her feet, shrugging off Chet's helping hand. Together they set off into the trees, walking slowly now. But Loren no longer saw the green of the leaves, nor the crystal clarity of the brook as they crossed it. She saw only black and blue, and the red of blood.

THREE

GEM HAD BEEN AN URCHIN CHILD WHEN LOREN found him on the streets of Cabrus, hungry and picking pockets in the service of a guild of young thieves. Annis had been a daughter of wealth and plenty, her every whim tended to by the comforts her mother's coin had afforded.

Their circumstances could scarce have been more different, yet they had surprised Loren equally since their arrival in Northwood—for both of them had spent every spare moment helping Mag around the inn. From tending to the stables to running drinks and meals to visitors when the common room grew busy, they took eagerly to even the meanest task. Neither had been raised in a life of honest work, and yet they took their roles as Mag's helpers very seriously.

They seemed to enjoy Northwood greatly. Loren told herself that one reason she had lingered so long was to give them a rest, which they greatly deserved. Even to her own ears, though, that excuse sounded thin and flimsy.

"With the cook's compliments," said Gem, arriving at the table with a tray, upon which he had balanced five bowls of stew.

"And the lady's," said Annis, swooping in with another tray that held five mugs of ale and two loaves of bread.

"Our blessings upon the cook and the lady," said Albern, scooping up his bowl and his mug. He tucked in with great abandon, tearing the heel from one of the loaves and dipping it into the stew.

The sun was nearing the horizon, and many within the town had joined the inn's tenants for supper and a drink. The common room buzzed heavily with talk and occasional bursts of laughter. Loren could hear the plucking of strings from somewhere in the back of the room as some minstrel readied to earn his dinner. But still her mind lingered on dark thoughts, and though her stomach growled at the smell of the stew, it tasted bland as paper upon her tongue. Chet tried valiantly not to show his concern, but Loren could feel it emanating from him like the glow of a torch.

"None of you will be surprised, I am sure, to learn that I have spent another day proving my worth," said Gem brightly as he ate. The first spoonful of stew did nothing to slow his words, and the food mashed noisily between his teeth as he talked around it. "Today I cleaned the hooves of all the horses in the stable, and laid fresh hay for each steed. Then I found that the dishes had stacked into a mighty mountain, and so I cleaned them all, every one, without even having to be asked. I hardly know how this place managed before I arrived."

"Oh, they must have pined for a dishwasher like yourself, master urchin," said Albern with a smirk. "Poor Mag must have spent her nights crying herself to sleep for want of such noble, scrubbing hands as yours."

"Just so," said Gem, missing the humor in the bowyer's tone.

Annis sniffed primly and dipped just the end of her loaf into the stew, nibbling on it with perfect manners. "Well, while you have been getting yourself filthy down here, I have been striving for cleanliness. I cannot guess when the rooms upstairs were cleaned last, and some of them stank of something which I am sure I would not like to know about. But they are clean now, and I have only knees and hands worn to the bone to show for it. Give me a few more days here, and I am sure I shall make the place fit for the custom of the High King herself, though why she should find herself in such a town as this I am sure I do not know."

Gem blinked and looked uneasily at Loren. "But . . . surely we will not be here that long," he said slowly. "I thought we would be leaving any day now."

Loren could see—or rather, feel—Xain's irritation from the other side of the table. She held her peace, excusing her silence with a mouth full of food, which she chewed slowly so as not to be obligated to answer.

Albern caught her unease, and likely Xain's dark look as well, for he shrugged and said lightly, "You shall all set forth when you are ready. There is no great rush. Certainly Mag enjoys your company."

"But she cannot enjoy the food we eat, nor the wine we drink, nor the rooms we sleep in, without so much as a copper penny taken in exchange," said Chet. Despite his words, he took a deep pull on his mug of ale before continuing. "I do not understand why she will not take our coin."

"It gives her pleasure to give you comfort," said Albern. "Do not ask about it again, or she might bring her spear from its retirement, and then you would be doomed."

"I can handle myself," Chet muttered.

"Not against Mag, I promise you," said Albern. "Years might have passed since she wielded a blade, yet I would wager all my coin upon her if she were to fight anyone in all the nine lands. You would too, if you were wise. When we were young she was called the Uncut Lady, and renowned as the greatest fighter in our company, and when she hung up her shield—"

"Every mercenary captain across the land poured a cup of wine into the dirt," Chet finished. "You have said that before."

"And do you doubt the truth of it?" said Mag. She had emerged from the common room's crowd to stand over the table. At the sound of her voice, Gem and Annis both turned to her with delighted smiles. But she fixed them with a stern look and gestured at the table. "Where is my plate? Where are my mug and my chair? Surely the two of you know better courtesy than this."

The children's faces fell. Gem scuttled off towards the kitchen, while Annis ran to fetch an empty chair. They were few and far between in the crowded room. Finally she found a drunkard slumped unconscious on a table and tipped him unceremoniously from his seat.

"Our apologies, Mag," said Annis as she pushed the chair up to the table. "We thought you were busy in the kitchen, and did not guess you would sup with us tonight."

"Sten finally rustled his useless hide out from the stables and came to relieve me," said Mag. "Tonight my company is yours, if you will have it."

"We will, and gladly," said Gem, who had returned with a bowl and a mug for her. These he set down with great reverence, as though he were serving a king. "And mayhap you can settle a matter over which I have spent much thought. None of us doubt Albern's words when he calls you the greatest fighter he has ever known. But how can that be, when you look no mightier than most of the people in this room? Why, your arms are not even so thick as his."

"If you think me a weakling, mayhap you will wrestle me, and see how long it takes me to pitch you into the dirt," said Mag, arching an eyebrow.

Gem stammered and stuttered and finally fell silent, looking down into his lap.

Albern laughed out loud. "Come, Mag, leave the boy alone. He has never seen you dance. You can't blame him for wondering, when he has only seen the sort of fighting you get from common street thugs and city guards." He leaned over to speak conspiratorially to Gem, as though he were confiding a great secret. "Not in the strength of the arm, little master, but more often in skill will you find the greater warrior. What use a soldier's brawny bulk when their blade cannot come within a foot of our Mag? The most dangerous fighters are the ones who dance with their foe like a lover, and who can stay on their feet and swinging long after the other man is ready to vomit his guts into the dirt."

"Surely you have seen the truth of that, Gem," said Loren with a half-hearted smile. "If all things in life depended on strength alone, you and I would have died in a ditch long ago."

Albern shook a finger at her and nodded "Just so. Why, once Mag and I and the company were fighting in the kingdom of Calentin, putting down the insurrection of some upstart who thought he could seize the throne because he had a flock of pretty knights at his back. One of these dullards came riding down on Mag with lance lowered, but she—"

The crash of a fist on the table threw them all into silence. Xain had slammed his hand down, and held it there now, his gaze roving across their faces. Loren's heart went to her throat as she remembered his madness in the mountains, when he had cast thunder and flame upon them with abandon, stricken with the magestone hunger just as he was now. Without thinking of it, she moved her hand to the hilt of the dagger beneath her cloak. From the corner of her eye she saw Albern's hand steal beneath the table, likely to his own weapon. Around them, the common room had grown quiet.

"If I must listen to one more of your tales, I will fling myself into the Melnar and drown," growled Xain. He shot to his feet and, seeing Albern tense, held up a hand. "Stay yourself, bowyer. I need only the girl. Loren, you have avoided this for too long. Come with me now, or do not expect to see me darken this inn's doorway again. If you are determined to sit here and pity yourself until the nine lands fall, then I will carry on with our task alone."

With that he stalked between the tables and out of the inn. A few of the patrons he passed by gave Mag a doubtful look, but she shook her head gently, and they let him pass.

"Something gnaws at that man," she muttered when Xain had gone.

"You speak more truly than you know," said Loren quietly.

Chet leaned over to murmur in her ear. "You need not go if you do not wish it."

Inside, Loren was fuming. Xain spoke to her as though she were some child, whimpering in the corner because she wanted second helpings at supper. He had been there in the mountains when Jordel had fallen. Then, he had wept as openly as the rest of them. If his mood had darkened since, and if his cravings for magestone scratched at the edges of his mind, he had no one to blame but himself. How dare he mock Loren's pain, speaking as if she had forgotten her duty?

But she only shrugged. "He speaks at least some truth. I should have had words with him days ago. If it will stay this foul temper that has seized him, I will have them now."

"I can go with you," said Albern.

"No," said Loren quickly. "Stay. Tell the children your story. Surely they will enjoy it." And she rose to follow the wizard into the city.

FOUR

Xain stood across the narrow street. A lamp on the building beside him bathed him in its sickly yellow glow. His nails scratched furiously at his sleeve, and his head darted back and forth in the darkness. When he saw her emerge, she thought she saw him sigh with relief. But she approached him slowly. If he was going to be so difficult, she was in no hurry to give him what he desired.

"I . . . I may have spoken harshly," he muttered once Loren was in earshot. "Forgive me."

"Mayhap," said Loren easily. "Still, you have me

here now, wizard. What shall we speak of? You make it sound most urgent, though you yourself have had days to speak to me. A conversation takes not one, but two at least."

"What we have to say—what I have to tell you, at least—I would not utter in anything above a whisper, and not at all here in the city," said Xain. Suddenly his voice was no longer bitter, or even exasperated. Instead he sounded afraid, and his words carried a darkness that made Loren shiver. She tried to disguise it as a sudden chill in the night air, and drew her cloak closer about herself.

"What, then? Do you mean to fly us into the air with your magic? For we are within the city still."

"At my best I could not do so, and I am far from my best. If it pleases you, Nightblade, let us take a stroll beyond the walls of Northwood."

Loren did not relish the idea of walking unknowing into the darkness with him, but his calling her "Nightblade" mollified her somewhat. It was a foolish daydream of her childhood, and only a few knew of it, though Gem kept trying to spread the tale of her—an effort she found more irritating than endearing, but she rarely had the heart to tell him to stop.

Xain pushed off from the wall and strode down the street, and Loren felt she had little choice but to follow. Rather than north, as she often went with Chet, Xain now took her east. There the gate lay open still, despite the late hour. Northwood had been removed from the wars of the nine lands for so long that it felt no need to lock its doors against them. The guard at the gate gave them a close look, peering at them in the weak light of his torch, but let them pass without question or comment. Soon they were in the empty darkness of the farmlands beyond the city, with only the tiny glow of candlelight through the windows of farmhouses to break the inky black.

From behind him, Loren saw the faint glow of Xain's eyes and heard him muttering words of power. A small spark of flame sprang to life in his hand, but almost immediately it guttered and died. Xain muttered a curse and tried again. This time the fire remained, hovering above his palm, though it was thin and wispy compared to the flames she had seen him cast in times gone.

"Your gift has not entirely left you, I see," she said.

"It weakens by the day," said Xain. "Soon even this small magelight will require all of my power and concentration. Then it will be a long time before my powers return to me."

"How long?"

"I do not know. I have never witnessed the recovery of one plagued by magestone sickness. They are, as you may know, strictly outlawed by the High King."

He barked a harsh laugh, and Loren found herself joining him. But she also thought, with some trepidation, of the small packet of magestones she carried in her pocket even now. Xain knew nothing of them;

she had made very certain of that. She did not like to imagine what he would do if he ever found out.

Soon even the lights of the farmhouses had vanished behind them, and Xain's was the only flame in sight. But the moons had risen already, and they gave Loren enough light to keep from stumbling—most of the time.

Finally Xain stopped and turned to her. Without a word he sat cross-legged upon the ground beside the road. With a furtive toss of his hand, he indicated for her to do the same.

"A moment," said Loren. She stepped off into the darkness, searching around in the grass. Though it was still green, it was dry, and from the hedge that ran beside the road she pulled a few dead branches. These she made into a little pile before Xain, and waved her hand at it. "Light this. It will save your strength, for if we must finally speak of dark matters, I would have all your concentration."

"My concentration? I find it difficult to think of anything else," said Xain. But he lit the tinder, and soon the branches caught above it. In no time they had a little fire going, and Xain let the flame die in his hands.

"First I should tell you what Jordel said just before he died," said Loren. "Though I know little of its meaning. He said the Shades' dark master had returned, and that Trisken was some captain of special significance. He said—as you and I saw—that magic is no proof against them."

The Shades were a secret order that Loren had only learned of a few weeks ago, when she and her friends had become lost in the Greatrocks and stumbled upon their stronghold there. Jordel had said precious little about them, only that they were an order somewhat like the Mystics—except the Mystics, who wore red cloaks, preserved order and upheld the King's law in the nine lands. Loren had never learned the Shades' true purpose, though she had an uncomfortable feeling that would soon change.

"All of this I had guessed already," said Xain, waving a hand in dismissal. "Any fool could have pieced it together."

"Then it was no great crime for me to wait so long to speak to you," said Loren, her irritation growing. "Tell me, then, what *you* know, and why it is of such great importance that we must meet out here where only the grubs in the dirt can hear us. Who is this dark master of the Shades?"

Xain looked at her a long moment. His eyes looked black in the darkness, black as they were when he cast his spells under the power of magestones. It made Loren shiver, though she refused to look away. Then Xain averted his gaze and picked at his sleeve again, and when he spoke it was not with an answer.

"What do you know of magic?"

Loren blinked. "Only a little. I heard tales as a child, and Jordel taught me some little more when we were searching for you. I know of its four arms, which you call . . . oh, I cannot remember their scholarly names just now. But they are firemagic, mindmagic, weremagic, and alchemy."

"Elementalism, mentalism, therianthropy, and transmutation," said Xain stiffly. Loren ground her teeth, but he went on quickly as though sensing her impatience. "Yes, every child in the nine lands knows this. Wizards are few and far between, but rare is the man, woman, or child who goes a lifetime without seeing at least one. Yet we are all of us ignorant. For there are two other branches, hidden, never taught to children. For in them lies the fate of us all, and a dark and terrible fate it is."

Loren felt as if the world around them had gone still. She had to struggle to hear even the crickets, for it seemed that everything had gone completely silent.

"What—" her voice cracked, and she stopped. She swallowed hard and tried again. "What are the hidden branches?"

"Ceremancy and necromancy," said Xain. "Life. And death."

Loren frowned. "Those . . . those are not magic. They are . . . they are . . . they simply *are*."

"So I, too, thought," said Xain. "Yet in Wellmont I spoke with Jordel for nearly a day, and he taught me the truth of things. Life magic and death magic are the source of all the other branches. They are the essence of power itself. My power, the power of all wizards, the power of magestones. All are interlinked, forever entwined with the two hidden branches."

"But there are no life wizards and death wizards," said Loren, irritated. "Surely we would know of them if there were. You were the first wizard I had met, Xain, but I had heard tales aplenty before then. Four branches I was told of. Not six. And nothing of two hidden branches."

"That was by careful design," said Xain. "And you are wrong: there are life wizards and death wizards. Or rather, there is one of each. The Necromancer, master of death. And the Ceremancer, though that one is more often called the Lifemage."

"Only one?" said Loren, more confused than ever. "Why, when there are a great many of the other kinds of wizards?"

"Because they are the source," said Xain. "They were the first, and from them sprang all the other, lesser powers. And though the first Necromancer and the first Lifemage died long, long ago, they were reborn. Again and again they returned, in later times and places, in new bodies, but always together, and always with the same powers. Life and Death, returning to wage their great and endless war for the fate of all men."

"I have heard tales of great warriors, wizards, and kings," said Loren. "And thieves as well. Yet never have I heard of either a Lifemage or a Necromancer."

"Many centuries has it been since they last lived in the nine lands," said Xain softly. "And in such times, the in-between times, the Mystics hide all knowledge of them. Every record is expunged, every tale snuffed out. They wish for no one to know of the Necromancer, for then followers might take root, and gather in strength in preparation of his coming."

Loren felt she understood at last. "The Shades. They serve the Necromancer. Do the Mystics, then, serve the Lifemage?"

"That is their true purpose. But they have forgotten. All but the highest and greatest among them, who guard the secret as carefully as the existence of the Necromancer. To know of one is to know of the other."

They fell to silence, and for a while the only sound was a light wind rustling the grass about them. Xain shivered and pulled his dirty grey cloak tighter. The weather struck him harder, as thin as he was.

As she began to digest his words, a thought came to Loren that made her heart skip a beat. "Then if the Shades are gathering in strength, does that mean the Necromancer is reborn?"

"That is what Jordel guessed," said Xain. He picked at the cuff of his sleeve.

"And while they grow in power, the Mystics do nothing to stop them," said Loren, stomach sinking. "Because they know nothing. Only Jordel discovered the truth, and he died in the Greatrocks. And now I have made us sit here and wait in a faraway city, when we should have been warning all the kingdoms."

Xain looked away. "You can hardly be blamed," he

said, though his voice was gruff. "We all keenly felt his loss."

"I should not have let that stop me. Jordel would not have." She brushed the fingers of one hand across the battered knuckles of the other. Almost she struck at the ground again, but she did not wish to open the wound. "I am sorry, Xain. I should have listened to you from the start."

Xain grunted and moved to rise. "I will not argue there. Only see that you remember this in the days to come."

Loren shot to her feet easily and lowered a hand to pull him up. "I will. Clearly you are too weak to do much of anything useful, and have chosen to be wise instead to make up for it."

He glared sharply up at her, but then the moonslight showed him her smile. A wry twist came to his lips, and he took her hand to rise. Together they strode back for Northwood, and Xain flicked a finger to douse the embers of the fire behind them.

FIVE

THE NEXT MORNING, THE TRAVELERS READIED THEM-
selves to depart. Though they had all seemed happy
enough to remain in Northwood, once spurred to action Loren thought they seemed relieved to be on the
move again. All of them except Chet had spent many
weeks riding from one place to another. A rest had
been welcome, yet now their feet itched for the road.

While Albern went into town to fetch supplies,
Loren went to the inn's stable to prepare their horses
for travel. Chet, for lack of anything better to do, came
with her. Midnight gave a great cry the moment Loren

approached, and she smiled to hear it. The horse was wise beyond the custom of beasts, and Loren thought she must know they were preparing to leave.

"Still your braying, you nag," said Loren, but she patted Midnight's nose with affection. "I have kept you waiting only a few days."

"Look at the way she nuzzles you," said Chet, looking Midnight over with appreciation. Loren had told him the tale already of how she had come to steal the horse. "She has taken you for her own, and no mistake."

"I took *her*, you mean," said Loren. She fetched a brush from the wall and took it to Midnight's coat, though she could see almost at once that the mare needed no grooming. "Though I suspect she thinks differently, I am her master and not the other way around."

She grew quiet for a moment and looked at Chet from the corner of her eyes. She had been meaning to ask him a question for some time. Now it had grown in urgency, but with the moment finally here, she found the words hard to say.

"Chet," she said slowly, carefully. "What will you do? Once we leave, I mean."

His eyes flew wide. He pushed himself from the wall where he had been leaning, and rested a hand on Midnight's flank. "Why . . . I mean to come with you, of course. Unless my company is not welcome, though I had hoped it would be."

Loren felt a rush of happiness, though she tried to still it. Chet had heard much of their journeys, but not all. Though he no doubt thought he understood his decision, he could not possibly imagine its implications.

"Of course you are welcome, always," she said. "And nothing would make me happier than for you to join us. But I would not have you come out of obligation."

"It was not obligation that made me leave the Birchwood," said Chet quickly. "I wanted to follow you. How often did we wish to leave the forest behind, when we were younger? How many lands did we see in our dreams, day after day, longing only to walk their roads with our own feet?"

"Yet in all my daydreams, I never foresaw the peril that has plagued me since I left," said Loren. "And though I would like nothing more than your company, I am loath to bring that peril upon you, and you unaware of it. Dark things hound our steps, Chet, darker even than I have known."

He paused, his hand scratching Midnight's side idly. "Things the wizard told you of? Is that why you make ready to go with such haste? Are you sure you can even trust his words? Mayhap your fear is misplaced."

"It is not," said Loren. "If what lies ahead is half so terrible as what I have left behind me, it will be a road far more perilous than any you have traveled to get here. I will walk that road with you—but only if both your eyes are open."

"They are," he said, shrugging. "I can handle myself in a fight, and have learned to ride a horse. What else would I do except take the road beside you, traveling as we always meant to?"

"This is not some fanciful journey. You must not come with me if you think so."

Chet smiled. "You have told me of the danger, Loren. That is enough. I still mean to come, unless you wish to lock me in these stables, or tie me to the trunk of some tree."

She gave a lingering sigh. "Very well. We will take you into our company, and happily on my part. But know that if you ever wish to turn aside and go your own way, no one will think less of you. And we shall have to find you a horse, unless you wish to be tied across the back of Midnight's saddle."

After readying Midnight and the other steeds to ride, they went back to the inn to see about a horse for Chet. There they found Mag already busy in the common room, her well-muscled arms glistening with sweat as she bussed trays back and forth from tables to kitchen. But she stopped at once when she saw they sought her attention, and came to speak with them at the bar.

"We need a horse for Chet," said Loren. "Do you know where we might find one from an honest seller, who will not give us some beast with a cracked hoof?"

"Why, beneath this very roof," said Mag. *"Sten!"*

Her roar was sudden and sharp, as could often be her way. It always made Loren jump a little. Her husband came hastily out from the kitchen, wiping flour from his great arms with a greased rag, his bushy eyebrows drawn together and his wide mouth muttering darkly.

"Sky above, Mag, how many times have I told you not to bray after me like some donkey?"

"And how many times have I told you how I love my little ass?" said Mag, though she stood a full hand shorter than he did. "See to the common room, will you? These two need a horse."

"The chestnut from that southern man?" said Sten.

"The same. And one last thing." She seized the front of his collar and pulled him down for a quick kiss. But when she tried to pull away, Sten wrapped his arms around her and lifted her from her feet, burrowing his thick beard into her neck. Loren and Chet looked away, shifting their feet. Mag squealed like a little girl, but gave him a sharp chop in the ribs at the same time. Sten groaned and dropped her like a heavy sack.

"The customers!" she snapped, though she could not hide her smile. "I will be only a moment."

Mag led them back to the stables. It held more than a dozen stalls, and most were full, four of them with the beasts Loren and her friends had brought. Near the back was a huge chestnut with a flowing golden mane. Loren had seen it as she came in and out.

"Two southern men came through here some weeks ago, from Idris or some such," said Mag. "They each rode a horse when they arrived, but had to sell one to pay for the rest of their way north. It is a good enough beast—no warhorse, but no swaybacked farm animal, either."

"Why did you buy it?" said Chet. "Do you often go riding?"

"Any innkeeper buys a horse for sale," said Mag. "A good bit of business, horseflesh. Often the folk who come through my doors need a steed to carry on their journey."

"And we will pay you handsomely for it," said Loren firmly.

Mag pursed her lips. "Not handsomely, though I cannot give him away for free. You know I will take no coin for your room and board, but a horse is another matter. Ten gold weights I paid. That is what I will take from you, and not one more. Just passing him on, so to speak."

"And if we were any other travelers, how much would we pay then?" said Loren, folding her arms.

"That I shall keep to myself, if it is all the same to you."

"It is not," said Loren. "But so be it. Ten gold weights, as you say."

After grasping wrists to seal the pact, Mag returned to Sten in the common room while Loren went to their room upstairs. She took from her coin purse ten gold weights and dropped them in a spare purse. After a moment's thought, she added five more. She did not know if it was a fair price—if anything, it seemed somewhat high. But the extra could pay for their food and rooms, for Mag had been far too generous. It left her purse somewhat lighter than she liked, but she would have to worry about that later. As long as they had enough to reach Jordel's brethren in Feldemar, that was all that mattered.

With Chet still by her side, she went back to the common room where Mag stood speaking with a customer. She threw the spare coin purse to Mag, who scarcely looked up as she caught it with a deft hand and carried on speaking. She did not open it to look inside. Satisfied, Loren went to her usual table in the corner, where Albern, Xain, and the children were already tucking in for lunch.

"I have fetched as many provisions as I thought the horses could carry," said Albern as they sat down. "It should see you at least halfway through Dorsea, though you shall need to stop for more supplies at some point."

"We will stop as rarely as we can afford," said Xain. "The fewer people who mark our passing, the better."

"Once you are deep into Dorsea, I think the danger shall lessen," said Albern. "In the south their kingdom is preoccupied with the war, and in the north they remain as untroubled as ever at the goings-on of the nine lands."

"Who is that man there?" asked Gem.

Something about the boy's tone raised the hairs on the back of Loren's neck. She looked over her shoulder to see Mag talking to someone new: a thin man with a hooked nose and spindly fingers, whose head darted about constantly as he spoke. He was altogether different from the simple folk she had grown accustomed to in Northwood, and it set her nerves on edge.

They all watched him for a moment, until Mag looked up from the conversation and caught Albern's eye. She tossed her head at him, and wordlessly Albern rose to approach her. Loren quickly found her feet and went with him, but when Chet, too, started to rise, she waved him back into his seat.

Mag wore a dark look as they reached her. "Len, tell them."

The thin man pinched his nose and sniffed. "There is a man. He is wandering about the city, searching for a girl in a black cloak."

Loren felt the blood drain from her face. Albern's mouth set in a grim line. The thin man nodded, pinching his nose and sniffing again.

"Aye, that is what I thought when I heard," he said, though Loren had said nothing. "Black cloak and remarkable green eyes, he asked for. Used that word, remarkable. Calls himself Rogan, which sounds foreign to me. He is dark of skin, like the girl with you, though from their looks I would not call them kin. Big. He carried no weapons, but he felt like one, if you follow me. When I heard him asking around, I thought to myself that I seen eyes just like that, and a black cloak as well, here in your place, Mag."

"Our thanks, Len. Drink up, and tell Sten it is my gift." He sidled off, and Mag fixed them with a hard look. "Is this Rogan some friend of yours?"

"I do not know that name," said Loren. "We should have left long ago."

"Stay your concern, at least for the moment," said Albern. "We know nothing for certain. Mayhap there is cause for fear, but mayhap this Rogan is some friend to Jordel."

"He said nothing of a red cloak."

"Hist!" Albern glanced over his shoulder. "Speak not so openly of our fallen friend's order where others may hear. And if this Rogan is one of them, and he sought us in secret, do you think he would show himself so openly?"

"We should go and see after him, and mayhap find our answers," said Loren.

"I think the same."

"I shall come," said Mag. "Len is a good sort, but his nerves can get the better of him. I may recognize the man's face where Len could not."

Loren ran quickly to put her black cloak away upstairs and fetch her dirty brown spare. When she returned, Chet again rose to go with her.

"Stay," she said. "Albern and I have something to look into. It will not take long, and too many at once may draw attention."

"Is it some trouble?" said Xain sharply.

"It may be, or it may be nothing," said Loren. "Rest assured, we will return in safety. Wait—but mayhap ready the horses, just in case."

She returned to the bar, where Albern still waited for her. Sten, too, was there, and through his beard Loren could see his frown of concern.

"Not long at all," Mag was saying. "Do not trouble your ugly little head over it."

"When have you ever given me cause for concern? I fear only for anyone who may think to tussle with you," said Sten. But the creases in his forehead deepened.

Mag placed a hand on his arm and stood on tiptoe to kiss his cheek. "See to the customers. Get those layabout children to help, if you need them." He let her leave him then, with no more than a long squeeze of her hand to see her off.

SIX

They set out into the streets, and though it was warm Loren quickly raised her hood to mask her face. Its shadow would hide her eyes—or at least, so she hoped.

Mag took them into the heart of the city. Northwood was no burg so great as Wellmont, or even Cabrus, the first city Loren had seen after leaving her forest home. Here there were hardly any buildings more than a single storey. The city was wide rather than tall, sprawled across the land with its streets twisting haphazardly in upon each other. Yet with unerring certainty Mag wove her way through them, until it was all Loren could do to keep up.

"Len said he was near here," said Mag, looking around in the lazy afternoon sun. "Stay close to the walls, and find shadows to stand in if you can."

Loren needed no second urging, already doing all she could to avoid being seen. Yet it seemed she need not have worried, for though the streets were well-peopled, not a single eye turned to her.

Search as she might, she could see no sign of the man Len had described. They searched every street and alley they could find, but had no luck for a long while, until Loren began to wonder if there was anything to worry about after all.

"There," hissed Albern at last. He seized Loren's arm and drew her against the wall of a smithy. Loren peeked out from under the very edge of her hood.

She saw him at last. Len had spoken truly: this man Rogan felt dangerous, and though he wore no armor his size protected him like a suit of plate. His arms were covered, yet under the sleeves she could still see his strength. Dark was his face, and he had scars across both eyes, though he had lost neither of them.

Something about him seemed familiar. Loren could not place the reason, and the more she searched for it the more she grew afraid. She knew she had seen something like him before. Not in Jordel, nor any of the other Mystics she had met upon her road.

Albern put words to her thoughts. "Do you see it? He moves like Trisken."

Loren thought her heart might stop. "We must leave. We should have fled the city last night. Why did I delay? We must leave."

"Albern, what is it?" said Mag.

"Nothing, or at least no great matter if we leave at once," said Albern.

His grip on Loren's arm tightened, and he very nearly hauled her down the street. Mag quickened her pace to match them. Loren glanced back over her shoulder once as they fled—and in a frozen, terrible moment, her eyes locked with Rogan's. Then he was gone, buried in the crowds that filled the streets.

"He saw me," she said, trying not to wail.

"We were too far away," said Albern. "He could not have remarked upon you, not dressed like this. You are not the only girl in the nine lands with green eyes." Yet he redoubled his pace. Now they were half running.

"Is it them?" said Mag. "The ones you fought in the mountains?"

"Mayhap."

"We have no time," said Loren. "I only hope the others have readied the horses."

Albern looked quickly back over his shoulder. "Mayhap I should come with you."

Loren wanted to refuse. Albern had sought to part ways with them and return to his home in Strapa, far to the south. But now she welcomed the thought of his company, for Albern was as skilled at using a bow as he was at making one. Indecision kept her silent, and she could not sort through her thoughts for the fear that filled her heart.

She saw Jordel's broken body on the valley floor.

She saw Trisken's bloodied grin.

The brute Trisken had commanded the fortress they found in the Greatrocks, the one filled with Shades that had inspired such fear in Jordel. Jordel, who had always been a solid rock for Loren to lean on. Trisken had fought them in the mountain's caves, and there they had cut him down with arrows and with swords. And Trisken had risen again, mortal wounds stitching together before their terrified eyes, and they could do nothing but run.

They had slain him at last. But in the slaying they lost Jordel, the greatest among them.

Mag's inn loomed above. Loren ignored the back door and burst in through the front, running at once to the table where the others sat. Gem and Annis looked at her in surprise, but in Xain's eyes she saw a dark recognition—he knew something was amiss.

"We are leaving," Loren said. "Now. Where is Chet?"

"With the horses," said Annis. "What did you see in the—"

"*Now*, Annis," snapped Loren. "Go with Gem and fetch our things, as quickly as your feet can carry you. Meet at the stables."

Annis and Gem caught Loren's panic like a fever and ran away upstairs. Xain tried quickly to rise, but stumbled and had to catch himself on the table. On thin and shaking legs he ran after Loren as she made for the inn's back door.

"A man in town searches for us," said Loren, before he could ask. "He is one of them, certainly. He holds himself as Trisken did."

Already pale, Xain's skin turned Elf-white. "We are too long delayed."

"We can be miles away before they learn we were ever here," said Loren.

"That is true enough," said Albern. "And unless they are mightier woodsmen than I guess, I shall see to it that they have trouble following us once we are beneath the eaves of the Birchwood."

"You will find Chet and me no slouches in that regard," said Loren. "We are children of that forest."

They struck the doors of the stable so hard the hinges nearly broke. Chet's gaze shot up from where he was inspecting his chestnut's bridle.

"Loren? What is it?"

"We are leaving," said Loren. "I hope you are ready to sit that saddle."

"I am," said Chet, eyeing Albern and Xain. "But I do not understand what—"

The sharp blast of a horn cut the air outside. Chet went quiet. Screams tore at the silence that followed, and somewhere far away, a bell began to toll.

SEVEN

Loren was on the verge of running back to the inn when Gem and Annis appeared at last, bags tucked under their arms and eyes wide with fright. Chet and Albern took the supplies and began throwing them upon the backs of the mounts, while Xain slowly gained his horse's saddle.

"What are these horns?" said Gem, his voice quaking. "I heard shouting."

"An attack," said Loren. "I knew he saw me."

The stable door flew open again. The party whirled to the sound as one. Loren drew her dagger without thinking, and Albern his sword. When she saw Mag and Sten, Loren relaxed for a moment—until she saw the blades they held in their hands, and the shields upon their arms.

"The city is under siege," said Mag. "We shall see you safely beyond the walls."

"You should go back inside," said Loren. "Wait until we have gone. They will pursue us beyond the city and leave Northwood in peace."

"That I doubt," said Mag. "There is already killing in the streets. And you have no time to convince me otherwise. Mount your horses. Quickly."

Loren began to reply, but Albern seized her and nearly threw her into the saddle. "You are nearly a match for Mag in stubbornness, girl, but not quite. Heed her."

Loren ground her teeth, but she stuck her boots through the stirrups. The others were quick to follow. With Mag and Sten on either side, she led the way through the streets, away north where the gate to the Birchwood waited. From the west rang the screams of the dying, and Loren heard the clash of steel.

"They would kill all these people just to find us?" cried Annis. "How can they hope to keep themselves a secret after this?"

"If none live to tell the tale, it will remain hidden," said Albern with grim finality. "Even if some spare few escape to spread word of the attack, most will assume it is an army of Dorsea."

"You mean to say it is not?" said Sten. Mag had heard the tale of their journey, but her husband had not, and knew nothing of the Shades.

"Time for that explanation later," said Mag. "We should hasten. If I were them, I would move to cut off escape to the north and east. With luck, we should gain the gate before then."

But just as she said the words, they came into an open square to find their foes before them. Shades in blue and grey stormed into view, mail shining and blades flashing with the sun. Folk fled before them, but the Shades cut most down as they ran. They were so intent in their slaughter that they paid no mind to Loren and the others.

"This way!" cried Mag.

She led them aside and down another street, away from the killing. Loren caught sight of Chet's face as they rode on. It was white as a sheet, his teeth bared in a grimace of horror. She gripped his arm as they rode, and squeezed until he met her gaze.

"Try not to look," she said. "Keep your eyes front, and your mind on where you are going."

He gave her a shaky nod. Beyond him, Loren saw Gem and Annis. Their mouths were grim lines, and their shoulders were set. The rest of them had seen so much death that even this wanton slaughter did not make them despair. She was unsure whether that was a good thing or not.

Mag took them through many twisting alleys, but

the next time they came into the open they happened upon more Shades. Here some citizens of Northwood had taken up arms, shovels and pitchforks turned to makeshift weapons. But the Shades were disciplined, and fought in coordination. One or two had fallen in the fighting, but scores of their victims littered the ground.

"No use. It will be a fight," said Mag. Her voice was a chilling monotone. It had turned flat and life-less—a terrible sound from the woman who had been so warm to them, so motherly to the children. Loren found herself shivering despite the afternoon's heat.

Albern drew an arrow from the quiver at his hip and turned to the rest of them. "Stay behind Mag and Sten. Stay your blades unless you have no other choice, for they will try to seize them and pull you down. Now, charge!"

Then, for the first time, Loren saw death made beautiful.

Mag struck, filled with battle-lust at the sight of her fellows killed in their own homes. She fought, blade lent the speed of her rage, her shield like a castle wall in motion as it warded their blows. Not once did her blade strike without drawing blood, faster than a serpent's strike, elegant and fluid as a flowing waterfall. Beside her Sten used his size and strength to batter his foes, knocking them back until he could find an open-ing for his sword. And behind her Albern let forth a flurry of arrows, each finding its mark, his archery like wizardry to Loren's eyes. But Mag's blade was coated in death, her fighting cry the wail of a banshee, and no foe came under her gaze and survived. In twos and threes they fought her, but they could not pierce her guard, nor could they stay her blade once it swung towards them.

The fight was over almost before Loren knew it had begun. The Shades who did not fall to their assault turned and fled through the streets, vanishing behind the buildings and into the alleys of the city. Mag turned to them, her face spattered with a mist of red. Loren saw flecks of it on her bared teeth.

"On!" growled Mag. "Do not stop moving, not even for a moment."

Wordlessly they followed. From the side Loren could see Albern's dark expression, and Sten looked sadly at his wife as they pressed through the streets. But Mag had no eyes for them, only for the road ahead.

Twice more they came upon Shades in the streets, and twice more Mag drove them back with a furious charge. Sten could barely keep up—indeed, even Albern's arrows seemed to strike a moment after Mag's lightning blows. Loren and the others tried only to stay out of the way, quaking in their saddles as they watched Mag slice through the heart of her foes like a scythe.

At last they came within sight of the city's north wall. But there they paused. More Shades came marching in through the gate, in rank and file. It was an army of them, a far greater strength than they had seen even in the Greatrocks.

"There are so many," breathed Loren.

"Surely not even Mag can defeat them all," said Gem. "Albern . . . what do we do?"

Albern hesitated. Sten had stopped in his tracks, and even Mag paused, as though the sight of so many foes had at last broken through her killing rage.

The moment's silence grew long. Loren tugged on Midnight's reins and began to wheel around. "Come. Mayhap they have not reached the eastern gate yet. We can try to—"

"They will have reached it," said Mag. She spoke in a battle commander's bark, but still it held no fire, no anger. Only emptiness. She turned to them, and Loren saw none of the warmth she had grown used to in the woman's eyes. "Come now, little children. Do you fear so few of them? Come with me, and you shall reach the Birchwood. I swear it."

"Mag!" But Albern was too late. She ran straight into the heart of the Shades, blade held aloft, glittering except where it was caked in gore. Sten came two steps behind, trying and failing to match her furious pace.

Albern drew another arrow. His quiver was half-empty. He turned to Loren and Chet with a snarl. "Make use of those bows on your backs, or give me your arrows, but do not stand here idle while she risks her life for yours." Then he kicked his mount's flanks and he, too, charged the Shades.

Gem, sitting behind Annis in their saddle, drew his short sword from the belt at his waist. Loren saw it shaking in his hand, but his eyes were hard. "Well, then," he said. "I had always thought to perish old in bed, but slain in battle seems a fair enough choice."

"Can you help them?" said Loren, turning to Xain.

He was shaking in his saddle, his hands looking almost too frail even to hold the reins. She knew his answer before he spoke. "My flames are nearly guttered out. I might conjure enough to stop one of them, or two. But even that little effort would exhaust me."

"Loren?" said Annis, eyes wide with fright. "What do we—"

"Between my horse and Chet's," said Loren. She drew forth her bow and nocked an arrow. "Gem, do not dare to strike at them except to save yourself and Annis. Stay close to the others, but above all, stay alive."

They rode after Albern. Loren drew the fletching all the way back to her ear, and sighted along the shaft. Mag stood against a squadron of foes now, and more were trying to circle around behind her.

Loren aimed for one of them, lowering her bow to strike him in the leg.

Blood dripping from his thigh, a trail of it for miles through the woods.

She tensed as the picture flashed into her mind, and the arrow went wide to rebound from cobblestones. Cursing, she drew another. Beside her, Chet loosed a shaft of his own. It flew true, skewering a soldier's calf. Beside them, Albern's bow was singing. Gem sat shaking in his saddle, holding his blade forth as if to ward any of the soldiers from coming too close. But they had no eyes for Loren and the others, only for Mag in their center.

Still she fought on, and her strikes had not slowed. The Shades could not get inside her reach, nor could they approach her from the side unawares, for Sten was with her. At her back he stood, guarding her rear as she guarded his, and if he could not kill as many as she could, still he could keep her from being outflanked. Any who threatened to break his guard soon found themselves with one of Albern's shafts in their throats.

So intent were the Shades on bringing the warriors down that they had drifted to one side of the street, leaving the other side open. And beyond them, Loren saw that at last they had stopped pouring through the entrance. The way to the Birchwood was clear, at least for her and Xain and the children. But despite their best efforts, Mag was hemmed in now, and the Shades were close to surrounding Albern besides.

"Albern!" cried Loren.

He risked a glance at her, and she pointed at the city's gate. Quickly his gaze followed, and she saw a light in his eyes. But then he turned back to Mag, and the light went dark.

Sten slipped.

A powerful blow to his shield sent his feet sliding in the blood that slicked the ground. His knee struck the dirt of the street, and a sword flashed around in a wide arc.

He jerked his head back, and for a moment Loren thought he had avoided the blow. Then she saw a red torrent gush from his throat.

Mag was behind him and could not see it, only that he knelt. She gripped his arm and tried to pull him up. Rather than rising, he fell onto his back, his lifeblood bubbling forth.

Mag screamed.

The sound of it was nothing human. Loren had never heard its like before. She knew at once that she would remember it for the rest of her life. For a moment the whole world held its breath. Chet froze with an arrow drawn. Even Gem stopped quaking. Xain had leaned forwards in his saddle, one hand outstretched as though to send forth flame or thunder.

But nothing came. Nothing but the scream, piercing and terrible and filled with rage.

Before it finished, she was already on her feet again, already killing. She pressed into their mass, hacking at them like a woodsman at a cluster of logs. Even with her back unguarded, they could not bring her down, but now at last their strikes found flesh. Loren saw deep red rents appear on her arms. *The Uncut Lady*, Albern had called her, but no longer. Yet she fought on.

Albern looked back at Loren, and then to the open city gate that now seemed leagues away.

Loren grit her teeth and spurred Midnight forwards to help.

"No!" cried Albern, and she reined up. "Fly, while you still can!"

She wanted to ride into them, and damn her vow not to kill. She would draw Mag from their midst, and the darkness protect any of them that tried to stop her.

A hand gripped her arm. She turned, expecting Chet—but it was Xain instead, and his eyes were grim. "Fly," he said. "Remember Jordel."

She ripped off her quiver and raised it, then tossed it to Albern. He caught it with a solemn nod. Then he drew his sword and threw himself into the fight, trying to cut his way through to Mag. But Loren would not watch. Midnight wheeled at her touch, and they spurred to a gallop. In seconds they had passed beyond the city and reached the Birchwood, and Northwood vanished behind the trunks of the trees—this time, mercifully.

EIGHT

THEY DID NOT STOP THEIR MAD RIDE WHEN THEY
reached the trees, but they had to when the sun went
down. Loren scarcely noticed, and it was Xain who
finally called them to a halt.

She did not understand for a moment, and she
looked at him in confusion. It was Chet who spoke
first.

"The moons will not rise for hours, Loren." His
voice trembled. "We can ride by their light if we must,
but pressing on now is folly."

Loren stared a moment longer before she heard the

words. Then she nodded and slid from the saddle, letting Midnight wander.

She set off through the trees, away from the others, eyes wide to catch every mote of starlight and avoid a stumble. But she did not see the forest around her. Rather, she saw only a ghostly and wispy aspect of it, just enough for her feet to avoid upturned roots and stones. Instead of the trees and the silvery starlight, she saw Albern's charge, and Mag's skin covered in wounds, and Sten's slashed throat.

It was some time before she could muster her thoughts. When she did, she realized she had wandered far from where the others had stopped. She turned to retrace her steps, and when she found their camp again they had started a small fire beneath the trees. Part of her wanted to douse it, to keep them hidden in case they were pursued. But she could not muster the strength to care for so small a thing.

Chet sat alone, outside the fire's light. His knees were pulled up against his chest, and his arms lay across them. He seemed to be looking at the firelight, but his gaze was far away, as though he saw nothing at all.

A sharp pang in her gut reminded her she had not eaten for hours. She went to Midnight's saddlebag to fetch some meat and bread.

Something went *clink* as she opened the saddlebag. Her brow furrowed. When she lifted the flap, she saw a small coin purse. It was her spare, the one she had given to Mag. Slowly she untied the strings and poured the contents into her hand. Ten gold weights sat there, gleaming in the firelight. She stared at them for a while. Then she put them back in the purse and put the purse in the saddlebag.

Her appetite had vanished, so she closed the bag again and went to sit by the fire. But by the time she reached it, she did not want to rest, so she kept walking past it and over to Chet. She had nearly reached him before he noticed her and looked up.

"You should eat," he said. "I suppose I should, too."

"I tried. Will you walk with me?"

He shrugged and stood to go with her. Together they went back into the darkness—only to her surprise, Loren found it easier to see, and she realized with a start that the moons had risen. She had spent more time alone than she thought.

Chet stopped and heaved a shuddering breath. When she looked to him, she saw his shoulders shaking gently. She laid her hand on his back and turned him around. Once he faced her again, she saw his cheeks wet with tears.

"They did not even seem to care who they killed," he said. "I saw children fall beneath their blades."

"So it often is when armies sack cities," said Loren. "Or so I have heard. I was there for the battle of Wellmont, but the city held. There was no killing in the streets."

He looked away and cleared his throat. When he spoke again, she could hear him trying to sound carefree, as though his tears were not there. "You all hardly blinked as you rode through it," he said. "I thought I would die of fright."

"We have seen killing before," said Loren. "Some of us more than others."

"I am sorry about Albern. I knew him only a few days, but he seemed to have a good heart. Mag and Sten, as well."

"They did," said Loren.

He swiped a hand across his eyes, but tried to make it seem like he was only wiping sweat from his brow. "Loren, we must get away from here. We should ride into Dorsea and vanish where no one will find us. If that army came to Northwood looking for you, and was willing to sack the city just to find you, they will not stop pursuing you now."

"That is why we must ride east, to warn the Mystics of their coming."

"Will they not expect that?" said Chet. "Will they not hunt us all along the road?"

"That does not matter," said Loren. "It is the duty I have taken upon myself. I have been hunted before."

"Duty?" said Chet. His voice had gone high and hysterical. "Why would you wish this upon yourself? I thought to travel with you, not die beside you. Oh, I know that all the nine lands may be dangerous, but this is another thing altogether. Did you not spend enough time, unhappy and trapped by your parents, out of some misplaced sense of duty?"

"That was nothing I chose," said Loren. "But this is my life now. It has been almost since the moment I left the Birchwood. Doom follows in my footsteps. That is why I urged you not to come with us. Even now I urge you to turn away, to let your tracks lead you home."

He stood there, looking at her in fear, and with a sinking heart she realized he was considering it. But at last he looked away and shook his head. "No. I said I would come with you. Who could call me anything but faithless, if I turned away because the road grew dark?"

"Who cares what anyone would call you?" said Loren. "I would happily have you by my side, but I would rather see you safe."

"And I you," he said. "That is why we should go, and now. Let others tend to duty. You and I have spent all our lives as its victims."

"I cannot," she said, in a small voice. "I owe it to him—to Jordel."

Chet looked as if he might say more, but then her stomach gave a gurgle. He stopped, collected himself, and shook his head. "We should eat. The road will grow darker still if we find ourselves starving upon it."

"I said I am not hungry."

"Hungry or not, I think you can swallow. Come."

They made their way back to the firelight. By the time they reached it, Chet seemed to have shaken off the darkness in his mind. Loren wondered if it had been so easy for her, the first time.

When she had first seen men killed in anger, it had been with the merchant caravan where she met Annis. Annis' mother, the merchant Damaris, had ordered a company of constables to be killed to preserve the secrecy of the goods she was smuggling. Loren remembered her horror at the senseless slaughter, at how the merchant had forced her to help dig graves for all the bodies. But looking back on it now, she hardly blinked at the thought of the constables dying. She had seen so much since then, so much worse, so much more frightening.

And yet she could not banish from her mind what had happened during the battle. She had chosen her target, and then had hesitated. The thought of her father's corpse had flashed into her mind, and the shot had gone wide. Mayhap, if she had been able to fire the arrow . . .

But such thoughts were ridiculous. There had been scores of Shades. Her arrow would not have made a difference. All the arrows in her quiver would not have made a difference.

Yet mayhap she *could* have done something. For one brief, thrilling moment, she had meant to charge in and rescue Mag by whatever means she could. She knew, looking back on it, she would not have hesitated to spill blood. That prospect terrified her—and yet it made her wonder again: why did she still hold so tightly to that ideal, when she had already taken a life?

That was different, she told herself.

Gem and Annis had eaten already, and lounged at the fire's edge while staring into its heart. Loren had not seen Xain touch his food, but then the wizard's appetite did not seem very great these days. He, too, watched the flames, but every few seconds he would look over his shoulder into the darkness beyond their camp. When he saw Loren and Chet return, his eyes flashed with interest.

"Good," he said. "We must discuss what we plan to do next."

"I myself am most curious about that," said Gem. "We have made our escape, and a narrow one. But what now?"

"We must warn the Mystics," said Loren.

"We know *that*," said Annis, "but where do we mean to go? South to Cabrus? The High King's Seat? I do not relish either of those choices, for my family would be thick about us. And you will remember that even Jordel did not trust all those of his order. How will we know the right redcloaks to speak to, and which ones will ignore our warnings to hang us as criminals instead?"

"If *you* will remember, Jordel told us where he meant to go," said Xain. "His stronghold of Ammon, in Feldemar. He told me where it lies, and that is where I think we must lay our course. His master lives there—a man named Kal, of the family Endil."

"And you think this man can be trusted?" said Loren. "Have you met him?"

"I trust few, Mystics least of all," said Xain. "But this, at least, we owe Jordel: to deliver his message to his master, and let the Mystics do what they may with the tale."

"But how shall we get there?" said Loren. "I have scarcely any idea how to make our way to Feldemar. I know only that it is north and east of Selvan."

"A far ways north and east, yes," said Xain. "Ammon is in Feldemar, and somewhat near the northern shore of the Great Bay. I visited that kingdom once in my youth. Ships travel to that area from all ports on the Bay."

"The King's road, then?" said Gem. "We could take it to the Seat, or Garsec, Selvan's capital."

"That would be like walking into the lion's den," cried Annis. "We would certainly be spotted, and then I would be taken by my family. The rest of you would not be so lucky. You would likely take long in the killing."

"No, Garsec and the Seat seem poor choices both," said Xain. "But there are other ports in Selvan, ports farther south along the Bay, from where we might sail. But traveling there would take a long while, and the voyage would be longer besides. No, I think we must sail from Dorsea."

Loren blinked, gawking at him in the firelight. "Dorsea? Have magestones addled your mind so much, wizard? They are at war with Selvan, and no safe place for us to wander. Especially since, as you have all pointed out so carefully, I speak like a child of Selvan birth. Chet is from my village, and most likely has the same accent."

"Yes," said Gem and Annis at once.

"Accent?" said Chet.

"That was true enough when we set out from Wellmont," said Xain. "But now the war is far away, in the southwest corner of the kingdom. Likely those in the northeast of Selvan have hardly heard of the fighting. Citizens of Dorsea will be even less concerned, so far away from the conflict. And so close to the border between the two kingdoms, we will find many families with both Selvan and Dorsean kin. Your quaint voices will scarcely bear mention."

"So that is our plan, then?" said Annis. "We will strike north into Dorsea, then travel east until we reach the coast? I daresay I like it better than the thought of riding to the Seat, where, if I have my way, I will never set foot again in this life."

"It seems a prudent course," said Gem.

Chet's eyes lit up, and he turned to Loren. "Mayhap—or mayhap there is another way. Traveling across the open country of Dorsea poses its own dangers, and we do not know the land. But there is another road to the coast of the Great Bay. And it is a road for which we already have two guides."

Loren caught his meaning at once. "The Birchwood."

"What of it?" said Gem.

"It runs all the way to the Bay. And Chet and I know it well. Mayhap we are not woodsmen so great as—" She stopped short just before she said *Albern*. "—as some others. But this is our home. I do not think the Shades can follow us beneath these trees."

"If there is one thing we should have learned by now, it is not to underestimate our foes," said Xain darkly. "Think of this. The Shades attacked North-wood from the west, but also from the north. They have been gathering in strength, much greater strength than we knew. Where did they all come from? They did not conjure so many soldiers from thin air. They are men and women of these lands, of Selvan and Dorsea and likely other kingdoms besides. And if they know we have fled into the forest, they will send trackers after us who know it as well as the two of you."

"You think any Selvans fight on their side?" said Loren angrily. "You think they would march into one of their own cities and murder their fellows in the streets? I think you know little of our kingdom."

"And you think too highly of your fellows," snapped Xain. "Mayhap they were starving, and the Shades gave them coin. Mayhap their homes were ravaged by war, and the Shades offered them safety. Mayhap they were dying from plague, and the Shades provided refuge. And mayhap their suffering was not at the hands of some whimsical fate, but their fellow citizens of Selvan. Do you think, then, that they would stay their blades?"

Loren fumed, though in the back of her mind she knew she had little reason for it. She had met evil men and women before. Few acted as they did for the joy of it. She turned away from Xain, refusing to answer him.

Chet frowned, but spoke to appease the wizard rather than to argue. "Still, we have a lead. I think we can evade them. And in any case, it would let Loren and me return home. If the Shades do indeed wander these lands, we owe it to our families to warn them." He stopped short, glancing at Loren from the corner of his eye. "And to our other friends, of course."

Loren turned to see Xain's dark eyes fixed on her again. Though she had never told him the full tale, he knew something of why she had left the forest. When he had found her there, a young girl who wished to flee her home, she had shown him the bruises her father used to leave upon her body. That was what had prompted him to bring her in the first place. He had to know she had little reason to return—not like Chet, whose father loved him, and who had had many friends in the village besides.

But still, Loren remembered some folk from her childhood with fondness, though it seemed many years since she had seem them last. Mayhap Chet was right. Mayhap they could warn the village and let them escape . . . but to where? She did not know, but anywhere had to be better than a kingdom overrun by Shades.

She met Xain's gaze defiantly. "Yes. We will make

for the coast by way of the Birchwood. Rest, all of you. We ride again at first light."

Xain glowered at her. "I will stand the first watch." She held his gaze a moment longer before she turned to fetch her bedroll from Midnight's saddle.

NINE

Dawn broke grey and cold, with the sun struggling to pierce the clouds and find them beneath the trees. Loren felt a sore spot under her shoulder. After days spent in Mag's inn, which was comfortable, if plain, the forest floor was an unpleasant reminder of life on the road.

"Do you think it will rain?" said Annis, who had already awoken. She was looking up at the clouds.

"No," said Chet. "The air is not right, and this part of autumn rarely gives rain."

"It gave us plenty in the Greatrocks," said Gem.

"Mountains are different," said Loren. "This is the Birchwood."

Xain still sat where Loren had seen him last night. She realized suddenly that he had not woken any of them to stand watch. The skin on the back of his hands was raw where he had been picking at it, and she saw him shivering as he rocked back and forth. He seemed unaware of the rest of them.

The magestone sickness must be terrible for him now. It had been weeks since last he had eaten the precious black stones, and the darkness took time to leave his body. Last time it had taken more than a month before his mind had righted itself, and his body had still been recovering its strength when she fed him stones again.

Now his countenance worried her. They could ill afford such weakness—the weakness of his body, or his judgement. For Loren knew his thoughts must be as frail as his skeletal frame. And she worried what the magestone sickness might spur him to do, especially if he imagined he was being betrayed. For Loren had shared much with him the night before, but she had not told him everything.

Could she now? Or would that only bring about the very crisis she hoped to avoid?

What would Jordel have done?

Her jaw clenched with resolve. No. Jordel had seen too much value in secrecy. He had valued Loren, and trusted her—but not enough. If he had told her more about her dagger early on, she would have had less trouble on the road from Cabrus. If he had told her about the magestones, she never would have given them to Xain. And if he had warned her about the Necromancer and the Lifemage, mayhap she could have found some way to save him from Trisken.

No. She would follow in Jordel's footsteps, but not too closely. Xain must trust her with his whole heart, and that could never happen while she hid secrets from him.

And what of your magestones?

That thought stopped her short. Could she tell him that she still had some of the stones? Did her desire for trust extend so far?

She glanced at him again. He had wrapped his arms about himself, and one hand picked at the other elbow.

No. He would go mad with hunger, she knew. She could not tell him—at least not now. That was not dishonesty, but mercy. And in the meantime, she would share all that she could.

Loren walked over to the wizard and motioned to him. "Come with me a moment. I wish to discuss the road."

His eyes snapped up to her, and for a moment she saw the fog of confusion in his eyes, as if he did not recognize her. Then they cleared, and he levered himself to his feet with some difficulty. Loren took his elbow as he stood, and then led him off east into the woods. Once they were out of sight of the others, she stopped.

"The road, eh?" said Xain. "The others are no fools—that boy of yours, least of all."

Loren gritted her teeth and chose not to correct him. "Last night you told me of the Necromancer and the Lifemage. But there was something else I did not tell you, something I was unsure I should speak of. But you deserve to know it, especially now. I am done keeping secrets between us."

His brow arched, and she saw interest spark in his eye. "Say on, then. It can hardly be darker news than I have heard already."

"It might be, in its own way," she said. "It concerns this."

She reached to her hip and drew forth her dagger. Xain fixed it with a wary eye. The black designs along its length were spiked and twisted—unmoving now, though Loren had seen them writhe like the tendrils of a living thing.

"Your dagger," he said. "From whence you took the name Nightblade."

"This blade was my parents'. I found it when I was a young child."

Xain arched an eyebrow. "And you stole it from them when you left?"

"It, and other things besides," she said. "Only I did not know what I carried with me. Nor do most who see it—except some very few, and to them it is an object of great terror."

Xain's brow furrowed, and he reached out for the

dagger. Loren hesitated, but then she handed it to him by the hilt.

"It is a fine weapon, elegantly made, to be certain," said Xain. "I do not recognize the craftsmanship. But I do not see what makes it more fearsome than, say, a sword. Especially when you will not even use it to defend yourself."

"To kill, you mean," said Loren sharply. "The dagger's power lies not in its steel, but in its magic. It was crafted and imbued with spells centuries ago, in the time of the Wizard Kings."

His eyes darkened. "That is an ancient weapon, to be found in the hut of a woodsman."

"Ancient, yes. And mightier than can be seen with the eye. Jordel recognized it from the moment he saw it, and eventually he told me its tale. It is a weapon of the mage hunters. A blade for hunting wizards. And killing them."

Xain sucked in a sharp breath through his teeth, and suddenly he held the dagger gingerly between thumb and forefinger. He handed it back to her, and Loren took it gratefully. Now the wizard looked at the blade with distrust.

"I have heard tales of such weapons," he said. "There were dark whispers of them—and of the mage hunters—that passed among the students at the Academy. If our instructors heard us whispering these tales, we were sharply reprimanded and beaten. Of course that only made the tales spread farther. I had heard that one such blade was found recently, some time within living memory."

"The High King Enalyn discovered it, or it was revealed to her," said Loren. "And she grew wrathful, and reinforced the Fearless Decree because of it. To carry such a weapon means death—not only for the wielder, but mayhap for the Mystics themselves."

"As it should," growled Xain. "They used these weapons to slaughter my kind in droves. No wizard could rest easily at night, knowing such blades were carried in the nine lands. Who knew but that some Mystic might not appear upon your doorstep the next morning, immune to your magic and intent on taking your life? They say it was a time of great fear for us, and the very reason for the dark wars of the Wizard Kings. After I heard of how they hunted us, I could find no fault with my forebears for beginning those wars."

He had begun to pace as he talked, and his voice rose louder and louder in its wrath. Loren stood back from him, and found her hand gripping the handle of the dagger more tightly. But almost as soon as the anger had come upon him, it fled. He sagged like a sack of grain with the bottom sliced open and placed a hand over his eyes.

"No," he muttered. "No, those are wrathful words from days I have left behind. I have eaten of the mage-stones and come back—twice now. I have seen what plagued the Wizard Kings, what madness took hold of their minds and led to the dark times."

"The Wizard Kings ate of magestones?" said Loren. "I had not heard that."

"You had not heard of magestones at all until you left the Birchwood behind you. Yes, many of the Wizard Kings consumed the stones with reckless hunger. Their power was all the greater, but so were their madness and their wrath. Those who abstained were no villains—at least no more so than any other kings—but as the kingdoms vied for power, wizards ate the stones in greater numbers."

He looked at her, and she saw in his eyes the same man she had first met under the trees of this very forest: bitter, yes, and quick with biting wit. But mostly sad, and frightened, and a little lost.

"Now I have learned of their madness. And it makes me wish there were more such weapons in the nine lands."

Loren gulped. "What, then, do you think I should do with it?"

"Keep it," he said. "I have lived my whole life a wizard, and until recently I gave little thought to what it must be like for the rest of you—those without the gift, and the curse, of our power. I can only imagine the fear you must feel, living in these kingdoms where magic runs rampant. Unless I miss my guess, you will cross paths with many more wizards in the course of your life. Keep it, and use it to your advantage."

He pushed past her and made for the camp, leaving Loren standing on her own. Just before he vanished between the trees, he turned and called back over his shoulder.

"I only hope I never make an enemy of you again, Nightblade."

TEN

THEY SET OFF SOON AFTERWARDS, MOUNTING THEIR horses and heading east through the trees. Despite the cast of the sky, the day soon warmed to a nearly unbearable heat. Loren cast her cloak back over her shoulders. Chet removed his own, stowing it in his saddlebags, and the children did the same. Only Xain still felt chilled, and clutched his cloak tighter as they went, trembling.

Loren set a good pace for them, but nothing too drastic. Though she thought they were most likely safe, she had not entirely discounted the possibility that they were still being followed. They could need their horses' strength for a sudden burst of speed. But they saw no sign of pursuit, and at midday she felt confident enough to let them stop for a meal.

It was a strange feeling, she reflected, sliding down from atop Midnight. For so long they had had Jordel to set their pace, and he had pushed them hard or let them wander, according to the urgency of their mission. Now they were without his guidance, and Xain, though older than Loren, was in no condition to set their course. Loren realized with a start that the others now looked to her for leadership. It was not an entirely comfortable feeling.

"So, do you know any songs?" said Gem, lounging in the grass and looking towards Chet.

"Gem," said Loren in a warning tone.

"What?" said Gem. "Albern knew songs, and was happy enough to sing them. He had a fine voice, too." His eyes grew solemn, and he looked down at his nails.

"I heard him sing," said Chet. "But I do not have his gift for it. There were only a few in our village who knew many songs, let alone had the voices to carry them. They guarded the secret jealously. I think they enjoyed the attention it earned them when we would have a dance."

Loren suddenly laughed out loud, and the others looked at her, startled. "I am sorry," she said. "But do you remember when Miss Aisley grew drunk on wine, and forgot the words of the song she was singing?"

Chet's crooked teeth flashed in a grin. "And she

had set her cap for Rickard, but she was so befuddled she seized Bracken instead and gave him a kiss so deep the old man nearly fainted."

Loren doubled over, and by now the children had caught their humor and chuckled along. She even saw Xain smirk. "Rickard would not speak to her for months, and Bracken kept hanging about her house day after day, and stayed a week longer than normal."

Their deep belly laughs rang out through the forest, echoing from the trees. Loren had almost forgotten what it was to laugh, and certainly at a memory of home.

Chet fixed her with a look, and it was as though he could read her thoughts. "You see? Not all our past is dark. I am happy we will see our village again. Mayhap, now that those who made it so terrible for you no longer dwell there, you will change your mind about it."

Loren thought she heard the words he did not say: *and change your mind about our journey.* She frowned; she did not wish to keep arguing about this with him, least of all in front of the others.

"I wish I could see Bracken again," she said, as a way of changing the subject. "When last he came, I was still just a little girl. I wonder what he would think of me now, chasing after the tales of Mennet he used to spin for me."

"Mennet!" cried Gem. "I heard many stories of him. He was my favorite. The other boys in Cabrus always said I looked just like him."

"We heard of him as well upon the Seat, but never as a hero," said Annis, sniffing. "He was a scoundrel, a lawbreaker whom the king could never bring to justice. I heard he slew maidens in their beds and took toys from children."

"Mennet? Never!" said Loren. "He took from evil kings who taxed their subjects too highly, and kinslayers and murderers. Always he made right what others had done wrong."

Annis looked at Gem, but the boy only shrugged. She looked to Xain, but he shook his head. "I care little for children's tales of a thief who likely never lived in the first place," said the wizard. "Everyone has heard of Mennet, but the wise know he is nothing but a legend."

Loren glared daggers at him, but Chet spoke first. "Still such tales may have worth. But I never loved them like Loren did. I loved the stories of kings and warriors, brave knights and cunning constables who brought down those who broke the King's law."

"Mayhap one day you will hunt me, then," said Loren with a smile. "For I am no friend to constables."

"Why do you think I left the village in the first place?" said Chet, feigning an evil smile and forming his hands into claws. She shoved him into the grass as the children laughed anew. It felt as though a dark storm that had followed them from Northwood was now blowing away.

They went to their bedrolls that night in far better spirits than the day before, and Loren insisted on standing the first watch to let Xain sleep. She did not know if he ever actually found slumber, and more than once in the night she saw his eyes glittering in the light of the fire. But she woke Chet as the moons were descending, and then fell into a deep sleep that lasted until just after dawn's first light.

But they were not long on the road that second day before something happened to darken their mood. The land rose sharply up across their path, forming a range of hills that were just shy of being proper mountains. But there was a clear path up, so they found its base and then Loren and Chet led them in the ascent.

They were halfway up the rise when Loren chanced to look out at the land they had crossed. And there, some leagues away, she caught a flash of movement that did not look like a bird or a bear. She called them to a halt and stood stock still, searching.

"What is it?" Gem said from his saddle. Loren hushed him with a sharp wave of her hand and kept staring.

Chet came to her side and spoke softly. "Did you see someone?"

"Mayhap," she mumbled. "Somewhat south of our course, and—there!"

She saw it again. There were several shapes moving beneath the trees. Even from this distance she recognized riders on horseback.

"I see them," said Chet. "They are many. Mayhap a dozen."

"A dozen what?" growled Xain.

"Riders," said Loren. "Mayhap a league behind us, but traveling in the same direction."

All were silent for a long moment. Then Annis said, half-heartedly, "We do not know they are Shades. They could be simple travelers, like us. Surely some people must travel through the Birchwood on their journeys, or because they do not like the roads, or simply because it is more pleasant than the lands beyond."

"We are hardly simple travelers," said Loren. "But mayhap you are right. We do not know that we are pursued."

"After the luck we have seen upon our road, do any of you truly doubt it?" said Xain darkly. "They are riding east. That means they come from the direction of Northwood."

They did not answer him, but carried on up the path. And their steps came a bit quicker.

ELEVEN

THEY SOON CRESTED THE RISE. THERE AT THE TOP THEY stopped and looked away west again, peering through the tops of the trees. But they could see no sign of their pursuers, if indeed they were being pursued. Quickly they rode down the other side of the ridge, and with many a backwards glance towards the top.

The Birchwood rose about them as they reached the bottom, and soon there was nothing but the sound of hoofbeats. No one talked as they rode, nor sang. When Loren's gaze did meet one of the others, she saw a hunted look that surely matched her own.

Often they glanced behind them, and after two hours of riding Chet reined his horse to a halt. Loren turned to follow his gaze. At the top of the rise they had crossed, they saw figures on horseback against the sky. At this distance, they were too small to be anything more than silhouettes. She could catch no colors in their clothing.

"They are making better time than we are," said Chet. "We should ride harder."

So they did, spurring their horses to a trot that they kept up the rest of the day. Deep in the heart of the forest, it was impossible to see very far in any direction, particularly behind. Turning from the path could lead the horse into a root or a tree. But now Loren thought she could feel eyes behind them, watching their progress, and it was all she could do to keep from staring backwards as they rode.

As the sun neared the top of the ridge far behind them, she searched for a stream. Fortunately, such were plenty in the Birchwood, and she soon found one to suit her purpose—shallow enough for the horses to walk in, yet deep enough that hoof prints on the bed could not be seen from above. Chet saw her aim at once and led them north in the middle of the stream, the water foaming white around their mounts' hocks.

"Ugh!" said Gem as a splash of water soaked his feet. The shoes they had bought for him in Wellmont were now worn and had holes. "This water is cold."

"Mayhap, but it will keep us safe," said Loren. "They cannot track us in the water."

"How long must we ride it?" said Xain. "I agree with Gem—I do not wish to sleep in a soaking bedroll, my wet clothes clinging to my skin."

"And I do not wish to sleep with Shades lurking in the forest all about us," said Annis. "We will ride as long as Loren and Chet tell us to."

Loren looked at her gratefully, and Annis gave her a smile. It was plain the girl was frightened, but her hands were steady as they gripped the reins, and her mouth was set in a grim line. Loren had not forgotten Annis' face in the Greatrocks when she confronted her mother. A spoiled merchant's daughter she might be, but there was pluck in her.

Soon the soft loam of the forest floor turned to hard and rocky dirt. The light was fading fast from the sky. "A cave," said Loren. "For the horses."

Chet nodded and led them out of the water. They searched about for a place they might conceal their mounts. Soon they found one: a cleft in the earth, wide and tall enough to ride inside, and with a corner behind which they could hide. There they hobbled the horses and left them with some oats, and then dragged branches to block them in and discourage them from wandering.

"Now back to the river," said Loren. "Quickly, all of you. Chet and I will follow."

"Why are you not walking with us?" said Gem.

"Enough questions, boy," said Xain. He gripped Gem's shoulder and pulled the boy along. "Do as she says."

Chet had a hatchet, and with it he cut two wide branches from nearby trees. With the limbs in hand, he and Loren retraced their steps to the river. Wherever the sparse grass had been disturbed, they used the branches to brush it back straight. With their boots they smoothed any soft spot in the forest floor where hooves had left a mark. Soon they found themselves back at the river, all signs of their trail removed.

"Now cross it, and strike out in the other direction," said Loren. "Hurry! Soon it will be dark."

"It is dark enough for me now," said Gem. But he had had enough rebukes for one day, it seemed, and he followed Xain obediently.

Into the forest they plunged, Loren letting Chet lead the way while she brought up the rear. Chet knew her mind without having to hear it, and led them to a rise in the earth that could be seen not far away. They came to its base, and Loren took the rest of them up the rise while Chet remained at the bottom and built a fire.

"Why are we climbing if we mean to camp at the bottom?" said Annis curiously.

"We do not mean to camp at the bottom," said Loren. "We mean only to build a camp at the bottom."

Xain's eyes flashed with recognition. "We have left a trail to it," he said. "If we are being followed, they will come to the fire. But from atop the rise, we can see them without being seen ourselves."

"Very clever," said Gem. "I only wish it did not mean we must sleep without a fire tonight."

"If we are right in our suspicions, it will be many days yet before we can light a fire at night again," said Loren. "Now quickly, let us find trees where we may sleep."

"Trees?" said Gem. "What are we, owls?"

"Leave *off*, Gem," said Annis.

Chet soon had a small campfire going, and he abandoned it to join them atop the rise. Together he and Loren found trees with wide branches that were hidden from the ground, and in them they built small platforms from branches they cut with the hatchet. Soon they had places for the children and Xain to lay their heads. For themselves they found two thick branches side by side, and lay lengthwise upon them.

Together they lay, arms hanging down just a few feet apart, and peered out into the darkness towards the campfire. Though a fair distance away, it glowed like the sun in the pitch-black night. All was quiet, save for the sounds of Gem and Xain rustling about, uncomfortable in their makeshift beds.

"Do you still think this course is wise?" said Chet quietly. "If they have caught up to us so early, what makes you think we can evade them until we reach our village, or the Great Bay beyond?"

"If they have tracked us this far, why do you think

we would evade them if we were to change our course now?" countered Loren.

He sighed. "Mayhap. But then again, if they see we have turned aside, they might guess that we no longer mean to warn the Mystics, and leave us be."

Loren thought of Trisken and the cruelty in his smile—the same cruelty she had seen in Rogan's eyes, in that brief moment on the streets of Northwood. "You do not know them," she said. "They are not the sort to leave matters be, nor to show mercy."

He did not answer that at first. After a moment he said, "Mayhap this is all needless worry, and the riders we saw behind us are not even following our course. But if you are right, and we are pursued, what do you mean to do?"

"Find some way to evade them, I suppose. I have not had time to think that far ahead."

"Well, mayhap it will be needless. I hope so."

Loren snorted, and thought she saw him smile at the sound. Then suddenly he thrust a finger ahead and whispered, "Look."

She tensed, expecting to see figures approach the fire. But he was pointing instead at the moons, which had just crested the horizon to shine their silver light across the tops of the trees. Below them, the familiar leaves of home had turned into something else, a thousand thousands of fingers of pewter rather than lively green, swaying in the gentle breezes of the night. Far away they heard the songs of whippoorwills and owls, prey and predator joined in a nighttime chorus. Loren let out a long breath, and for just a moment felt the tension of the day's flight leave her. She looked back to the moons. Merida, the smaller, was especially bright, while Enalyn was partly hidden behind her sister.

"Merida leads the way tonight, her lantern searching the Birchwood for her mother and father," Chet said quietly.

"Enalyn follows cautiously, urging her sister back home to await their return," said Loren.

"Always I have wondered if I would live to see it, the day when the sisters at last find their way to those who search for them. I wonder what it would look like, a sky with no moons."

"It would be a sadder thing, I think," said Loren.

"I think you are right."

They were quiet for a while after that. Even Gem had stopped rustling above them, though Loren still thought she heard the occasional noise from Xain.

Finally Chet spoke again. "This part of the journey is not so bad."

"You are right. It is the times before, and after, that make up for it."

He snorted a brief laugh, and then grew dour. "I . . . I cannot stop seeing the streets of Northwood," he said in a voice scarcely above a whisper.

Loren looked at him. He was easier to see now in the moonslight, and she saw a faraway look in his eyes that she felt far too familiar with. "It may be some time until you can."

"Was it the same for you?"

"That I cannot tell you, for I cannot see inside your mind," she said. "But I can tell you that, when I first saw soldiers killed by other soldiers, I dreamt of their lifeless faces for days afterwards."

"What made it stop?"

Loren thought of the long road since. "Seeing many things worse."

He did not look comforted, and turned his face back to the moons. Seized by impulse, Loren reached out and took his hand in hers. Almost at once she felt unsure of herself and began to draw back. But his fingers tightened, not in restraint but in comfort. So she left her hand where it was. He did not look at her, nor she at him. Together, they only watched the moons.

Then a shadow passed in front of the fire below.

They pushed forwards to peer into the night. There—she saw it again. A dark figure crossed the light, and then another. Now she could see them illuminated in the orange glow. Six figures she counted, and she caught glimpses of their horses in the trees beyond. She saw at least one cloak of grey, but none of the blue-and-grey uniforms the Shades normally wore. Still her heart sank, for she knew the truth: whoever the figures were, they were hunting her and her friends, and had at last found signs of their prey. A moment later, they stomped out the fire and cast dirt over it, and vanished into the darkness beneath the trees.

Loren let out her breath in a sharp *whoosh.* "You left no trail that might lead them up this rise?"

"None," said Chet. "With any luck, they shall think we doubled back and made for the river again. They will follow it farther north, and by the time they realize their mistake, we shall be leagues gone."

"With any luck," said Loren. "But my travels have not given me reason to rely overmuch on fortune."

"Let us wait an hour, and then wake the others," said Chet. "If we wish to make use of our lead, we cannot spend the night here."

"You are right. Close your eyes now—I shall wake you when the moons change places."

Her gaze followed Chet as he curled up closer to the tree's trunk, propped between the branch on which he lay and the one just next to it. Soon his eyes were shut in slumber, his lips slightly parted and deep breaths wheezing between them. She turned her eyes outwards again, but she rubbed her thumb across the palm of her hand, and kept doing so until she woke them all an hour later.

TWELVE

THEY ROUSED THE CHILDREN FIRST, WHO WOKE WITH many grumbles. When Loren swung herself up to rouse Xain, she found him already awake and staring at her in the moonslight. She suppressed a shiver.

"They followed us to our camp," she said. "When they found it empty, they left. Now we mean to ride on, while darkness still hides us."

He nodded and rose. Together the party climbed down from the tree to land softly upon the grass. Loren and Chet led them off into the trees, with Xain bringing up the rear. Her gaze roved the woods before them, searching for any sign of movement. Most likely Chet was right, and the Shades would follow their trail all the way back to the river. But she was keenly aware that they could be walking into a trap.

They saw nothing all the long way back to the river, nor after reaching the other side. Swiftly Loren led them to the cave where they had hidden the horses. She heard Midnight's gentle nicker and breathed a sigh of relief. They fetched their mounts and gained their saddles before making for the river again. Once they had crossed, Loren spurred them on as quickly as she dared in the dim moonslight.

All night they rode, until the sky before them grew grey and finally broke with dawn. They rode a little farther still, until they found a stream where they might water the horses. Finally Loren called them to a halt.

"Well?" said Chet. "We have seen no sign of them, and have gained many leagues. Do you think they will abandon the chase?"

"I doubt it," said Loren. "We should guess that they will be at least as tireless as we are, and mayhap more so. Then we cannot be surprised, except pleasantly."

"What do you mean to do, then?" said Gem, yawning wide. "Ride on until we collapse? I do not think that will help our cause. I am blessed with great stamina, but even I tire eventually."

"Yes, we are all well aware of your great endurance," said Annis, rolling her eyes. "Never have I called you the Prince of Snores under my breath."

He narrowed his eyes at her. "Good."

"Children," said Loren in a warning tone. "I am not ready to let us rest. Not yet, at any rate. If indeed we mean to lose them, we must ride at least a little longer. Eat now, and stretch your legs upon the grass. But then we must continue, and quicker than before."

Annis and Gem began to grumble again, but she ignored them and went to fetch her breakfast from Midnight's saddle. Then, because the mare had run hard all night, she fetched an apple from the bag and fed it to her. But Chet seized his hatchet and walked off into the woods. Curious, Loren went after him.

She found him a ways off, looking at the lower branches of a young oak. He chose one and gripped it firmly, then began to hack at it near where it joined the trunk.

"What are you up to?" she said.

"I hope we have left our pursuers behind," he told her. "But then again they might find us, and next time it may come to a fight. If it does, I would see us armed. But we have no blades to hand, nor would I wish to use one if we did, any more than you. I thought I could make us some staves. Indeed, it would be nice to have a walking stick in any case, for when the ground grows rough."

Loren smiled. "A wise thought. I am glad to find you so helpful, for I had thought you saw this road as folly."

"Oh, I do," he said quickly. The branch came off

the oak at last. He stood it up, measured the right height, and began to cut away at the other end. "I still think we should abandon our course and ride north, or south, or anywhere other than where we mean to go. But as long as I am trailing in your footsteps, I might as well try to make that road less perilous. Who knows? If indeed they are still following us, mayhap we might find help in the village. A score of woodsmen could help us fend them off in short order."

Her spirits dampened, and she looked away. "Chet, that is a poor idea."

He shrugged. "Why? They know the Birchwood better than anyone. Do you think they could not drive away a dozen fighters, even these Shades?"

She turned away. "I do not wish to argue. Just let us hope we have lost them."

Leaving him to his work, she went back to the others. The children sat in the grass and ate. The horses had taken their fill of the stream and now grazed along the ground.

"Where has Chet gone?" said Annis.

"He is fashioning staves for us," said Loren. "In case we should come upon any more trouble."

"I shall keep my blade, if it is all the same to you," said Gem. "I am still practicing the stances Jordel taught me, but I think I could take one of these Shades in a fight."

"Of that we are all very certain," said Xain, rolling his eyes. Loren smiled. Though the wizard still looked thin and haggard, it was encouraging to hear him jest, even so feebly.

They sat and enjoyed the morning sunlight for a time, until Loren began to think she would have to go and fetch Chet to ride on. But just then he returned, and in his arms he carried five staves of different sizes. One he threw to Loren, and she caught it easily in her hands. Three others he dumped on the ground before Gem, Annis, and Xain, and kept one in hand.

"Here you are. Some fine walking sticks if we must dismount—or weapons, if we are forced to fight."

"I told Loren already, but I prefer my sword," said Gem. He nudged his staff away with a toe, though Annis had taken hers and was hefting the weight of it curiously. Meanwhile Xain had scarcely glanced at his.

"But a sword can rarely prevail against a staff," said Chet. "A blade is a fine weapon for a battle, I will give you that. But if you are not standing in rank and file, you should take the weapon with the longer reach."

"Fah!" said Gem. "Do you think you could have stood against Mag, if she carried her sword and you a staff?"

Chet pursed his lips and cocked his head. "Mayhap not against her. Yet the point stands. Here, I will show you. Take up your blade, and come for me."

Gem looked suddenly doubtful. "I—I do not wish to hurt you."

"I doubt very much that you shall. But move slowly, if it comforts you to do so."

The boy stood and adopted his first stance. Loren still remembered the day Jordel had given him the blade and shown him the forms, back when they rode together through the Greatrocks. Gem had taken to the training with gusto, but even to Loren's eye he still seemed very much a novice. She leaned back, her hands planted in the grass, watching with amusement.

Gem stepped forwards and swung, a wide and slow arc that Chet could easily have sidestepped. But instead he lashed out with his staff, so hard it knocked the blade from Gem's hand. The other end of the staff came around to rest on Gem's shoulder.

"And you are bested," said Chet.

Gem greeted the words with a glare. "I was moving slowly."

"Then try it faster."

He did. This time he struck with much greater vigor, though Loren could tell he still withheld himself. Chet struck back faster than before. He did not even aim for the sword; he merely swung the staff at Gem's head. The boy yelped and leaned back, away from the blow, his own stroke turning weak and ineffectual. Chet flipped the staff at the boy's ankle, and Gem tumbled into the grass. Annis cried out and flung herself back as his short sword flew through the air, landing where she had just been sitting.

"I am sorry!" said Chet, face filling with remorse as he dropped his staff and ran to her. "Did it strike you?"

"I am fine," said Annis, though she looked at the sword with distrust.

But Gem had grown angry, and he leaped up from the ground to jump at Chet from behind. Before Loren could move to intervene, he had wrapped his arms around the older boy's neck, his legs wrapping around Chet's waist to try and restrain him. Quick as blinking, Chet seized the boy's spindly arms and lunged forwards, flipping Gem over his shoulder to land hard on his back. All his breath left him in a *whoosh,* and he lay there, gasping.

"A fair attempt at an ambush," said Chet without a hint of anger. "Mayhap later I can teach you wrestling to go along with your sword training."

"It would please me greatly if you would fling yourself into the river," said Gem through wheezing gasps.

"Enough," said Loren. "Gem, take your staff or not, as you will. But the rest of us should carry ours, for we have no other ways to defend ourselves. Xain, can you carry yours on your own?"

"I am not so feeble as you seem to think," snapped the wizard, glaring at her. But the weakness in his voice betrayed his words. Still, he snatched up the staff where it lay at his feet, then used it to lever himself up. He stood there, leaning heavily on the stick, looking for all the world like some wise old sorcerer from tales.

"Now he looks a proper wizard," said Gem, grinning. Xain's frown deepened, and he twisted his fingers. A globe of flame sprang to life and crashed into the ground by Gem's head. The boy shrieked and rolled away.

THIRTEEN

THEY MOUNTED AND RODE ON. THE BREVITY OF THEIR rest and the long ride since had left them all weary, but the beauty of the Birchwood in summer did much to raise their spirits and keep their wits sharp.

Fifteen autumns Loren had spent beneath these trees already, but until recently she had thought her sixteenth would pass elsewhere. When she fled south, she thought the forest had revealed all its secrets to her. Now it was as though she looked upon it with new eyes. The green leaves, the gentle brown of the branches and trunks, seemed more beautiful to her than they ever had when she dwelt there. The birdsong came more pleasant, and the rolling slopes of land seemed more gentle and inviting. Many dark months she had spent elsewhere in the nine lands, in dirty and crowded cities, along the soggy banks of the Dragon's Tail, and in the unforgiving crags of the Greatrocks. Now, returned to her childhood home, she could see in it the beauty she had never noticed before.

Her unexpected attachment for the forest grew throughout their ride, and it remained with her when she called a stop for the night. As the next day passed much the same, she felt homesickness growing in her heart, and she remembered Chet's pleading words. A desire grew in her to lengthen the visit to their village, as Chet wished.

She shook that thought off. That sort of thinking had kept them in Northwood for far too long, and might have brought about that town's death. It had almost seen them all killed, and would have, if not for the sacrifice of Mag, Sten, and Albern. She owed it to their memories, and to Jordel, to press on. Once they warned the Mystics, and Jordel's order knew of the coming danger, mayhap then she could return to the Birchwood and live in peace—or visit for a time, and then resume her journey as she had often dreamed, this time with Chet at her side.

Three days she wrestled with these musings while they passed ever farther east in the wood. Sometimes they would find rivers or streams, and then Loren would guide them along through the water for some miles in case anyone was still on their trail. But eventually that wary practice seemed less important, and they would simply cross. Soon the land sloped down again, and when the trees grew thin they could see a wide bend in the Melnar many leagues ahead.

"That loop is only a few days' journey west of the village," said Chet, and Loren could hear the eagerness in his voice. And now, she felt that eagerness echoing in her own heart.

Faster they spurred their horses on, for it seemed that even the children caught the mood. Only Xain remained reluctant, scowling and shivering atop Jordel's charger. Soon they found a narrow road. It was little more than a dirt path worn by hooves and boots, but Loren thought she recognized it as the one that ran all the way to their village. At midday they stopped again to eat. Loren wanted to keep going, to ride on until she saw the familiar houses of home ahead, but that was a foolish thought. Even on the road, it would take them some days yet to reach the village.

As they sat in the underbrush beside the path, Loren felt a prickling on the back of her neck. She faltered as she ate, looking about and wondering at the feeling. Then she noticed that Chet, too, had stopped eating, and was looking off into the shadows beneath the trees.

"What is it?" said Loren, quietly.

He shook his head. Then she heard it: silence. The

birds and beasts around them had fallen quiet. The only noise was the wind and the creaking of trees. Gem and Annis watched with wide eyes; Gem looked as if he would burst, but still he managed to keep his mouth shut. Xain was watching Loren, his eyes narrow.

"On the horses," whispered Loren.

They mounted as quickly and silently as they could. Loren led them north into the trees, for she had no wish to follow the road now. She scanned all around for another river or stream. Inwardly, she cursed herself for losing her caution. If they had kept hiding their trail, mayhap they would be home free now.

They found a stream and began to ride south along it. After a time it passed under the road they had been on, where a slender wooden bridge crossed it. They did not slow, but rode beneath the bridge, ducking their heads to pass under its bottom rafters.

Still the forest around them remained silent. The babbling whisper of the stream was now a grating sound against the quiet, and she was painfully aware of how loud their horses' hooves were. Even her pulse thundered so loud that she wondered if their pursuers could hear it.

Soon she grew frustrated. The water slowed their steps, and if the Shades were close behind, a stream would do little to deter them. She leaned over to whisper in Chet's ear.

"We should cross the river and make for the road

again. I think speed will save us now, more surely than silence will."

He looked back over his shoulder. "That would mean turning around, mayhap into the waiting arms of those behind us."

"Then let us cut east, and turn north if we feel it is safe."

He shrugged and pulled on the reins. The party passed between the trees again. Still all remained too quiet. Now it was maddening.

Loren was half-ready to turn and scream into the woods, when suddenly the Shades struck.

Arrows whistled out from the trees, but none struck true. Annis screamed, and her horse reared. Gem barely stayed atop the beast.

"Ride north, and quickly!" said Loren.

They spurred their horses and fled. Loren whispered thanks for Midnight's sure steps and quick reflexes, but she watched the children's horse with worry. Annis was sure in the saddle, but her mount was easily frightened. Often it tried to break from the others, and Annis had to wrestle it back into line.

But it was Chet's steed that nearly doomed them. An arrow came flying from their left and passed within a handbreadth of the beast's nose. The horse screamed and lurched left. Chet pitched from the saddle at the sudden change in direction. He landed hard on the forest floor, and Loren's heart stopped. But he scrambled to his feet quickly, lifting his staff. His bow lay in the dirt a few feet away—thankfully unstrung, or surely it would have snapped.

"Chet!" cried Loren. She wheeled and went to him, reaching down a hand to pull him up. But it was too late, and figures in blue and grey appeared beneath the trees.

Another volley they loosed, but all arrows went wide. Then they leaped from their saddles and attacked with swords held high.

Loren dropped from Midnight's saddle and landed catlike beside Chet. Her hands shook, but she managed to string her bow. From the quiver at her hip she drew an arrow. With shaking hands she fitted and drew it as Albern had taught her. But still she could not aim for the heart. The shaft went wide, though it did make the Shade she aimed at dive to the side.

Then the Shades were on them with swords, and Loren snatched up her staff from the ground. Together she and Chet managed to ward off the warriors' blows. They used the trunks to their advantage, ducking behind them and letting the Shades' swords bounce harmlessly off the wood.

One of the blades stuck in the bark. Chet lunged forwards and slammed the butt of his staff into the man's head. The Shade fell to the ground in a heap. But another came just behind, forcing Chet still farther back.

A high, thin scream ripped the air. Gem came running into the fray with his sword held high. Behind

him came Annis, blanched with fright but still gripping her staff firmly. Gem's wild swings proved little
danger, but at least distracted one of the Shades long
enough for Loren to take him unawares. She struck
him first in the gut, and then on the back of the head
with a sharp overhead swing. But then his companion
pressed forwards, and Loren had to give ground before
her.

The woman knew her way about a blade, and
though Loren could keep her at bay, she could not
knock the sword from her grasp. Whenever Loren
lunged to strike, the sword would be there to block it.

Gem leaped to the attack. The Shade blocked his
first stroke, and then delivered a powerful backhand
blow. He crashed into the trunk of a tree.

"Gem!" said Loren.

Her hands loosened on the staff. With a cry the
Shade kicked out, knocking it from Loren's grip, and
then she swung her sword hard. It missed Loren, barely, and she danced back out of reach. But then the
Shade swung again, and this time let go the sword,
which flew spinning towards Loren's face.

She dropped on instinct and heard the blade whistle by overhead. By the time she rose to her knees,
the Shade was already on top of her. Loren was borne
to the ground, one arm across her throat. The Shade
whipped a knife from the back of her belt. Loren barely
caught the woman's wrist in time, choking for breath
as she fought to push the knife away.

Annis screamed and swung. In her panic she struck the Shade in the back, not the head. But it made the woman grunt and loosen the pressure on Loren's throat for a moment.

Then the air rang out with a sharp *crack,* and a bolt of lightning from Xain struck her in the chest. Loren felt the bolt through her body, rocking her with a sharp and sudden pain.

The Shade lurched back with a cry. She reached for Loren again, but Chet had defeated his foe, and he struck Loren's in the chest with his staff. The Shade fell to the ground. Loren flipped up and on top of her, one hand gripping the woman's throat.

"Killing children in the woods? Is that the manner of person you are?" she screamed.

The dagger was in her hand before Loren knew what she was doing. She raised it high. Only at the last moment did she stop herself.

The woman's eyes had rolled nearly all the way back, and her hands feebly tried to pull Loren's fingers from her neck. Loren could see where her nails had dug into the skin, turning it an angry red under her grip.

She screamed again and turned the dagger. The pommel came crashing down on the woman's head. The Shade's skull slammed against the ground, and she lay still. Only then did Loren's fingers loosen.

When she looked up, she found Chet staring at her in silence. The look on his face nearly made her weep. It held no anger, nor shock, nor even fear. It was sorrow—the same sorrow she had seen in his eyes when he sat beside her in Northwood, and held her as she trembled and cried, murmuring that it was not her fault.

Quickly she turned away. "Annis, fetch rope from my saddle. Now!"

She started to drag the Shades to the base of a beech tree. After a moment's hesitation, Chet moved to help her. Soon Annis came running with the rope, and then ran to revive Gem with a splash from her water skin. Loren bound all the Shades' wrists behind their backs before tying the bindings to each other in a circle around the tree. When they woke, they would be able to rise if they all stood together, but they could not move away.

"It will not hold them forever, but long enough for us to make our escape," she said. "Now get the horses back, and quickly. With luck they will not have run far."

Chet's mount had fled after throwing him, but they soon found it a little ways to the northwest. The other horses were nearby, and the travelers swung themselves into their saddles.

Loren feared to look at Chet as they made ready, but finally forced herself to do it. He was studying her from the corner of his eye, and he looked away quickly when he saw her turn towards him.

"We cannot return to our village," said Loren. "If

they followed us this far, it is folly to believe they will not stay on our trail. We will only bring their wrath down upon our home."

Chet said nothing. Xain watched him for a moment before looking to Loren. "Where, then, do we ride?"

"North. North to Dorsea, and then east to the coast." She spoke again to Chet. "But that does not have to be your course. You could go on alone, for you can hide your tracks better than the five of us could. They would not follow you, and you could return home in peace. No one will speak ill of you for doing so. Indeed, I would call you wise."

Still Chet said nothing, and now all the others noted his silence. Gem watched him, mute, an angry bruise growing on his cheekbone.

"That is a fine dagger you have," Chet said at last. He kicked his horse and rode north, and was soon out of sight among the trees.

"Do not get used to seeing it," Gem called after him.

After a long and doubtful look, Annis spurred on after Chet. Xain still sat, waiting and watching Loren.

"Turn your eyes, wizard," said Loren. "They should be on the road ahead."

He shrugged and pulled on the reins, and together they went after the others.

FOURTEEN

Now their steps felt hounded, and traveling through the woods no longer gave Loren any sense of peace. All that day, she could not banish thoughts of their fight with the Shades. Over and over she saw in her mind's eye the dagger held aloft, ready to plunge into the soft flesh of the woman's throat.

For she *had* been ready to strike, that she knew. Fueled partly by her worry for Gem, whom the Shade had attacked, and partly by the thrill of the fight, she had very nearly taken the woman's life.

But you did not, she tried to tell herself.

Yet it had been a near thing. So near, in fact, that she could almost imagine the feeling of the dagger sliding through skin.

And why stop yourself? came a voice in her mind.

She had been a killer before she first left the Birchwood, though she had only recently learned that fact. Along all the road south, and then west and north and east again, she had counseled peace to her companions. She had called Jordel bloodthirsty, and admonished Gem and Annis when they wished violence on others. Now those words became a bitter ash in her memory, and she half wished she could take them back.

More than the dagger, though, she saw Chet's sorrowful eyes. He had not moved to stop her. He had not even cried out. He had only watched, and if Loren had struck, he would have let her. What would she have seen in his eyes, she wondered, if indeed she had killed the Shade?

They stopped as the sun set and evening came over the Birchwood. Still Loren could not meet Chet's eyes, so she made a show of adjusting Midnight's saddle.

"We will rest here for a time, but we should ride again once the moons rise."

"Another midnight ride," said Gem. "They seemed romantic at first, but repetition has dampened their appeal."

"You may stay and sleep the night here, if you wish," said Loren, much more harshly than she had intended. Gem balked and looked away without an answer.

"Loren, he meant nothing," said Annis quietly.

"I grow weary of his complaining. I will return in a moment."

She hobbled Midnight and walked away, hoping they would think she was going to make water. In truth, she only wanted to be alone. Soon she came upon a clearing, the other end of it invisible in the dimming twilight, and sat with her back against a tree. Sightless she stared into the darkness, her hands fiddling in her lap, trying to banish the anger and the melancholy that plagued her.

"You cannot lie to me, you know."

Chet's words came from nowhere, and frightened her half to death. She jerked to her feet. He stood by the tree she had rested against, leaning there with arms folded. Loren shoved his shoulder hard.

"Do not sneak up on me like that!"

He gave a smile, but it was tinged with sadness. "You would prefer I tramped around the forest like an ox? I thought we sought to go with stealth."

"You know what I mean. Go back to the others. Leave me be."

"Why? What ails you?"

She glared. "Why, nothing at all. It is only that murderers chase us through the forest, and twice they have nearly killed us. No matter what we try, we cannot evade them for long. Indeed, it is only by the greatest miracles of luck that we are alive at all. So as you can see, it is nothing. What could I possibly be worried about? Clearly our fortune is such a blessing that we need not concern ourselves with any worldly troubles."

He did not answer, but only looked back at her, and now the stars shone bright enough for her to see him. He had the same look he had worn earlier, when she nearly killed the Shade.

"Stop that," she snapped.

"What?"

"You look at me with pity. I do not ask for it, I do not need it, and most importantly, I do not *want* it. Save it for Xain, who suffers greater than any of the rest of us."

"I do not pity you, though I will admit it pains me to see you suffer the way you do."

"I do not suffer!"

It came out as a shout. She drew a deep breath and spoke in a more measured tone.

"I do not suffer. Yes, I am worried, and if you do not understand why, you are a fool."

"You cannot lie to me, as I have said already."

Her teeth ground together, and her words came with great effort. "You think I am lying? Very well. Tell me the truth."

"I saw in your face the moment when you almost killed that woman."

"I did not almost kill her."

"You cannot—"

"I am *not* lying!" She no longer cared how loud she was. "I am not a murderer!"

"I know it. You stayed your hand, and for that I am proud of you. I know few others—in fact, I know no one—who would have shown such restraint in the heat of a fight."

Her anger fled like a gust of southern wind, and like the wind it left her cold. She slumped, shoulders sagging, and sat down again. Slowly Chet came and sat before her. She thought for a moment that he might take her hands, but he did not.

"Ever since I left the forest, I have told myself I was better than those who would kill without thinking," she said quietly. "There are so many times when it would have been easier, but I refused. And I chastised those who I thought took lives too easily."

"You were not wrong," said Chet. "Not even now. You have been sorely tested, and you faltered. But you did not fail. I only wish you did not have to take the test at all. Do you understand now? I wish you could abandon this quest, and not only because I fear for your life. I do not want to see your mind broken by whatever madness runs rampant in the nine lands."

Loren shook her head. "To turn aside now would make me a coward. If we do not act, the madness you speak of would gather in strength until all things were swept away before it. Mayhap, if Jordel were still alive, I could leave it in his hands. But he died, and now I feel as though right and wrong slip through my fingers, pooling together upon the ground until I can no longer tell one from the other."

"All the more reason to go," said Chet. "I do not believe in a darkness so great that we cannot outrun it."

"You do not know what I have seen. These Shades are not the worst of it. They are but servants of a dark power, a wizard they call the Necromancer."

"Who is he? I have heard nothing of it. And besides, what is one wizard in all the nine lands?"

"He—if he is a man, for we do not know—is not just a wizard. He is the master of death itself. The nine lands will fall before him if he is not stopped, and only the Mystics can resist him."

Chet looked away, thinking. Then he said, "Very well. You say you must tell them, for the memory of your friend. I pledge my help in that. Let us give this warning, and then they may fight their war. We need take no part in it. We can return home, or go to any other land you wish."

Loren met his gaze. "I do not know that for certain. But if no more is required of me once I have brought these tidings, then I will go with you."

"Promise me that—"

"No," she said quickly. "I will not promise anything. I will promise only to try. That must be enough."

The moons shone in his eyes as he studied her. Finally, he nodded. "It is."

She sighed. "Good. Then let us return to the others and ride on."

"In all haste," he said. "For the sooner we reach Feldemar, the sooner I mean to ride with you away from all this, if I must tie you to my saddle to do it."

She kicked his shin, leaving him to hop painfully back through the trees to the horses.

Loren let them stop again when the moons set, and in the three hours of darkness before dawn, they slept in restless fits. Xain stayed on watch once again, but when Loren rose, she thought she might as well have stayed with him. She had found it hard to get any sleep at all.

Dawn came with no sign of pursuit, but still they rode north as quickly as they could. Now they had resumed their earlier caution, so whenever they reached a river they would ride in it for a mile or more before getting back on course.

Just after they stopped for a midday meal, Chet called them to a halt and pointed. Far above the trees ahead, they could see thin wisps of white smoke rising.

"Signs of a village," said Loren.

"I thought we turned away from your home," said Gem.

"Not *their* village, you dolt," said Annis. "Do you think there is only one in all this great expanse of forest? My tutors used to tell me there were hundreds, all within a day's ride of each other, but who never saw each other at all, more often than not. They say that living so far from any other people, the tongues they speak can change throughout the generations, so that sometimes when they meet each other they must talk with their hands."

"That is ridiculous," said Loren. "We knew of other villages within the Birchwood, and would meet with them on occasion. We never had to speak with our hands."

Annis shrugged. "Mayhap you did not go deep enough into the woods."

Xain had been grinding his teeth, but now he spoke. "Will you all be silent? Do we make for the village, or avoid it?"

"I say we go there," said Chet. "They will be friendly, and mayhap we could pay to spend the night under a roof, rather than the stars. It would be wise to replenish our supplies in any case. We lack for nothing now, but that may not always be so."

"The wise man keeps his larder full, even in times of plenty," said Xain. "Very well. Lead on, huntsman."

"Hold," said Loren. "What if the Shades come to the village after we have gone? They will learn of our course, and can guess where we mean to go."

"What if they have reached the village already?" said Gem quietly.

That gave them all pause for a chilling moment. Annis looked into the trees distrustfully.

"I doubt very much that they reached it already," said Chet. "Or if they did, they at least did not attack it, for then I think we would see darker, thicker smoke, from the burning of the homes."

"Mayhap," said Loren.

"And mayhap your other concern may be turned to advantage," said Xain. "If we meet villagers, we may tell them we are heading west. The Shades, if they come after, will think we are doubling back, or making for some other destination. It may throw them off our trail."

"It might," said Loren. "Or it could endanger the village terribly. If the Shades believe they know something of our whereabouts, they may strike the village down in wrath."

"If the Shades believe the villagers are hiding something, they will strike regardless," said Chet quietly. "Therefore let us give information willingly, and with no sign of deception, so that they may pass it on freely. That may be their greatest chance of avoiding slaughter."

She could not deny that, though it was a chilling thought. "Very well. Only let us approach the village from the east, so that we lend credence to the lie."

"A fine plan," said Gem, licking his lips. "I enjoy all that talk of wise men, but I like a full larder best."

FIFTEEN

It took them several hours more to finally reach the place, a group of homes built in a part of the wood that had been cleared for the settlement. As they came closer, approaching from the east as they had planned, Loren saw signs of the inhabitants all around—a small shed built out in the trees, a woodsman's saw and axe lying near a tree, and even some food that had been abandoned.

But when at last they came within sight of the village, they saw that all their caution had been in vain.

At first Loren saw nothing amiss, for the place was

quiet. There was no one in sight, and the only movement was the same thin white wisps of smoke they had seen from afar, rising lazily from the chimneys.

They saw the first body only moments later.

It was a woman, or had been. A wound gaped in her back, her guts spread out on the forest floor around her. She lay face-down, and had clearly been crawling.

Annis screamed before Gem's hand shot up to cover her mouth. Loren's stomach twisted, and her teeth clenched. She turned her eyes quickly away. Beside her, Chet had gone the same shade of Elf-white as he had been when they fled Northwood.

"Xain, stay here with the children," said Loren. "Chet, come with me."

"It could be dangerous," he said, still pale as a sheet.

"Someone could be alive. Mayhap they need help. Stay if you want, but I will not."

So saying, she leaped from Midnight's saddle and pulled her bow from her back. After a moment she heard the heavy *thud* of Chet's boots landing in the grass, and then his soft footsteps as he came after her. That was a relief, but still the hairs on the back of her neck rose ever higher the farther she advanced.

The village had become a charnel house, with bodies strewn about everywhere. As in Northwood, no one had been spared. Their blood had pooled together, and the bodies lay prone in it, like weary travelers cooling their brows in a river of red. Some had been maimed, their limbs lying close by, while others had been skewered or flayed open. But of the attackers there was no sign, nor were any of the homes cast down or burnt.

"Why did they leave the village standing?" whispered Chet. He walked a half-pace behind her and to the side, his staff held in his hands before him like a spear.

"Why should they not?" said Loren. "The Shades have no interest in this place. Likely they were searching for us."

"But we left them vanquished in the woods days ago."

"Only four. You and I saw more than that when they came by our campfire, and I would guess that there are many, many more in the woods. Likely they have divided themselves into several parties, roving through the Birchwood in search of us."

A sharp cry made them both jump. But they saw no threat, nor indeed any source for the voice. It sounded again.

Loren saw where it came from, and she felt the need to retch.

One of the corpses was not a corpse at all, but still alive. He was a young man, probably no older than Chet. At first she thought he was standing against the wall of one of the homes. Then she saw the metal spikes, and the angry red wounds in his hands. He was not standing. He had been nailed there.

"Get him down," she cried, running forwards. She grasped the head of one of the spikes and pulled as hard as she could. It barely budged. Chet tugged the other spike, and it came out easily. The young man sagged, screaming as all his weight was put on the other hand. The spike ripped out before they could remove it, passing all the way through the flesh. Another scream tore the air.

His eyes had been gouged out. The wounds were burned, as though with a red-hot poker. Blood gushed from his hands, but there were no more cuts on his body, only deep burns and many, many bruises. He lay there whimpering like an animal, and Loren nearly retched again as she saw both his legs were bent at odd angles.

"No more," he said. "No more, I beg of you."

"It is all right," said Loren, though the words came from nowhere, and she knew them for a lie. "They have gone. We are here to help you."

"Who are you?" He reached for her arm. "Who is that? Is that Dinna?"

"No, it . . ." Loren struggled for the words. "I am only a passerby. No one else is here. They are all . . . they are all gone."

He broke into sobs at that, though no tears came from his ruined sockets. Loren whipped off her cloak and rolled it up, gingerly lifting his head to place the cloak beneath it. The boy only kept weeping.

"Loren . . ." said Chet gravely. She knew his mind without needing to hear the words. They had no healing for these wounds. Nor would any healer in the nine kingdoms.

With a look to Chet to silence him, she gently put her hand over the boy's. His fingers tried to close over hers, but the pain of his mangled hand was too much, and he gave up.

"Who did this?" she asked him, her voice soft and gentle.

"Loren!" repeated Chet, this time in astonishment. But he fell silent as she gave him another hard look.

"They were soldiers," said the boy. His voice gurgled a little in his throat. "I do not know. They had weapons, and armor. Their captain was a beast."

Loren felt a chill of premonition creep over her. "What did he look like? Was he dark of skin?"

"Yes, dark as the night," said the boy. "He called himself Rogan. He asked us for a girl, a girl in a black cloak, and . . . and something else."

Loren's throat had gone bone-dry. She swiped the back of her sleeves across her eyes and went on in a shaking voice. "What then? How did the fight begin?"

"There was no fighting," said the boy, his sobs deepening. "He gathered all of us together here. We told him we knew nothing of the girl, and he started killing us. We tried to run, but they chased us down. All but the children."

She and Chet looked at each other. "What did he do with the children?" said Chet.

"He took them," said the boy. "He said he was their father now. Then some tried to fight him, those whose children he tried to take, but he and his men killed them, too. He killed them, and when I tried to help, they . . ."

The boy bit his lip and sucked in his breath, but then he broke down and began to cry again. Loren put her hand on his shoulder, one of the few places on his body the Shades had not mangled, the only comfort she could think to give him.

"I told him I did not know where she was, that none of us knew where she was," he said as he wept. "Finally he told me he believed me. But he did not stop. He never stopped."

Eventually his cries subsided. Loren leaned forwards, fearing he had died. But his lips moved again, barely able to whisper now.

"Who are you?"

Loren could not answer past the tightness of her throat.

"Are you the girl?"

She would have given anything not to have to answer him. But she could not stop herself.

"Yes."

"The one he sought?"

"Yes. I am sorry. I am sorry."

He turned his head away from her. A short while later, his chest shuddered in a breath, and then he lay still.

Chet came to Loren's side and put a hand on her shoulder. She threw it off and walked away. He let her go, slowly turning and going back to the others. Loren walked out of the village on the west side, to the edge of the forest, shaking as silent tears ran down her face.

In fury she stared off between the trees. She wished they were there, Rogan and the Shades and all of them. Let them fight her here and now, and be done with it. Who knew but that villages just like this one were being ransacked all throughout the forest? What death had she rained upon her homeland by her reckless flight into this wood?

A small voice, a voice of reason that sounded very like Jordel, told her that she could not hold herself responsible for this. But the white-hot anger in her gut refused to listen.

She stayed there, alone, until the tears passed and the sun had nearly set. Then she went back to the others, circling wide around the village so she would not have to pass through the death and blood once more. They had retreated into the trees, and were sitting silently in a circle. The children were staring at the ground, while Chet watched nothing at all. Even Xain had a grim look, his mouth twisted with more than its usual bitterness.

"We will rest here for the night," she said. "The Shades have come already. They will not be back, at least not for a time. We will ride on before first light."

"Should we . . . I mean to say, the corpses . . ." said Gem.

"We cannot bury them all, not without spending many days here."

"The Shades will have done this in other places," said Chet.

"I imagine they will have."

"Can we not warn them? Or can we not, at least, give the Shades reason to pursue us instead of killing innocents who have never even heard our names?"

"How do you mean to stop them, Chet?" said Loren, growing angry. "We could march into their midst and offer ourselves up for sacrifice. But as long as we are outside their grasp, they will hunt for us wherever they think we might be found."

"So you mean to let them?"

"We do not let them do anything," said Xain. "Did we invite them into the Birchwood? Did we tell them where to find this village? Did we tell them to put these people to the sword?"

Chet shook his head. "There must be something we can do."

"There is not," said Loren. "As is too often the case, we can only flee, and survive, to someday deliver a greater stroke that might secure victory."

Loren thought of when she and Jordel had left the city of Wellmont under siege. Others had begged the Mystic to stay, to aid in the defense of the city. He had refused, and when pressed, he had grown angry. At the time, Loren had thought him somewhat heartless. Now, at last, she understood. The wrath was a mask, a bandage meant to cover the gaping wound of his guilt. Doubtless Jordel would have fought upon the very walls of Wellmont, and given his life in defense of the city without a second thought. But he had known, or suspected, that a greater battle lay just over the horizon, and so he needed Xain to survive. How long must he have traveled the nine lands with that burden, letting ill deeds go unchecked in the service of stopping a far greater evil?

Loren looked at them all, at Chet and Xain and the children, their faces turned to her, angry and hurt and expectant.

"I will take the first watch. Rest, all of you. Even you, Xain. Tomorrow is another long ride to an uncertain end."

SIXTEEN

The days afterwards passed like bitter months of winter: cold, reluctant, and lingering in the mind long after passing. No one spoke often, nor laughed, nor told any jokes, for the memories of the village in the forest plagued them. They slept only a few hours at a time, when neither the sun nor the moons were there to guide their way. Often as they pressed on, their heads would sag against their chests for a moment, only to snap upwards at a jostle in the road.

Xain's condition was growing slowly worse, and though Loren tried not to pay it too much mind, she could not ignore it entirely. Fortunately, it was not as bad as it had been in the Greatrocks. Then he had been driven to madness, half the time forgetting who and where he was, and the other half filled with a murderous rage that he sought to unleash upon Loren and the others. This was more of a quiet wasting away, a slow breaking down of his body. Loren often saw him wincing as he dismounted, and his skin had begun to bruise easily at even a light touch. But he spoke no word of complaint, and always matched the pace Loren set, and so she kept her thoughts on the road ahead.

Five days after they found the village slaughtered in the Birchwood, they came at last out the northern side of the forest and down into the kingdom of Dorsea. Early on that day, Loren noticed that the trees were sparser and shorter, and seemed less hearty than those in the south. The ground turned from soft loam and grass to a brown and brittle dirt, which kicked up much dust that took long to settle.

Dorsea itself, when they reached it, was much the same. The land was not quite mountainous, but rolling and hilly as far as the eye could see, browner than it was green. What vegetation there was came in small, scrubby bushes and spindly trees that sucked what water they could from the earth.

"To the west and to the south, Dorsea is much like Selvan," said Xain. "But here, it is half a desert. The land may be tilled, but not easily, and so the people are as hard and stubborn as the land upon which they feed themselves. Still, adversity has made them somewhat kinder than their western and southern brethren who, like all fat and happy people, begin to turn their eyes outwards to what more they can claim for their own."

"I know much of Dorsean greed," said Loren. "It is what brings them to war with Selvan, over and over again." Chet nodded firmly.

"You speak with many dramatics, and little truth," said Annis, rolling her eyes. "Why, I have met many merchants from Dorsea, and members of the Dorsean royal family, and they were no more or less crafty than any other inhabitants of the High King's Seat. Those from Selvan included. You are a gem among women, Loren, and you seem a decent enough fellow, Chet, but you must know that not all people of your kingdom are so good and kind-hearted as you."

"It is no less foolish to claim great knowledge of all people, when you have spent all your life upon the Seat," said Xain. "It could be said, rather, that the wealthy and the powerful are much the same from one kingdom to the next, though the people they rule may vary wildly. But this is idle philosophy, and we have little time for it. Let us press on."

Now they were in open territory, and a land about which Loren knew little. Xain took to guiding them, for as he told them, he had traveled Dorsea well as a young man.

"Do not tell me you hail from this kingdom?" said Annis in surprise.

"It is hard to say where I hail from," said Xain, "especially since my first answer would have been the Seat until recently, and they will no longer claim me as their own. But as for where I was born, that is Wadeland to the east, though I left it as a young boy when my parents found I had the gift of elementalism."

"And how did they find that out?" said Gem, leaning forwards with interest. "Were you bandying about the horses one day, when you accidentally set the stable boy on fire?"

Xain chuckled—an odd sound from him these days, and one Loren welcomed. "Nothing so crude as that, though I can hardly blame you for thinking so, since you are a commoner and know little of the practices of the wealthy. When a child of royalty nears his sixth year, he is required by law to see a representative of the Academy. Wealthy families, even those who are not related to the nobility at all, or only distantly, such as my parents, pay in coin for such a representative to visit them. These representatives know how to test for the gift, and they put the child through a series of trials, meant to discover if any of the four branches have presented themselves in any strength."

"I took the trials," said Annis, sounding as if she were trying very hard not to boast. "They found nothing. What do they do, I wonder, if a child shows the gift of more than one type of magic?"

"That is impossible," said Xain. "Wizards are gifted with only one—even the most powerful among us."

With those words he fixed Loren with a look. She thought, as he must be thinking, of the Lifemage and the Necromancer, and the two branches of magic that had lay hidden for centuries. How did the wizards of the Academy detect them, if they even could? She doubted if they would ever know.

SEVENTEEN

THEY MADE CAMP ON THE WIDE PLAINS OF DORSEA
that night. They found a crag of a hill in the midst of
the flatlands, and settled down to the north of it, so
that it might block the light of their campfire from
anyone who would follow them out of the Birchwood.
Loren knew there might be Shades in Dorsea already,
and they might be seen from the west or north. But as
they had seen no sign of their pursuers for days, the
warmth of the fire seemed worth the risk.

Chet took the first watch. Loren had half expected
Xain to volunteer, as he so often did now, but the wiz-

ard looked weary and worn. Almost as soon as they had built a fire he curled up in his bedroll and slept. Loren hoped that was a hopeful sign. When he had suffered from the magestone sickness in the Greatrocks, he had gone through a time of great anguish and pain, followed by a bone-deep exhaustion. If he had come to that point already, it meant his recovery from now on would be less taxing.

Loren's thoughts were still much occupied with their fight against the Shades in the Birchwood, and the village full of corpses, and she feared that sleep might well elude her. But it was a warm night for autumn, and the soft glow of the fire quickly lulled her off to a deep slumber, one without dreams or dark thoughts. She woke feeling refreshed, more so than she had in all the many miles of their journey since Northwood, and as relaxed as if she had spent the night on one of Mag's softest mattresses.

Then she saw the moons in the sky above her, and realized with a start that it was still the middle of the night.

She looked about in confusion. Had a noise woken her? If so, it was gone now. Only dying embers remained of their fire, and the others were all curled in their blankets. The world was silent, save a faint whisper on the air and far-off birdsong.

When she lifted her head, she saw Chet sitting by a rock near the edge of their camp. His head was bent down into his chest in slumber, and her mouth twisted in annoyance. It was foolish, and she would have words with him—but in the morning. For now, she would simply take the watch and let him sleep. They were all of them weary.

But when she rose, she saw the Elves.

There were six of them, standing glowing in the starlight, only a few paces away from her sleeping friends. She knew them at once from the tales she had heard all her life. Those tales were told in quiet whispers in the night, for it was said that to speak of the creatures too often was to invite their wrath. The stories always came from survivors, of which there were precious few. When humans came upon Elves in the nine lands, more often than not they did not survive to speak of it.

They were all of different hues, but shared white clothing and the same raven-black hair, which hung long, down to the smalls of their backs, wafting gently with every movement. They wore no armor and carried no weapons, clad only in the white robes, the edges of which frilled and floated as though underwater. Their eyes were as pale as their clothing, a thin and ghostly gossamer with no pupils or irises, so that it was hard to tell where they were looking.

Except that they were looking at Loren, and somehow, in the deepest part of her soul, she *knew* it.

She was frozen, unable to move so much as a muscle. What should she do? What *could* she do? Her first thought was to rouse the others, to get to the horses as quickly as they could and ride for their lives. They were powerless if the Elves should choose to harm them—even Xain, were he at the height of his power, and he was far from that now. Elves could not be reasoned with; they could not be talked out of slaughter if that was their intent. Indeed, so far as Loren knew, no one had ever spoken to Elves, nor knew the words that they used.

But she and her friends could not run, not now. They could never move fast enough. Even if Loren left the others to save herself, the Elves could be upon her in an instant. They would kill her, and all the rest of them, if that was their whim. And she could do nothing to stop it.

A thought came into her mind. *The dagger.*

It was on her belt—she never removed it, even when she slept. But she immediately dismissed that furtive instinct, for it was ridiculous. Mighty knights and kings had tried to battle Elves, but none ever survived. What could such a tiny knife do against them?

The dagger.

This time the thought came more insistent, like a shout in her mind. And with a start, Loren realized that the idea was not her own. The Elves had given it to her.

She studied them. They had not shifted so much as a muscle. Only their clothing and their hair moved, wafting gently as though in a breeze, though the night held no wind. They had not spoken. The words had come directly from their minds to her own.

Loren reached for her waist, desperately hoping that this was not a terrible mistake. If they thought she meant to fight them, they would kill her for certain. As quickly as she could, she drew the dagger and then flipped it about, holding it by the blade, hilt forwards. One tentative step she took towards them, then another. When she was a few paces away, she knelt and placed the dagger on the ground.

Then they moved at last—or at least, one of them did. It stepped away from the others and came forwards, and watching the movement of its limbs was like watching a courtly dancer. The Elf was pure grace, and ease, and at the same time it imparted a terrifying power. It held out a hand, its fingers curled as though around the dagger's hilt. Loren pictured that hand circling her throat, and she quailed with fear. Then the dagger appeared, as if from nowhere, in the Elf's hand. If it had reached for the blade, or moved it with some magic, Loren had not seen it. One moment the dagger was not there, and then . . . it *was*.

The Elf turned to the others and lifted the dagger. It flashed in the light of both moons, which were directly overhead, and Loren thought she saw the silver glow of the Elves reflected in its steel as well. And then the Elves began to sing.

Loren burst into tears. Her knees failed her, and she fell to the ground in a heap. She buried her face in her hands, wailing, giving no heed to the sound of her voice or whether it might wake the others. The sound of the song was too beautiful: incomprehensible, for it was sung in no tongue she had ever heard; soul-shattering, for Loren felt that when it ended its grace would break her mind and leave her wishing always to hear it again. She felt as though it were transforming her from the inside out, changing something deep within her, something beyond explanation or hope of memory.

The song stopped. Loren lay there, still a wreck, aching to hear just one more note. And then, though they had sung to the dagger in chorus, as if in reverence, the Elf took the blade by the tip and dropped it in the dirt.

The dagger. The thought came to her again, and this time Loren knew it for the Elf's. She struggled to hands and knees; the thought of standing seemed more than her body could bear. Slowly she crawled forwards, searching the ground for the blade. But she was too far beyond the fire, and her eyes were filled with tears besides, and she could not find it.

A hand gripped her shoulder, and where it touched her she felt an incredible warmth. It was not a warmth of the body, but of the soul, and where it ran through her it filled her with hope and courage. But the hand was uncaring, uncompromising, and it lifted her to her feet without waiting for her to act. She found herself standing before the Elf, looking into its gossamer-white eyes, and then she realized that the glow in those eyes was the same glow she saw in Xain whenever he reached for his magic.

This is the end, she thought. The Elf would kill her now, for she had moved too slowly. She only hoped it would leave the others be.

The dagger, came the thought, impatient. The Elf was holding it now, its hilt towards her.

She found her hand wrapped around the hilt, though she had not meant to move it. The Elf released the blade, and then her shoulder, and the world seemed darker and more horrible than it had before she felt its touch.

The stones. And now in her mind's eyes she saw the magestones, the small packet wrapped in brown cloth that rested in one of the pockets of her cloak.

"What?" she said out loud.

She caught a movement—just the barest twitch of a muscle in the Elf's jaw. Then it seized her again. Loren wanted to burst out in hysterical laughter at the feeling of it, the power and the joy. But the Elf, uncaring, reached into her cloak and seized the packet. From the brown cloth it drew one of the stones, and then broke it in half to hold before her eyes.

The stones.

Loren took the stone between thumb and forefinger, gingerly. And in her mind's eye, she saw herself putting the stone in her mouth, crunching down upon it, and swallowing the dust. Her eyes widened with fear, and she thought of Xain.

"No," she stammered. "I cannot—"

The Elf seized her throat. She felt its skin upon her

own, no longer dampened by the cloth that had protected her when it took her shoulder. Her mind threatened to collapse upon itself. She saw herself, *all* of herself, the bone and sinew and flesh beneath the skin, and a bright white light at the center of it all. But it was all of it distorted and misshapen, turned about so that she could see every angle of it at once. And from each part Loren saw what looked like a thin thread, a silvery wisp of *something* that ran off back and forth in all directions, in *every* direction at once and none of them, and through time as quickly as through the many leagues they had traveled, and would travel still. With the sight came *knowing,* and she knew that she beheld the skeins of time, laid out before and behind her, and all of the many twists and turns that had led her to where she stood now. And farther, beyond the place where the camp lay, she saw those threads touching others, one at a time and then great clusters all in a group, and twisting endlessly around each other in a pattern that covered all the nine lands.

The twisted, broken thing that was Loren's body twitched, and from its mouth croaked the words, "I cannot . . . I cannot . . ."

Then the Elf placed the magestone in her mouth and released her, and the world was as it had always been.

Loren swallowed hard on instinct, and she felt the half-magestone slide down her throat unbroken. She gasped, for she *felt* it creeping through her. She thought it might be like a black corruption, or some great sickness sliding through her veins. But it was nothing so terrible. It was . . . a sharpening. Her mind had been a dull blade all her life, and the magestone slid through her like a whetstone, honing its edge.

With a start she realized she could see all the world around her, clearly as if it were day—except that she could see *better* now. She saw the pores on blades of grass, and the threads that made up Gem's bedroll, and the hairs that clung stubbornly to Xain's thinning scalp. Although it was a poor kind of sight next to the vision of the Elves, this was something her mind could comprehend, and she found it beautiful.

She looked at the Elves in wonder, and the glow that poured from them seemed thrice as lovely as before. But now their eyes were black, black like Xain's when he had cast darkfire, and she quailed under their gaze.

The Nightblade, came the thought in her mind. *The one who walks with death.*

Then their eyes turned from her. All of them looked skywards, to where the moons continued their long path across the sky, west towards the horizon where they would finally set. As one the Elves turned, though Loren did not see their feet move, and they began to wander off into the west. Back and forth they strayed, but always westerly, and though they did not seem to hurry, they were out of sight beyond the horizon in what seemed like no time at all.

When the last glow of their presence faded from

sight, Loren went suddenly weak and fell to the grass again. She still felt the glamour of their presence in her mind, but without it there to sustain her, she was exhausted. What was more, the night vision of the magestones had faded. The world was black around her again, black save for the silver moonslight—a light she already knew would remind her, for the rest of her days, of the Elves.

At the sound of her dropping to the ground, Chet started awake where he sat against the rock. His head jerked, his eyes blinking furiously, and then he beheld her.

"Loren!" he said. He tried to rise, but he was still groggy and nearly toppled over. "I fell asleep. Sky above curse me, I am sorry. I hardly thought myself tired, but then a deep weariness overcame me, as though . . . what is the matter?"

She looked at him, and only then realized that tears still trickled down her face, leaking from the corners of her eyes to leave their tracks upon her cheeks. Hastily she wiped at them with her sleeve.

"Nothing," she said. "Nothing. Go, sleep in earnest. I will take the watch."

"I have slept enough—too much, it seems." He still looked worried, and he peered at her in the night as though trying to read her expression. "I can keep the watch, for a while longer at any rate."

"No. I cannot sleep now. Rest yourself. I . . . I wish to be alone for a while."

She could tell he was still worried, for he did not look away from her for quite a while. But he did not argue, only turned and went to his bedroll. Soon he was asleep like the rest, and Loren marked that Gem's snores had resumed, loud as ever.

Loren took the other half of the magestone the Elf had fed her. She put it between her lips and bit down, and then swallowed, though her stomach clenched with fear to do so. But the magestone went down the same as last time. Only now, she saw nothing, and the night was dark as ever.

Brow furrowing, she reached into her cloak for the magestone packet again. But in reaching for it, her hand brushed against the dagger's hilt once more. The night sprang into stark daylight, a vision beyond vision where even the horizon seemed near.

Her hand jerked back in surprise, and the vision vanished. She stared at the dagger a moment. Then she took it again, and could see as bright as day.

Jordel had told her that her dagger held many magicks, and one day he would teach them to her. He had died before he could teach her this one. But had he meant to teach it to her in the first place? Did he know the dagger held this power, or was it some secret of the Elves? Or had Jordel known, but withheld it, because of the magestones?

Would they act on Loren the same way they had acted on Xain?

That thought came with its own terrors, and she

shoved the magestones as deep in her pocket as she could. Then she pulled them out and stood, intending to throw them into the darkness. But at the last second she stopped. Mayhap she was wrong. Mayhap the magestones would have no ill effects, if she was not a mage. Mayhap the dagger itself protected her.

She could not know, not at least for a while yet. And until she knew, it seemed foolish to throw away such a great amount of wealth—and a great amount of power.

Loren put the magestones back in her cloak and leaned against the rock once more. She put her hand on the dagger, then removed it, over and over again, watching the world turn from night to day each time. After a time the vision faded, and she saw nothing more with the dagger in hand than she did without. But her thoughts went on wild journeys long afterwards, recalling all she had seen when the Elf touched her, and the words it had put into her mind.

Nightblade. The one who walks with death.

Those words stayed with her the longest.

EIGHTEEN

Loren woke Chet an hour before dawn, when the sky was just beginning to grey. He roused slowly, but when he moved to wake the others, she stopped him.

"Come with me," she said. "I have something to tell you, and I would not tell the others. Not yet, at any rate. Come."

He did as she asked, though she could see the questions in his eyes. Loren led him up the side of the hill, until they sat on a flat shelf in its northwest side. From there they could see the camp down below, and the open plains for many leagues to the north and west.

All the land was empty, as far as they could see, though Loren wondered if she would see anything different if she was to eat another magestone. But that was something she was not yet ready to test.

Loren told Chet everything that had happened, as best she could remember it—for already the memory had begun to fade, a grey and hazy thing, like a dream half-remembered. But all she had to do was recall the Elves' black eyes when she had eaten the magestones, and she knew with certainty that they had been real.

When she first mentioned them, Chet went white as the Elves' robes had been, and made the sign of the plow over his heart. Loren doubted that would have helped, for she guessed that the Elves cared little for such superstitions.

She did not tell him of the magestones, for she had never told him that she still had a packet of them with her. But she told him all the rest of it, and how it had felt when the Elf touched her, which she said was because she had not fetched the dagger quickly enough. By the time she finished her tale, Chet was looking down at the ground between his feet in thought. Loren waited a while, but when he still said nothing, she began to feel uncomfortable.

"You must promise not to tell the others," she said.

He looked up in surprise. "Why not?"

She paused, for in truth she had not thought overmuch about it—she only knew she did not want to tell them. "I am not certain. Only it feels like something that was for me, and me alone."

He chuckled. "Why tell me, then?"

"I had to tell *someone*," she said, sighing. "The memory fades even now, against my wishes. I was terrified for every moment of it, and feared that we might all of us be killed where we lay. Yet at the same time it was beautiful, like something from one of Bracken's tales, and I would not be the only one to know it happened. And somehow . . . I feel that if I were to tell them, they might not believe me."

"I believe you," he said quietly.

"I hoped you would. Come. We have rested long enough, and should put as many leagues behind us as we can."

They went down the hill again and woke the others. But when Loren shook Xain awake, his gaze locked with hers.

"What happened to you?" he said, eyes wide with wonder.

"What?" she said, feeling a chill run down her spine. "Nothing."

"Your eyes . . . something is different about them," he said slowly. He sat up straighter and peered at her more intently. "Something I feel I should recognize, but I cannot."

Loren swallowed, and thought she could feel Chet's eyes on her back. "Nothing," she said. "Mayhap it is a symptom of the magestone sickness."

Xain stared a moment longer without answering. Then he sighed and turned away. "Mayhap. I am weary, and feel as if I have hardly slept a wink."

When she turned, Loren saw that Chet was indeed looking at her with worry. But she smiled at him, and he looked away, and they readied for the day's travel.

The ride went swiftly. They turned their horses due east around midday, for the land seemed flat and easy, while to the north and south it was rocky and harsh. Three more days they rode this way, and each night Loren went to sleep thinking of the Elves, and woke to memories of their faces in the moonslight. The party gave a wide berth to any villages or farms they spied from afar; doubtless someone would mark their passing, but they wanted to leave as little information in their wake as they could.

On the fourth day, Loren found Xain studying their saddlebags with worry. Her earlier optimism about his recovery seemed to have been justified, for he was slowly regaining his strength. But now he was looking at their supplies, and seemed displeased.

"We do not have enough to reach the coast," said Xain.

"We thought we might not."

"That worry was far off when we were still in the Birchwood. Now it presses close. I would counsel that we should stop at the next village we see, only I fear that if the Shades still follow us, it could freshen the trail."

"We have seen neither hide nor hair of them for days now," said Gem, piping up from behind Annis on their horse. "And I would welcome a change from the endless, unbroken brown of this kingdom, and the wilting scrub brush that covers its landscape." He had taken to complaining day and night about Dorsea, never tiring of pointing out its flaws when compared to the lush green of Selvan, until Loren had to grit her teeth to keep from cuffing him.

"He is right, Loren," said Annis. "And I try not to complain, but I too would welcome a stop. This road is lonely and dirty and boring."

"Very well," said Loren. "We shall rest in the next town we see. Mayhap we will even spend the night in an inn."

"It will seem poor compared to Mag's," said Chet quietly.

They all rode in silence for some time after that.

They did not have to wait long, for later that afternoon they saw a small cluster of brown houses near the horizon. Loren stowed her black cloak in the saddlebag, for it was far too distinctive. But despite misgivings about the wisdom of such a stop, Loren found herself nudging a bit more speed out of Midnight. The mare seemed to catch her mood. The town sat on a small stream that headed to the northeast, and likely ran all the way to the ocean many, many leagues away.

The sun was nearing the horizon as they reached the place. From a ways off they saw some folk at the town's western end, waiting, or so it seemed. But once they got close enough to be seen more clearly, the villagers turned and shuffled off back to their homes. As they left, Loren saw weapons in their hands: staves and simple cudgels, no blades or spears. It gave her an unquiet feeling.

"Did anyone else find that odd?" Chet said, and she knew he had seen the same thing.

"Again you forget that we are in Dorsea now," said Xain. "Villages and towns cannot afford to be so friendly as in Selvan. And we would not do well to mention it, either, for that and your voices would mark us as foreigners."

The village was a small place, but a road ran through it parallel to the river, and there was an inn at the southwestern end. They caught a few glances as they rode past the homes, but the villagers seemed filled with curiosity rather than suspicion. The inn was low and squat, only a single storey high, with the rooms around the outside of the building and all their doors leading straight to the common room at the center. A fat and bearded innkeeper greeted them cordially at the door.

"Evening, good folk," he said. "You will need rooms for the night, I imagine?"

"We will," said Loren. "And stalls for the horses, if you have the room."

"That we do, though you have a couple of fine steeds there. Likely they are used to finer quarters than ours."

Annis smiled down at him. "We value hospitality more than feather pillows, and yours seems in plentiful supply, good sir."

The man grinned wide at that, and he gave Loren a low bow. "Always a kindness to have guests of such fair words under our roof. My boy Ham will take your steeds. Get yourselves inside for a pint."

They dismounted, and Loren raised a questioning eyebrow. Annis smiled, suddenly shy. "Dorseans hold hospitality as a high virtue, and disdain finery, which they see as unnecessary luxury," she said. "Or so I was taught upon the Seat."

"Mayhap you should do all our talking while we are here," said Chet. "He grinned wide enough to split his head open."

Annis ducked her head, cheeks darkening with embarrassment. They found a table inside, and soon the innkeeper came personally to bring them supper. After they had eaten for a while, and had drunk of his ale, which was fine enough (though nowhere near so good as Mag's) he asked if he might sit with them for a time, and they happily obliged. He introduced himself as Crastus, and did not ask for their names in turn, though they had prepared false ones.

"Where might you be headed? If my asking is no discourtesy, I mean," he said once he had settled down and taken a swig from his mug.

"Southeast, for the Seat," said Loren, for they had discussed this story before they entered the town. "Bridget here has a cousin in a courtly position who means to take her for a handmaiden. We are friends of her father's, and promised to see her safely to her destination."

"I have family north and west of here," said Crastus. "From where do you hail? Mayhap I know the place."

"It is only a tiny village, many leagues north of the King's road and deep within Feldemar," said Loren smoothly. "Too small a place to warrant a name."

"Like our own village," said Crastus. "Do you know the family Mennet? They are my kin, and are from around about those parts."

"Mennet?" said Loren, Gem, and Chet all at once.

Annis' eyes widened, and she pursed her lips. With a quiet look to Loren, she urged them all to silence. "I have met many Mennets through my father, though it pains me to say I cannot remember their names," she said. "You must forgive my friends their surprise. They are travelers, as you can plainly hear by their tone, and not from Dorsea by birth."

At that, Crastus gave them all sharp looks. "I should say not. Were I a wagering man, I would lay a gold weight that you three come from Selvan. The dark fellow there has hardly said a word, so I would make no guess as to him."

"From Selvan stock, but born in Feldemar," said

Annis, cutting off Gem, who had begun to open his mouth. Loren kicked the boy under the table. "And certainly they hold no truck with that kingdom now, what with the goings-on in Wellmont."

Crastus eyed them a moment more. But then he shrugged and went to his mug again. "Ah, it is no worry of mine. As long as the fighting stays far, far away, I care nothing for it. Though you might wish to keep your words to yourselves, for some hold more tightly to their kingly bonds—more tightly, I would say, than seems reasonable."

"Thank you for the warning," said Loren. "Is that why we saw some men waiting for us when we rode in, bearing weapons?"

"No, that is something else entire," said Crastus, leaning in to speak in a hushed voice. "Some say there have been Elves sighted west of here."

The others' eyes all widened—all but Loren, who tried to keep her face calm. From the corner of her eye she saw Chet looking at her.

"Elves!" said Gem, giddy. "Truly?"

"I would rid myself of that smile if I were you, boy," said Crastus. "Elves are no playthings for children such as yourself."

"I have heard they are beautiful—though, to be certain, few enough have seem them and lived to describe it," said Gem. He had done nothing to follow the innkeeper's advice, for his smile remained.

"Aye, and that is because they will kill you without

a second thought," said Crastus. "I pray they stay far, far away from here, that I do."

Loren cleared her throat and took another bite of her dinner. She had become aware that Xain, too, was looking at her now, and his brow had furrowed in thought.

The conversation turned to other things, and soon Loren rustled them all from their tables to go into town and get the supplies they had come for. Food they bought, and oats for the horses, and from the river they filled their waterskins to bursting. All these they put in their room, ready to be packed and loaded in the morning.

Night had fallen by then, and they met back in the common room for a drink before bed. Crastus joined them once more, and began to tell them a story of a time the king of Dorsea himself had come through the town, and tried Crastus' ale and proclaimed it the best he had had in years. The innkeeper was a fair tale-spinner, better at it at any rate than his ale was to drink, and Loren was leaning back in her chair enjoying the story when a man poked his head in the front door and gave a sharp whistle. Some rose from their seats and moved to the door outside.

"What is that?" said Xain, eyes suddenly sharp.

"Another party spotted coming in," said Crastus. "Probably just more travelers like yourselves, but half these boys will go and fetch their weapons expecting Elves. As though swords would help if indeed those demons decided to put our town to the torch."

He went on with his story, but Loren gave Chet a worried look. It might be more travelers, or it might indeed be the Elves. What if Loren had done something wrong since they saw her last, something she could not understand? From the look in his eyes, Chet seemed to understand something of her worry.

"You will forgive me, Crastus, but I think I shall take a stroll for the night air," she said, standing from her chair. "I have had more of your fine ale than is good for my head, and I wish tomorrow's ride to be a pleasant one."

Crastus looked somewhat miffed that she would miss the end of his story, but he waved them off, and she and Chet walked into the darkness. Quickly they made their way through the city streets to the west, and soon came to the edge of the town. There stood many of the villagers, more than had waited for them when they came riding in, and all of them held their weapons at the ready. Loren felt her pulse quicken, but she could not see beyond them yet. Grabbing Chet's sleeve, she pulled him to the side, moving around the men so she could see into the west.

She did not see Elves, or at least not the silvery glow she had seen from them before. At first she saw only torches, like a dozen orange eyes coming at them through the darkness. When the torches neared, she finally saw the figures carrying them—and then blanched, for they were soldiers on horseback, wearing armor and clothing of blue and grey.

NINETEEN

"Shades," she whispered.

"We have to go," said Chet, and she could hear the panic in his voice.

"This village . . . the people . . ." said Loren. But she did not know what to do. Certainly they could not do anything from here, without their horses and the others. "We must tell Xain and the children. Come."

Now they ran as fast as they could, feet pounding along the dirt streets, their cloaks flying behind them in the night. They nearly ran over one or two passersby, who shouted after them, but they never slowed to listen. The front door of the inn slammed into the wall as they threw it open, and everyone in the common room fell silent and turned to look at them.

"Riders," said Loren. "Dozens of them, with arms and armor, coming from the west."

She found Xain's gaze and held it, and he understood at once. He rose from the table, while Crastus stood and began shouting orders at the townsfolk in the room. Loren and the others ran to their room for their supplies, while outside the Dorsean villagers mustered themselves in case there was a fight.

"They found us," said Gem, voice quivering.

Annis took his hand. "That is unlikely. If they were so close behind us, we should have seen them days ago. Likely these riders came from the south, or some other direction entirely. They do not know we are here, and will remain ignorant if we leave at once."

"That is our course," said Loren. "Bring your things to the horses as quickly as you can. Gem and Annis, see to mine, and help Xain with his as well. Mount up as quickly as you can, and ride east."

Chet gave her a look. "You speak as if you will not be with us."

"I will be just behind you," said Loren. "I must find out what the Shades know—if indeed they are aware we are here already. Once I find that out, I will come running out the eastern end of the town, and you had best have Midnight ready for me."

"That is far too dangerous," said Annis. "And it

is a worthless piece of information next to your life. Whether they know we are here or not, our path seems the same: ride for the east until our horses drop."

"It makes all the difference," said Loren. "If they know where we are, we must learn how, or we will never evade them. And there is no time to argue this. To the horses, *now.*"

She went running from the room, but Chet was on her heels. When she turned to him, he shook his head. "There is no time to argue with me, either. I will come with you. I am as sneaky as you ever were, and two are safer than one."

Loren nodded, and they went off. First Loren went to Midnight and took her bow from the saddle, strung it, and slung it on her back. Then she led Chet back the way they had come through the village. By the time they reached the west end again, the Shades had come to a halt just beyond the buildings. There were more than she had seen before, scores and scores of them.

She shook in her boots as she recognized Rogan at their head.

Chet joined her in cover behind the edge of a house, Loren thanking her stars that they had not been seen. Rogan sat high in his saddle, his horse covered with thick plates of armor the same as he was. His helm left his face exposed, but chain mail hung from the back of it to cover his neck. She remembered the tattoo on the back of Trisken's neck—the tattoo that had kept him alive, and which Jordel had destroyed in order to kill him, though at terrible cost.

They had missed some words between the Shades and the villagers already, but now Rogan was speaking. "We will not turn back. All my life I have heard fine tales of Dorsean hospitality, and I will not be greeted with anything less. Or would you have me spread tales of your dishonor to the neighboring towns?"

"We have no room for so many," said a man from the village. He was somewhat older than Loren, though still young and hale, and he stood forwards from the rest of them as though he were their leader. "If you must rest for the night, we shall not begrudge you that—only do it beyond the town's borders, in the fields outside."

Rogan studied him. Tall and strong the man might have been, but before Rogan he looked like a child. The Shade captain rolled his shoulders, and when he spoke it was as though he had not heard.

"We are looking for someone," he said. "A girl. She is young, and clad in a black cloak. If you came close enough, you might remark upon her eyes, for they are a bright shade of green. Has anyone seen such a girl?"

There was quiet for a moment, and some of the villagers shifted on their feet. Loren saw Crastus among them, and his boy Ham standing next to him, look at each other. But no one spoke any word.

"Come now," said Rogan. "She would have passed through recently, no more than a few days ago, if she came here at all. Certainly someone would have remarked upon her passing?"

"As I said, take your horses back out into the plains and stay the night there," said the man who had spoken before. "If you wish, some of your men can come and buy supplies in the town."

Rogan pursed his lips. Then, with more speed than Loren would have guessed from his massive frame, he slid from the saddle. The townsfolk took half a step back at that. He came forwards, and Loren saw the axe slung across his back. It was huge—the head of it was at least half again as wide as Loren's torso, and she doubted she could wrap her hands around the haft.

The villagers were backing up slowly now, but the man at their head did not falter. Instead, he took a step forwards and hefted the club in his hand. Even he must have realized how frail he looked before Rogan, but he did not turn away.

"Leave here, now!" he said, and his voice was strong. "You are not welcome!"

Rogan's hand flew to the haft of his axe, and it sprang from his back in a flourish. He did not strike the man with it, but swung it into both hands and sent the butt into his chest with a *thunk*. The man fell to the ground, gasping, and Rogan seized the back of his collar. He dragged him up to his knees, and then brought the axe around again until the blade was pressed to his throat.

"I will ask again, since hospitality has failed us all,"

said Rogan. "I look for a girl in a black cloak, with green eyes. Who has seen her?"

The rest looked at each other, and for a moment Loren thought they might answer. But Rogan did not wait. The axe jerked, and the man's throat spilled blood out into the dirt. Some in the crowd screamed, and they all drew back as though from a burning flame.

"Take the town," said Rogan. "Collect the children."

Chet was tugging at her arm, but Loren stood unmoving. She felt the urge to run with him, to flee to the others and leap atop Midnight's saddle and ride off into the night. But these people would die under the swords of the Shades, and all to find her.

She remembered the boy they had found in the Birchwood. *Are you her?* he had asked her, for he could not see Loren through the sockets where his eyes had been.

Loren threw off Chet's arm and stepped out into the open, drawing her bow from her back. "Rogan!" she cried. "I am here!"

Everything stopped at once. The villagers looked at her in fear, their faces orange in the light of their torches. But Rogan looked at her like a wolf looking at a meal, eyes glittering.

"Loren, of the family Nelda," he said, almost sweetly. "We meet at last. I have eagerly awaited this moment."

"Let them be," said Loren. "Whatever your quarrel with me, they are no part of it."

"Whatever our quarrel?" said Rogan, and then he threw back his head with a laugh. "Loren, do not feign ignorance with me. It says you think ill of my wisdom, and that is the height of bad manners. Do you think we would let you live to reveal what you know to the Mystics who hold your leash?"

"No one controls me. No one commands me," said Loren. "And you cannot win, whatever you might do here. Word of your coming will already have spread through Selvan at least, and has likely already reached the Mystics' ears. They will find you, and crush you in your infancy, before your plans ever bear fruit."

All of Rogan's false courtesy vanished in an instant. He had the look of a brute then, his thick layers of muscle enshrouded in the plates of his armor, and the gore that kissed his axe was full of dark promise. But his eyes were bright, and filled with a wisdom that frightened Loren all the more.

"Our infancy? You think we are new to this king-dom? I drew blood before you first drew breath. I serve death itself. I am shadeborn. My master is my father, and in his name I will lay all the nine lands low."

"I think you boast overmuch."

"I think we are alike in that. You say you have spread word of us, but I think you lie. You have no friends in the nine lands, Loren. The Mystics them-selves hunt you to put you to death, and the constables would throw you in a dark cell if ever they laid their hands upon you. No one else will help you. We killed

— *168* —

your companions in Northwood, and your woodland kin in the Birchwood. We even found the village where you were whelped and raised, and put it to the torch."

"*No!*" cried Chet. He rushed forwards as though he would charge Rogan, alone and unaided. But Loren seized him and held him, and when still he struggled, she twisted his arm back until he winced.

"He baits you," she hissed. "Leave it be. He is probably lying."

"You saw what he did to that village," said Chet. His voice sounded as though it might break. She knew he was thinking of his father, who had remained behind when Chet had left.

"Your companion shows more spirit than you do," said Rogan. "A promising protégé. Sadly, he is too old for my purposes. But there are many others here who will serve the master well. Take them. I will deal with the girl."

The Shades at his back moved at last, jumping from their horses and charging at the villagers. The townsfolk raised their weapons, but as in Northwood, they were a rabble facing trained soldiers, and they were cut down. Loren saw them hack apart men and women both, until the ones left standing turned to flee.

But they did not kill the children. Her heart stopped as she saw them pause, lower their blades, and seize any child they saw by the arm. Then they threw them over their shoulders and began to carry them back to the horses.

One of them took Ham, the innkeeper Crastus' son. The boy screamed with tears pouring down his cheeks as the Shade carried him away.

"Loren!" cried Chet. She saw that she had stood frozen too long. Rogan was almost upon them. Instinct took over, and she snatched an arrow from the quiver at her hip the way that Albern had taught her. She drew and fired, aiming low, and by good fortune the shaft buried itself in the joint between his thigh and his hip. Rogan sank to one knee with a grunt, but soon fought his way back up, snapping the arrow off where the fletching stuck out.

"Run!" she cried, and then turned to follow her own command. They vanished between the buildings in the village, Rogan limping after them.

"Fly, little girl!" came his booming voice through the night. "Fly, and leave these innocents to die in your place. The bodies at your feet will stack higher and higher until they wall you in and there is no place left to flee from us."

She had hoped the Shades would come after them, but she should have known it was a futile wish. They stayed and cut down everyone before them, even those who did not fight. Panicked glances behind her showed her more children being carried off, slung over the Shades' shoulders, or simply dragged screaming by their scrawny limbs.

Just beyond the village's eastern edge, they found the others waiting for them, eyes wide with fright and horses ready to run. Together Loren and Chet climbed into their saddles. For one brief moment they stopped to look back. Some of the buildings were burning, burning in a bright red blaze that spread from roof to roof. The air was filled with the screams of men and women, silenced with sharp violence, and the screams of children, which lingered on and on until they faded into the dark.

"What happened?" said Gem. He sounded as though he might start crying at any moment.

"I cannot say it," said Loren. "If you value our friendship, never ask me again. Turn now, and ride."

They did, while the nameless village died at their backs.

TWENTY

THEY PUSHED THEIR HORSES NEAR TO BREAKING, though they saw no sign of the Shades' pursuit. The burning town was a memory behind them before long, but Loren thought she could feel the heat of the flames all the rest of that night.

Dawn came bleak and hopeless, and after a brief pause to survey the horizon behind them, she let them dismount to eat.

"I do not understand," she said, pacing while the others sat. "I do not understand. He barely even chased us. Why stay to kill those villagers?"

"He is a cruel man," said Gem. "Cruelty does not always need a reason."

"He is *not* some simpleton," said Loren. "I have seen savagery so strong it is almost madness. We all have. Rogan is different. He is cunning, and wise. He does not kill just for the joy of it, but for some greater purpose."

"Trisken loved his cruelty well enough," said Xain. He rubbed at his throat as though at a phantom pain. The brute Trisken had given him many dark memories when they fought in the Greatrocks.

"Rogan is *not* Trisken," said Loren. "He is something worse."

"If that is true, then all the more reason he would stay to kill those who cannot defend themselves," said Annis. She was looking up at Loren with concern, and with empathy, neither one of which Loren was glad to see. She was not some child who needed consoling.

"I think you look for reason in madness," said Xain. "Those touched by a berserker's fury do not act the way reasonable folk do. You cannot hope to control them as you normally would."

Chet's head jerked up. "What would you do then, wizard? Put them down? We are not killers." He spoke harshly, surprising even Loren. Xain glowered at him without answer. Chet stared a moment longer, and then returned to his meal.

They downed their hasty breakfast and rode on.

That day was no hotter than the last, yet the sunlight seemed harsher, and the wind of their riding seemed to bite at Loren's skin. She was likely imagining it; the village, and Crastus, and Ham, were only the latest fuel thrown on the fire of her guilt that had been building since Wellmont. It made her irritable, and that made her cross with the others. When they stopped to relieve themselves, or water the horses, she did her best to avoid them. Soon they took her hint, and rarely spoke unless it was absolutely necessary.

By evening the children were nearly dead in their saddle, and Xain was slumped across his horse's neck. Though she felt she could ride for days if she must, Loren realized she could not force them on forever. She found a high rise in the ground and led them there, where they could rest while keeping a watch on the land all around them. The others threw themselves into sleep at once, and Loren stood watch all night. As the moons made their way across the sky, she kept her eyes upon the plains, for when she looked at the campfire she saw the burning of the village.

Three more days passed without incident. Whenever they saw signs of other people, Loren went to great pains to avoid them. The others followed without question or comment, though Loren sometimes took them many miles out of their way and slowed their progress considerably. But she would not endanger any other lives, not if there was a way she could possibly avoid it.

And then, in the middle of the fourth day, they crested a rise and came at last to view the sea.

In truth it was only the Great Bay, and not the wide ocean itself. But the Bay stretched for leagues and leagues beyond counting, wider than some of the nine kingdoms were long, and so it seemed as vast as the ocean to Loren. Indeed, it took her breath away when she first saw it, the sun cascading off its breadth and glowing like a thousand precious jewels. For just a moment, she forgot the dark thoughts that had plagued her for the last many days.

"The Great Bay," said Xain. He straightened in his saddle, and his voice took on a new strength. "Where the first High King, Roth, first came to the Underrealm from the northern lands, which are forgotten. Many long months has it been since I last glimpsed its blue expanse, and I never thought the day would come when I would miss it. Yet while my heart sings to see it, my mind is less convinced. We may be in more danger now than before."

"I think I feel the same," said Annis in a small voice. "The world has been emptier without the sound of the sea, but now I can only think of how close we are to my family."

"And to the Academy," said Xain. "My face would be most unwelcome there."

"Where do we go now?" said Gem.

"We must find a port," said Xain. "There are many along the coast, although we will not be able to see them until we are much closer. There we will find passage on a ship to Dulmun, and then ride to Feldemar."

"Should we turn north, or south?" said Loren.

"Neither," said Xain. "Our best choice is to make straight for the coast. It will be faster to ride the road that snakes all along the Great Bay, than it would be to turn our path now."

So they rode on, their horses' hooves devouring the miles. But the Bay was farther away than it looked, thanks to its great size, and by the time the sun set they had not even closed half the distance. The next day they rode as quickly as they could, eager to reach the water now, but the coast hardly seemed to draw nearer. Instead the massive blue stretch of water only took up more and more of the horizon.

"How large is it?" said Gem.

"Larger than you can imagine," said Xain. "Large enough that you cannot see either side, standing on a boat in its center. From the middle, it would take two days of hard sailing to find a coast. And it is only a fraction of the size of the great sea beyond."

But at long last they could see the coastline approaching, and by that evening they had reached it. Then Loren saw the black and rocky sand of its beaches, where waves came crashing with thunderous roars. She sat there in her saddle for a moment, watching, wondering that there could be so much water in the world.

"Come, let us water the horses," said Chet.

"No!" said Xain sharply. "Do not let them drink from it, nor should you do so. The waters of the ocean are filled with salt, and though they hold no poison, they can have much the same effect. If you tried to drink your fill, your thirst would only grow, and you would retch and spill anything in your stomach. It is all too easy to die of thirst upon the sea, though you are surrounded by all the water you could imagine."

Chet drew back, giving the waves a distrustful look. But Gem sat up in his saddle and said, "Is it safe for swimming?"

Xain looked at him, perplexed. "Yes, if you remember not to swallow the water."

With a whoop, Gem leaped to the ground and ran off, throwing off his belt, breeches, and tunic, his lack of smallclothes thus rendering him stark naked. He flung himself into the water with a scream, thrashing about in the waves. Annis looked away and lifted her chin demurely.

"At least he will come out cleaner than he normally is," she said.

Loren bid them to rest and eat. She drank from her water skin. It was strange, having to resist the urge to fill it, but she had no wish to taste the water and test Xain's claim. Before long Gem came running back out of the waters, hugging his arms about himself, and scooped up his clothes.

"It is cold!" he cried. "Colder than I thought it would be, anyway. Does the ocean think it is winter?"

"It cares little for our seasons," said Xain. "A great current sweeps through the Bay, up from the south and around and then back out to the north, and it brings the ice with it."

"Gem, for pity's sake, clothe yourself!" said Annis. Loren found herself smiling, and shook her head. The merchant's daughter had always had such strict ideas about decency, ever since Loren had first met her. It seemed that was one thing, at least, that had not changed in the long months since.

Gem shrugged and began to pull on his clothes again. "You are right about the salt. I got a little in my mouth by accident, and it nearly made me retch. I had never heard this of the ocean."

"Urchins of the city streets would have little cause to know it," said Xain.

Loren looked to Chet to see him smiling at her, and she gave him a little smile back. But then his face froze, his eyes focused over her shoulder, and he hunched forwards. She looked behind her.

"Chet, what is it?"

"I saw something. Something moving—a man, I think."

At once she reached for her bow, and Chet for his staff. Xain got to his feet, though it was a slow and painful process.

"That dune," said Chet, pointing. "Towards the southern side."

"Remain here," said Loren to the children. "Chet

and I will look to see what it was. Do as Xain tells you."

She tossed her head, and together they ran west. Loren took them in a wide circle so that they came to the dune from the northern side. In a few minutes they had reached it, and they slowed as one. Forwards they crept, an inch at a time, silencing their footsteps with long practice. Loren found the going difficult, for the sand shifted beneath her feet and left her stance uncertain. But the sound of the waves helped to mask the noise.

They crept around the edge of the dune with deliberate slow steps, until Loren saw it: a figure in grey and blue. She froze, ducking back, but she had not been seen. It was a man, similar to Xain in age and appearance, with long dark hair that went to his shoulders. The beginnings of a beard dusted his chin, but it looked to be there from neglect, rather than by design.

Loren met Chet's gaze and made two quick motions with her hands. Then she went left, staying behind the thin scrubby bushes that clung to the coastline, until the man was between her and the dune. Meanwhile Chet climbed up the sandy slope until he stood above the Shade.

The man was looking out, away south and west where Xain and the children were, though they had hidden themselves. He leaned forwards, straining to find them again, when Loren sprang forwards with a cry. The Shade wheeled, grasping for the sword at his belt. But then Chet attacked, his staff cracking down on the man's shoulder. The Shade fell in a heap, and when he saw Loren standing above him with an arrow drawn, he did not try to rise again.

"Mercy!" he cried. "Mercy, I surrender!"

"Fetch the others," said Loren, her voice like steel. She had heard cries of mercy from the Dorsean villagers as the Shades slaughtered them, and found her heart unmoved by the man's pleas.

Soon Chet returned with Xain and the children. The wizard came at once to stand over the Shade. Loren kept her arrow trained on him, though she relaxed the draw to half.

"Where are your companions?" said Xain.

"I have no companions."

At once Xain knelt, wrapping his hand around the man's arm. Flames sprang to white-hot life, and Loren heard the sizzling of skin. The man screamed. In Xain's other hand appeared a knife, and this he pressed to the man's throat.

"Where are they?"

"Xain," said Chet, a warning sound in his voice. But Loren met his eyes and shook her head.

"I lost them," said the Shade, gritting his teeth as he spoke. "A storm struck the coast, and its thunder made my horse bolt. By the time I got control, I could not find them."

"Where are you bound, and for what purpose?"

"North, to find them again."

"And us?"

The man did not answer. Flames sprang forth again. Loren saw the sweat that beaded on Xain's face, and knew it did not come from the heat of the fire. This must be taking a terrible toll on his strength. But the Shade screamed again, and this time he had an answer.

"We were searching for you!" he cried. "We sought a girl with green eyes, and a wizard, as well as two children. When I spotted you from afar, I saw that you matched the description."

"What were you to do when you found us?" said Xain. The flames in his hand died, but Loren could still smell the cooked flesh and burnt cloth beneath.

"Stop that," said Chet.

"Chet, take the children away from here," said Loren.

"What?" he said, looking at her in disbelief.

"Take them away," she said. "Quickly."

He looked a second longer, and for a moment Loren thought he would refuse. But then he ushered the children away. He returned a moment later while the Shade was still answering Xain's question.

"We were not to engage you in battle. If we saw you, we were to send two messengers at once—one west, to find our captain, and another south, to the Seat."

"The Seat?" said Xain. "Who is your master there?"

"I do not know," said the Shade at once. When

he saw the baleful look in Xain's eye, his arm flinched and he screamed. "I do not know! I swear it! Our sergeant knew, but she never told me. Only if the messengers were to be sent would she give them the name."

Loren thought it sounded like the truth, and just the sort of wise cunning she would have expected from Rogan. Xain studied the man for a moment, and it seemed he thought the same.

"I believe you," he said.

Then he plunged his dagger into the man's neck.

"No!" cried Chet, rushing forwards. Loren stepped into his path and stopped him with her hands on his chest.

"It is done," she murmured. "You can do nothing."

"He surrendered. That was murder!"

Xain looked up at them, eyes dark. "Mayhap. Or mayhap it was justice. Have you forgotten the screams of the village we left behind? I have not."

Even now, the man's fingers grasped at his own throat, trying to close the gaping hole there. Dark red seeped between his fingers, staining the already-dark sand beneath him. Loren wanted to look away, but could not move her eyes. She wanted to join Chet in admonishing Xain, but felt she had no place. What words had the Elves placed in her mind?

The Nightblade. The one who walks with death.

She thought they had meant she carried a doom with her, but mayhap they had meant Xain.

"I have forgotten nothing, wizard," said Chet. "But your sort of justice is the kind that brings war and death to all the nine lands in the end." He looked at Loren, eyes filled with fury, urging her to join him.

"He had no choice," said Loren. "We could not have let the Shade go south, to tell his compatriots where we were."

She hated the look on his face then: the shock, the disappointment. Most of all, she hated the sadness, and the sorrow. Loren was almost as surprised as Chet was to hear the words coming from her lips. Had she not once spoken just as Chet had? Did she not believe as Chet did? She knew she had, once. But she was no longer so certain.

"We had best move on," she said, turning away from them. "Let us go back to the horses. Quickly, for the night will not be long in coming."

TWENTY-ONE

By the time they stopped for the night, they could see the glow of fires from a town far ahead. It was on the horizon, and Loren guessed they could reach it in just a few more hours' ride.

"We should reach the town tomorrow," she said.

"Why not ride after the moons rise, and get there tonight?" said Xain.

"And then what? We could not find a ship at night. And if the Shades have come this way they might have gone to the town, and then they might hear of our presence before we could leave."

He nodded, saying nothing more, and they found a spot near the shore to camp. Loren would not let them start a fire, for finding the Shade that day had made their pursuers seem altogether too near.

She took the first watch, and sat it atop a dune overlooking the bay. From above, she could just see the sleeping forms of her friends in the silver moonlight that reflected off the water. One of the shapes moved, and then rose to climb the dune towards her. Her heart sank as she recognized Chet. She did not wish to face him just now. But as he neared, she scooted over to let him sit on the sand beside her.

He was silent at first, and she avoided looking at him. She focused on the cool breeze coming in off the water, for autumn was much warmer here in the north. But she held no illusions: he had come to speak to her, and she knew it. It was plain in the nervous twitching of his hands, the way he turned his head to her often, and then turned away when he saw she was not looking.

At last she found herself growing impatient. "Out with it, Chet," she said.

He folded his hands over each other. "That man today. The one that Xain killed."

"Yes. I was there."

"I do not blame you for it. You could not have stopped it, nor could I. But I did not expect you to speak against me."

"Did I speak against you? Once the deed was done,

there was nothing more to be said. We needed to carry on."

"You did not only urge haste. You said Xain had no choice. Those were never words I thought to hear from you. What he did was wrong. The man was our prisoner, and was half-dead from lack of food and water besides. He was no threat."

Loren stayed silent. In truth, she did not know what answer to give. Chet turned towards her, edging closer.

"I know you agree with me. Yet you spoke in Xain's defense. You cannot tell me you have grown as bloodthirsty as the rest of them."

"It is no thirst for violence. It is wisdom. We cannot leave enemies all about us, aware of our plans and intent on our harm. I have done that ever since I left the forest, and it has brought nothing but tragedy to my friends, and myself."

"You would never have said that in the Birchwood."

She looked at her hands as they lay in her lap. They were fidgeting, fingers twisting themselves about her thumbs. "Mayhap not. I used to think as you do. Always I would chastise the others when I saw them as violent, when they would kill or urge me to take a life. Still I will not do it with my own hands."

"That is not enough, and you know it. I think you were right before."

"But I am responsible now—for them, for the fate of the Mystics and the Shades both." She looked at him, his light brown hair glistening in the moonslight. "And for you as well. Those who hunt us will kill without a second thought. You saw that yourself. I may not approve, but neither can I stop to slap the wrists of those who would embrace violence to answer violence."

He looked back out across the bay, and she could see from the twitching in his jaw that he was holding back harsh words. She did not like to see such frustration in his eyes, any more than she liked to see him look at her with pity or sadness. She knew that, if she were to see herself six months ago, she would have looked at Jordel in much the same way when she thought he killed too freely.

"I have known you all my life, and most of yours. I was there when your father . . . when he treated you the way he did." His fists clenched together. "Often I was on the very brink of raising my own hands to stop him, however I could. Always you warded me off, either with words or with the look in your eyes—eyes that have always been able to say so much, even when I felt like the only one who could hear you. And it enraged me. You never lifted a hand to him yourself. If you had, no one in all the nine lands would have said a word against you. You had every right to do it. Yet you did not. I thought it foolish for a time. I felt the way you say you feel now.

"And then I grew older, and somewhat wiser, or so I thought. I felt I finally understood why you acted thus. Because to raise your hands to him, or to lift your axe and end him, forever, would be to lower yourself to his level. If you killed him, though anyone would have called it justified, you would only have beaten him by becoming him. And that was far, far worse than suffering. That was how I was able to still my fists all those long years. Because I knew that you were winning your own victory by proving yourself the better person, though it might take all your life to do so. Or so I thought. Was I wrong?"

Loren wanted to say he was. Since she left the woods, she had seen so much—Damaris' slaughter of the constables, and all of Auntie's horrors in Cabrus, and the terrible battle in Wellmont, and Jordel's death in the Greatrocks. The world seemed filled with evil, evil far more potent than her father's simple, stupid hatred that rotted the core of his soul. That evil she could have borne forever. But she could not stomach the thought of letting a much greater evil envelop the kingdom she called home.

And yet, she wondered, what good would it do to defeat those dark forces, if doing so meant she must accept the darkness into herself? She still believed that those who killed for a just cause could turn to killing when it suited them. That was mayhap the source of all wrongs that plagued them; for even Rogan had had a curious light of righteousness in his eye, when he slit the villager's throat and let his lifeblood pool in the dirt.

"I do not know the answer you want," said Loren. "Or rather, I know what you wish I would say, but I do not know if I can say it with any ring of truth. I have seen so much and traveled so far, Chet. And I am tired."

"Forget the road. Forget what you have seen. Try to remember how you felt when you lived with me in our village. And try to remember why."

She cast her mind back, all the long way to when she was a child, when her father had first pressed her into doing his labor, when she had first felt the crushing blows of his fists. And she remembered fleeing from the work, and his beatings, and escaping into the woods with Chet to sit in a clearing and listen . . .

"Mennet," she said. "It was Bracken's tales of Mennet. I was just a young whelp, and I wished great harm upon my father. And Bracken listened to me, and he heard me, and then he told me of Mennet, the thief who could bring down a king without spilling a drop of his blood. Yet now they tell me Mennet was nothing more than a legend."

"I do not believe that, and I do not think you do, either," said Chet. "And even if it is true, why should we care? I have heard it said that even false tales may have great value."

"But how can we know which have value, and which are simply stories for scared little children hiding from their parents in the woods?"

"Is there no value in that?" said Chet, his voice soft.

He reached out and took her hand, as he had never done before, for it was always Loren who reached for his. "The value of a tale is what we take from it. The choice is our own. That is one lesson I learned from none of Bracken's tales—or mayhap all of them at once. And that belief kept me from falling into despair as I grew older, and thought you might be something more than only my friend. When I wished to wed you, though your parents would never have let me."

She held his hand, and felt his thumb dragging across her palm. And then she did not know what she was doing, but she leaned across the space between them and touched his cheek, and met his lips with her own.

The shores rustled down below them, and the wind whispered, and the moonslight sang its own song that seemed sweeter than all the rest.

Loren leaned away again, relishing the smile she had put upon his face. She matched it with one of her own, though smaller, and stood.

"I suppose I have much to think upon," she said. "But we will be no good to the others if neither of us sleeps. And I find myself weary, so I will leave you to the watch. Wake me when the moons are straight overhead."

She went down the dune and away from him, but not too quickly, and it was a while yet before she could close her eyes in sleep.

TWENTY-TWO

As they drew closer, Xain recognized the town, and told them its name was Brekkur. They could smell it long before they could make out the guards who stood above the gate. It was a fishing village, and the pungent odor wafted far upon the coastal winds.

The walls were wooden, not stone, and looked newly built. "That is likely because the town is growing," said Xain. "Many such towns wax and wane with the seasons, and in summer they fill to brimming with fishermen. Then they take down their walls and erect them again farther out, only to bring them in close once winter sets in and people flee for warmer climes."

They found little resistance at the gates. Loren guessed that the towns must have received no word of the Shades who marauded across the kingdom. It seemed an ill omen that so wanton a slaughter could be carried out with not so much as a whisper of warning reaching the coastline. But then again, they had seen only the killing of a rather small village, and likely that was of no great consequence to the kingdom at large.

In any case they were soon making a careful way through many shacks and stalls, put up against the ramshackle huts that were the town's permanent structures. Behind each one stood old vendors, leaning forwards to hawk their wares to Loren and the others. Many had fish, but others offered hooks, nets, and lines.

"Do they think we are fishermen?" said Gem, sniffing as one particularly malodorous old woman came too close.

"Most are, who come here," said Xain. "In summer these places are like farms for seafolk, who spring up out of nowhere to ply the water and return filled with bounty, which is then brought all across the nine kingdoms in preparation for winter."

"But fish will not keep that long," said Annis. "Even in the kitchens upon the Seat, which were often stocked with ice, they did not last long."

"They do not need to," said Xain. "When food is suddenly plentiful, and may be traded for, the citizens of towns and cities in all directions may turn their attention to other things. And so for a while, Dorseans near the coast eat mostly fish while they turn to crafts like smithing and clothes and such. Thus summer is a happy time for the common folk, for they may turn their hands to things of beauty rather than the meager business of survival. Though you would likely have never noticed, in your fine halls where food was always plentiful and you never had aught to do but your embroidery."

The words came surprisingly harsh, and Loren looked at Xain with worry. He ducked his head almost as soon as he had spoken, and looked away from Annis as though with shame. His shoulders were shaking in the stiff breeze that blew in from the sea, and Loren guessed the sickness was wracking his body harder than normal.

"I am sorry," said Xain quietly. "The sickness . . . it plagues me, though I weary of giving you that excuse."

"I know," said Annis.

"I will still my tongue."

"You need not," said Annis. Xain paused and turned to look at her. She shook her head. "I know how it hurts you. It is a cruel punishment."

"For cruel crimes," said Xain, frowning.

"You were not in your right mind," said Annis. "And I know that, though I have often tried to pretend otherwise."

The wizard's jaw clenched, and he turned away, bowing his head. His shoulders shook harder for a moment, and Gem looked away uncomfortably. Loren reached across the gap between them and took Annis' hand. The girl tried to give her a smile, but in her eyes Loren saw barely-restrained tears.

The conversation, however, had made Loren realize something else: she had suffered no ill effects from eating the magestone on the night the Elves had visited her. The day afterwards, she had mayhap been a bit weary, but that she attributed to the fright of seeing those otherworldly creatures. Now, though, she had had no cravings to try the stones again, nor had she felt any madness creeping into her mind the way it had crept into Xain's from the very moment he had eaten them. It seemed, then, that the illness struck only mages who ate the stones—or mayhap her other guess had been correct, and the dagger somehow protected her. Either way, it was a great relief.

They came to the docks soon enough, and Xain began to inspect the ships with a practiced eye. Loren had not forgotten when they sailed together on a riverboat down the Dragon's Tail, or how practiced Xain had seemed with boatcraft. She had wondered at it then, but she was grateful for it now. Several smaller boats he passed by at once. He spent a few minutes longer studying a large ship with its sail unfurled for cleaning, but then inspected the waterline and turned away, shaking his head.

They were riding slowly down the docks, in no particular hurry, when they came to a great ship with two masts. Loren found it breathtaking, though she knew little of sailing. It towered above them, and a long wooden ramp ran down from its deck to where they stood on the dock. Upon its prow was fixed a carving of an eagle, wings behind it as though it was diving. Its beak was split in a scream.

"You have an eye for ships, I see," came a voice.

Loren looked down to see a solid-looking man on the dock before them. He had spoken to Xain. Close-cropped black hair covered his head, from the top of it down to the thin beard that barely left his chin. His shirt seemed altogether too small, sleeves buttoned tightly around thick muscles that were well browned by the sun. His breeches and tunic were all faded, clearly from long wear in the sun and ocean wind.

"This is your vessel?" said Xain.

"He is," said the man with a nod. "The *Long Claw*, we call him, and I have commanded him across the Bay, and beyond, for nigh on a dozen years now."

"You are a man of Dulmun, judging from your speech and the make of him." Xain spoke with curious interest, his voice more alive than it had seemed in many weeks.

"You have an eye for many kingdoms, I would guess," said the man. He stood forwards and thrust a hand up towards Xain on his horse. "I am called Torik."

"A pleasure, Captain," said Xain. He took the larger man's wrist, but said quickly, "Gentle, if you will. I have taken a spell of something on my journey here, though it is nothing catching, I assure you."

"A man must be bold to admit when he is ailing," said Torik with a grin. "Though I cannot say as I would let such a man on my crew."

"Fortunate for us both, then, that I am not searching for such a position," said Xain with a smile.

They both laughed, which surprised Loren—Xain's dour mood seemed to have vanished in an instant. She remembered the last time he had surprised her like that, when they met the riverboat captain Brimlad in the town of Redbrook. Something about sailing seemed to put him in good spirits.

Torik threw an arm towards the gangplank. "I would guess you seek passage, and that is something we have plenty of room for. If you wish, I can take you aboard and show you his quality."

"I can see it for myself from here, but gladly will we take your offer," said Xain. He turned to the others. "Come aboard. I think this ship will do nicely."

"You have not even asked him where he is sailing!" said Gem.

"He makes for the High King's Seat, and then to Dulmun," said Xain. "It is the usual route for Dulmun ships that sail from the coast of the Great Bay. Is that not the truth, Captain?"

"Certainly enough," said Torik. "Give your horses

to the boy. He will take good care of them, on my word."

A young deckhand came running up, reaching for their reins. Another stood nearby, expectantly, and Torik caught his eye.

"Run up and tell the boys guests are coming aboard. Make sure they keep the sheep guts out of sight."

The boy's eyes widened, and he scampered up the gangplank. Annis looked uncertainly at Loren. But Xain spoke first to reassure her.

"In Dulmun, a ship is considered blessed if its decks are regularly polished with the insides of a sheep. But worry not, for you have already heard the captain means to keep such gruesome sights from you."

"I am not afraid of sheep guts," Annis snapped.

If Loren had thought the ship impressive from the dock, it was doubly so once they stood upon the deck. The mast seemed to stretch out of sight into the sky, and the vessel was longer from one end to the other than some of the largest buildings she had been inside. A large crew ran about, pulling lines and doing other things she could scarcely guess at. Torik led them all about, pointing things out here and there. She was soon lost in the many strange words he used, though Xain nodded his head appreciatively and seemed to listen with rapt attention.

"Now let me take you into his hold," said the captain. "We have many fine cabins down below—and some not so fine, if you are short on coin. I can show you where you would stay, if indeed you wish to secure passage."

An open hatch awaited, with a staircase leading down. Loren did not find the darkness below very inviting, but she swallowed her misgivings and followed the captain. The passage hooked around immediately, leading into a long hallway with doors on either side. It looked for all the world like the upper floor of an inn, like many she had stayed at in her travels. Metal grates in the ceiling let the light in, and the place seemed far cozier and more inviting than she had expected.

"If you will all step in here," said Torik, throwing open a door.

Still looking about in wonder, Loren led the way inside, with the others close behind.

The door slammed shut behind them with a *snap.* The air filled with the hiss of steel, and Loren saw half a dozen swords pointed in their direction. Behind them stood broad men and women in red cloaks.

She gave a shout and reached for her dagger. Beside her, Xain muttered words of power, and his eyes glowed white. But the magic sputtered almost as soon as he reached for it, and his shoulders sagged. At the other end of the cabin, which was spacious enough, Loren saw a Mystic woman with her hands twisted to claws. Her eyes glowed white, and Loren felt herself unable to move, held in the mindmage's grasp.

"Stay your hands," said the woman. "You will find you have no choice in the matter, after all."

"Stand down," said a deep and booming voice. "We will not harm you as long as you keep your hands away from your blades."

From behind the Mystics came another, and with one glance Loren knew him for their leader. His shoulders were broad, and his beard long. Many lines of care and worry criss-crossed his face, deep as the scars she saw there also. The other Mystics parted way before him, as if on instinct, or as if some invisible force surrounded him and pushed him aside. He marched forth to stand before Loren, glowering down at her. She felt her resolve crumbling despite herself, and slowly moved her hand away from her belt. It moved easily now, for the glow in the Mystic wizard's eye had dimmed.

"You will forgive us our surprise," said the Mystic. "Or mayhap you will not. It is no matter either way. I am Kal, of the family Endil, chancellor of the Mystic Order, and I have been searching for you for some time. Word has it, you were last seen traveling with Jordel."

Loren was so surprised that for a moment she could not speak. From the corners of her eyes she saw the others looking towards her, wondering. Her mind raced, trying to guess the right words to speak to save them all. In the end she did not know which lie to tell, and settled for the truth instead.

"I am Loren, of the family Nelda," she said. "And yes, it was our honor to travel at Jordel's side, for a time. We have come to Dorsea at his bidding."

"I am not one to take a woman at her word," said Kal. "If you rode with Jordel, where is he? And why would he send you, rather than come himself?"

"If I may show you proof?" said Loren. She reached slowly for a pocket within her cloak. The Mystics by Kal's side tensed, but he stilled them with a look. Loren retrieved Jordel's Mystic symbol, the badge of office she had seen on his chest the first time they met. She had retrieved it from his body when he died, thinking she might one day have use for it. That day seemed to have arrived at last.

Kal's eyes widened as he beheld the badge, and then narrowed to slits. "Jordel would not have given this into your hands, not even if you were his messengers."

He said it flatly, and yet Loren heard the question behind the words. "I am the bearer of ill news, I fear. Jordel fell in the Greatrocks, passing from this world to the next. We have carried on in his memory."

It was not that Kal moved, or made a face at her words. In fact no muscle in his great body so much as twitched. Yet she saw the words strike him like a hammer blow, turmoil raging in his eyes, though he made no sound. Indeed, he gave no sign that he had heard her at all. Then finally, at last, he reached out and took the badge from her hand, gently, as though lifting a babe from her arms.

"Sheathe your blades," he said. The air whispered with steel again, and in a blink the Mystics were standing at attention, any hint of threat vanished. Even the woman in the back had loosed her hold on her magic.

For a long while Kal looked at the badge in his hand, turning it over and over in the firelight. Then he thrust it back out towards Loren, where it lay in the palm of his hand. She reached out to take it, and put it in the same pocket where she had carried it all this way.

"Very well, Loren of the family Nelda," said Kal in a gruff voice—gruff, but soft at the same time. "Come and sit. It seems we must have words, and not a few of them, I wager."

TWENTY-THREE

KAL BROUGHT THEM TO A SMALL TABLE IN THE CABIN, which Loren quickly guessed was his own. There were only two seats besides his, so she took one and gave the other to Xain. The children and Chet sat around the edges of the room, on the floor. Two of the Mystic swordsmen remained, as well as the wizard, but all the fight seemed to have gone out of them.

"I was Jordel's master," said Kal. "Taught him from a young pup, I did. And when he took his knighthood and went on his journeys, I would often command his stronghold of Ammon in his stead."

"Ammon!" said Loren in surprise. "But that is where we are bound."

"So I guessed," said Kal. "I thought nothing of it when I had not heard from Jordel for some time, for often his duties would take him far, and word takes time to travel. Then I heard he was exiled by our order. Still I feared to leave Ammon, for I thought he would make his way there, and I wanted to be there when he returned. But when more weeks passed, and still I got nothing so much as a letter, I decided at last to act. Too late, it seems. We left Ammon two weeks ago, and just arrived here. I had put word out through the ship's captain that we sought you, and he recognized you the moment you showed your faces on the dock."

"It was good fortune, then, that we came when we did," said Xain.

"I will call nothing good fortune that begins or ends with the death of Jordel, nor has it somewhere in the middle," Kal snapped. "And I will hear the tale of that now, as quick as you can, girl."

At Kal's urging, and with Xain's help, Loren told him the whole tale of their journey: how she had first met Jordel in Cabrus, and how he had urged her to confide in him from the first. Then she told him of how Jordel had smuggled her out of the city and into the south of Selvan. When she told of how they rejoined Jordel in Wellmont, she stopped and looked warily at Xain.

"I know he is Xain Forredar, and called by some

an abomination for eating magestones," said Kal in a brusque tone. "I see also that he suffers from magestone sickness. You may as well carry on with the story, for I suspect that has some part in what took place after."

Still Loren looked to Xain. But he only shrugged, so she went on, keeping nothing back. When she spoke of the magestones, she made the whole thing sound like her idea, hoping to divert some of the blame from Xain. But she could think of no way to gloss over the wizard's madness on the King's road, when he had coated Vivien and the other Mystics in darkfire. Kal's face grew stony at that, and she heard the other Mystics in the room shift. But she barreled on, telling them how Jordel had insisted they spare Xain's life, and then the road they had taken into the Greatrocks.

When she came to the Shade fortress in the mountains, her voice faltered and she bowed her head. But the cabin only sat silent for a moment or two before Kal slapped his hand on top of the table.

"Say on, girl. Do not stop talking for favor of weeping, for you are not so young as all that. There is no shame in grief, only do not get it on my rugs."

So she told him all that they had seen in the mountains, helped here and there by Xain, who had some knowledge of the Shades from what Jordel had told him in Wellmont. They came at last to the battle on the bridge, where Jordel had given his life to stop Trisken. Then she did weep, though she kept telling the tale. Behind her she heard Annis and Gem quietly sobbing together. Even Xain cast his head down in sorrow.

The journey from there she told much more quickly, for she had no great wish to dwell on the death of Wellmont, nor of the villages in the Birchwood and the plains of Dorsea. When she had finished, Kal studied her a long while, obviously displeased.

"These are dark tidings," he muttered under his breath. "Far, far darker than I had imagined."

"Would that they were anything but," said Loren. "They have been a heavy burden, and are delivered at great cost."

"Aye, and too slowly," said Kal. "What madness made you wait in Northwood for so long before you set foot upon the road again?"

Those words were like a punch to Loren's gut, and behind her she heard Chet shifting where he sat. But Kal raised a hand to wave off their hurt looks.

"Spare me your doe's eyes. What is done is done, and no use in anyone harping on about it—even me. Only you cannot blame me for wishing I had known of this sooner."

"Jordel always urged us to haste," Loren said quietly. "I should have heeded those words, even after he was no longer there to say them."

Kal's fist clenched on the table, and he rapped his knuckles twice in quick succession against the wood. It was a moment before his muscles relaxed, and looked as though he did it with great effort.

"Jordel was a bright and eager young knight, and it was my job to teach him to hunt mages."

Xain stiffened beside her at that. Loren saw the Mystic wizard sit up a bit straighter, eyeing Xain suspiciously. But Kal went on with the story as though he had not noticed, and only a glitter in his eye told her that in fact he had.

"I have never been called aught but a hard man. That is what is best for the soldiers in a commander's care, and anyone who says different will have corpses on their conscience. Jordel took it as well as any mage hunter I have trained before or since, and never once a hint of insubordination. And more, when I would tear apart one of his fellows for being a blamed idiot, Jordel would take them aside afterwards. He would piece them back when I had shattered their fragile pride into splinters. He had a way of making the soldiers feel they could succeed, that they could become mage hunters even when I knew they never could. But once in a while—a long, long while, mind you—he was right, and I was wrong."

He shifted to lean forwards in his chair, planting his elbows on the table and glowering at all of them. "And now I am saddled with his latest flock of novices. What is more, we have a task that is likely too great for me, and certainly too great for the likes of you. Yet we have little choice but to use what strength we have. And the appearance of the Shades may prove a boon. Mayhap now, at least, my useless compatriots will get off their arses long enough to do what they have been meant to do for centuries."

Loren balked at that, and looked uncertainly at Xain. But he seemed just as confused as she was. "Who do you mean?" she said.

"Why, the other Mystics, of course," growled Kal. "Useless layabouts though they are, now that we have some proof, mayhap they can trouble themselves to lift a finger where they never could before."

"I have met many Mystics," said Loren. "Never one I would call a layabout."

"Oh, they get riled up enough when they think a wizard has taken magestones," said Kal. He was fairly spitting now in his disdain. "But they have all but forgotten our purpose—the very purpose that drove Jordel, and which brings you here now. Even the so-called greatest among them, the ones who imagine themselves my superiors, would sooner bury their heads in palace intrigue than seek to find the dark master."

Loren shuddered at the word. "You mean the Necromancer."

"Aye, that one," said Kal. "The dark master, the lord of death, and a thousand other prettier names that they have worn through the ages. For more than a score of years I have warned of their return, and never will anyone listen. Mayhap now that will change."

He sat up straighter, and reached for a flask that hung on a strap from the wall. The stopper came out in his hand, and he took a long pull. "Right. You lot have got more road ahead of you, though less than you have left behind. You will be the ones to bring warning of the Shades to the lord chancellor—fop that he is—and the High King."

"What?" said Loren, incredulous. Beside her, Xain looked ready to fall from his chair. "What makes you think they will listen to us above you?"

Kal's frown, which Loren was already learning was perpetual, deepened. "For one thing, I have no time to sail for the Seat. Now that I have learned of Jordel's fate, I must return to Ammon with all possible speed. Our actions in the northern kingdoms must be coordinated, in Dulmun most of all. It is the oldest kingdom, and likely our greatest point of strength if indeed the Shades should make open war. Moreover, every redcloak at my command must be dispatched, at once, to find where the Shades may be gathering in strength. Worst in all this news is that they have been able to accomplish that, and all of us unaware of it. That speaks to traitors within our ranks, and rooting them out will be a dark business."

"The lord chancellor will never give us an audience," said Loren.

"He will if I tell him to," said Kal. "But such audience would be useless. He would still never raise the Mystics to war. Not unless the High King herself commanded it."

"And there you speak madness," said Xain with a harsh laugh. "If an audience with the lord chancellor will be hard to come by, one with the High King will be impossible. Not unless you wish to see my head on a spike on her palace wall, and our tale still untold."

Kal's mouth twisted in a grim smile—an expression that looked utterly alien there, and made Loren squirm in her seat. "Yet that is the great beauty of it. Who better than you, Xain Forredar, to get the High King's attention? Doubtless you will be brought straight to her throne room if you show your face upon the Seat. It is a much faster route than any other courtier, who would have to wait weeks or months for a meeting."

"They will kill him," said Loren angrily. "And then what help will he be to your cause?"

But to her surprise, she saw a grim resolution settle on Xain's face. He sat straighter in his seat, and his hands were steady on the table.

"He sees it. Here, boy, drink up," said Kal, and he slid his flask into Xain's hand. The wizard took a long drink. "I think you have little reason to fear, girl. Those who hate Xain upon the Seat are many—the dean and the lord chancellor among them—but rumor has it the High King is not among their number. She may have issued the decree for his arrest, but she has put no word in writing calling for his death. That was done by the Academy when that young whelp Vivien told them about the magestones."

"You guess that the High King will pardon him?" said Loren with a snort. "That is quite a risk to take— and with someone else's life, I might add."

Xain dropped the flask on the table with a sharp *clack*. "Yet it is a risk I will take."

Loren stared at him, incredulous. "Xain, you cannot be serious."

"I am, Loren. Kal is right—it is the fastest way to see the High King. There, I will be able to tell her my tale. Whatever may happen afterwards is not important."

"It is important!" Loren cried. "I did not drag your wasted hide across all of Selvan and half of Dorsea only to see you throw your life away now. And what of your son, Xain? Have you lost all hope of recovering him?"

He stared at her, his eyes cold and dark. "Do not dangle my son before me in hopes of changing my will," he said, voice harsh. "There are duties higher than even the bonds of family, and the promise made to a dying friend is one such. Especially when that promise was made in payment of sins forgiven."

His anger left him as suddenly as it had come, like a thunderstorm vanishing from the summer sky. "By my hands many have burned," he said, quiet now. "Jordel forgave me that, though the ones I slew were his brothers and sisters. Now I must earn that forgiveness. And if fortune smiles, mayhap Enalyn will at least let me see my son. One last time, at least, before the end."

TWENTY-FOUR

As Kal told them often and loudly, they had little time to waste. Still, he allowed them one day on the ship to recover from the road. Besides, the *Long Claw* needed to be restocked for the voyage, while Kal had his own plans to make for the return to Ammon.

"I shall be taking another ship," he told them. "No use delaying my own passage home just to go to the Seat, when there is much work to be done back at the stronghold."

With them he was sending four Mystics—good soldiers, he said, ones he trusted. From what she had seen of him so far, Loren thought that his trust did not come lightly, and was grateful for his offer. He brought the Mystics by later on the same day they had arrived, while they were preparing themselves to sleep in the cabins belowdecks.

Three of them Loren recognized from Kal's cabin, though when she had seen them first, they had been behind swords. Their leader was a man named Erik. He was a hale warrior, with red hair and a beard almost as great as Kal's own. With him were a huge young man named Jormund and a woman named Gwenyth. Though Erik spoke easily enough, and in fact was far more polite than Kal, the other two hardly said a word when they were introduced.

The fourth Mystic was another mage, a woman named Weath, who Kal told them was an alchemist. Almost from the start, she and Xain fell into animated conversation. Among a blur of words Loren hardly understood, she gathered that they had attended the Academy at around the same time, though Weath had completed her training with the Mystics. But they soon excused themselves to continue their conversation elsewhere—or rather, they were forced to leave when Erik nearly threw them out of the room.

Erik then sat with Loren and shared with her a bottle of wine, for he had many questions. In particular, he wanted to know of the Shades: their strength and the composition of their troops, their strategies and any weaknesses he might exploit. Loren felt that she was little help, for she had no mind for warfare or strategy. But when she told him of Trisken, and the man's ability to cheat even mortal blows, Erik took a great interest.

"It was the tattoo on his neck," Loren explained. "It held some dark enchantment. I would wager the Necromancer put it there, for it had the power to stay death itself. But when Jordel destroyed the tattoo, Trisken could at last be killed."

"And you say it was on the back of the neck?" said Erik. "Do they always place it there?"

"I do not know for certain," said Loren. "But Rogan, another man like Trisken, goes to battle with mail hanging from his helmet, which protects the same area. It seems a safe wager."

"You are certain Rogan has the same power?"

"I shot him in the hip with an arrow. He snapped the shaft off as it if were a fly's bite, and came for me again." Loren shuddered at the memory, and at the baleful look she remembered in his eye.

"I have seen men do much the same in battle when their blood is up," said Erik.

"Not like this, I promise you," Loren assured him.

Whenever he paused to think of more questions, Loren asked him about himself and the others with him. She learned he bore the title of knight. But when she asked if that was true of the other Mystic warriors she had met, he shook his head.

"The greater part of Mystics are simply that—Mystics. They follow orders and fight at the command of others. In time they may be promoted to a knight, like myself, and then to the rank of captain. Captains answer to chancellors, who answer to one grand chancellor in each kingdom, who answer only to the lord chancellor himself. The lord chancellor answers to no one, save the High King."

The others bore no rank—not even Weath. That confused Loren, for it seemed a wizard such as she would be more than a match for Erik in battle, even if he was a mighty warrior.

"It is not only strength in battle that determines worthiness of rank," said Erik. "If that were so, the lord chancellor should never have risen to his position. That one is no warrior."

"How did he rise, then?" said Loren.

Erik looked around, though no one else had come into the room since they began speaking. "There are many rumors, and little known for certain. But he hails from the family Drayden, and their influence is powerful in the nine lands. The dean of the Academy hails from that black clan as well."

Loren shuddered, for she had heard that before. Annis, whose family of Yerrin was fearsome enough, had feared to do more than whisper at the dark machinations of the Draydens.

When at last Erik had exhausted his questions, and Loren had no more for him in return, he took his leave. Loren found herself alone in her cabin, for Gem and Chet had gone to the deck, while Xain and Annis had left her some time ago. She rose from her seat, pacing back and forth. There were two hard decisions to be made, and they had weighed heavily on her ever since Kal had first told her of his plan.

Just as she had made up her mind to go and put her thoughts to action, there was a sharp rap at her door. Before she could answer, it swung open to reveal Chet. His face was troubled, and he shut the door silently behind him as he came in. Then he came to stand before her, and though he looked as if he wanted to reach out and take her hands, he did not.

"You mean to go through with this mad plan, then?" he said.

Loren met his gaze and nodded. "I have no choice, Chet."

"We all have a choice. You told me you had a message for the Mystics, a message that might let them save all the nine lands from peril. That message is delivered now, it seems. Yet still you march by their orders."

She found herself annoyed at that, but she let it pass. "The message has not yet reached as far as it must. You heard Kal, and I know you saw the wisdom in his plan. Without the High King's order, the nine lands may wait forever for the Mystics to act."

"Xain is already determined to go and tell her of this, whatever the consequence he himself may face. Yet you, too, are a criminal under the King's law. You might face the same penalty."

"That is unlikely. I would be surprised if word of my doings have even reached the Seat."

Still he did not look satisfied. But Loren had only just mustered the courage to go and do what must be done, and she had no time to console him now.

"I hope you will come with me still," she said. "But I will understand if you wish to wait here. Stay on the coast, and I promise I will return to you the moment the High King has been told of the Shades' threat. I mean to visit Ammon after, if only to see Jordel's home. Beyond that, I have no aims—mayhap we can return to the Birchwood, where I am certain your father awaits your homecoming."

"Would that I could believe that," he murmured, looking past her as his eyes grew far away.

"I believe it. But now I must go and speak to Annis. You need decide nothing until tomorrow."

She moved past him. At the last second his hand jerked out to brush against hers, and she let her fingers trail against his for a moment longer than she needed to.

Upon the ship's main deck she found Annis. The girl sat on a large coiled rope, which formed a perfectly sized seat. She was watching Gem, who had somehow persuaded one of the Mystics to practice his swordplay with him. The boy had stripped down to the waist, and his bare feet danced upon the planks of the boat while he swung back and forth with his blade.

Though her mind had been made up, she quailed

the moment she saw Annis sitting there. The girl looked up and saw her, and in her smile Loren saw the same quiet panic she herself felt. So rather than speak, she only sat next to Annis on the deck, and together they watched.

Gem's weeks of practice seemed to have paid off, for he matched the Mystic blow for blow. The man was one Loren had not yet been introduced to, but he was thin and wispy, and seemed a perfect match for Gem's small frame. Only now that she watched him, Loren saw that his frame was not so small as it had once been. In the months since she had met him, he had shot up like a beanstalk. And from all their many adventures, as well as the sword practice that he had thrown himself into after Jordel died, thin and sinewy muscle had developed where once there had been only skin clinging faithfully to bones.

She looked to Annis by her side, and saw that the merchant's daughter, too, was no longer the child she had been when first she had met Loren. She was neither so plump nor so short as she had once been. And her eyes as they watched Gem showed something Loren recognized, something that might not yet be womanly, but was not entirely childish, either. It was a disconcerting feeling, to recognize that two people she held to be her closest friends in all the world should have grown so much in such a short space of time, and she herself hardly recognizing it.

Annis caught her looking and blushed, turning her

eyes away from Gem as he practiced. "Am I staring so boldly?" she said. "I do not mean to—you probably think me a fool."

"Sometimes you can be," said Loren, nudging the girl's knee. "But not just now."

Annis slapped her hand, but the girl's smile could not banish all anxiety from her eyes. She opened her mouth as if to speak but then closed it again. When she finally found her voice, Loren could tell the words were not the ones she most wanted—and needed—to say.

"What do you think I should do? About Gem, I mean."

Loren shrugged. "Whatever you wish. Your feelings are your own."

"You could give me *some* advice. After all, you and Chet . . ."

Loren felt her cheeks burn just a bit. "That is not the same. We have known each other all our lives, and Chet wished to marry me for years. You and Gem only met a little while ago, though indeed it seems much longer." Her smile dampened, and she spoke more softly. "But I do not think that is what chiefly troubles you, Annis."

For a few moments the girl attempted to feign ignorance, but the mask soon fell. She hung her head, her thick black hair cast down about her face. "No, it is not."

"We are going to the Seat," Loren prodded. "From all that you have told me, many of your family are there as well, and even more of their agents. For all we know, Damaris herself might have returned by now."

"I doubt that," Annis said quickly. "I do not think the Seat is much safer for her than it is for me just now, if indeed the Shades' influence reaches so far as it seems."

"And yet . . ."

"And yet."

"If you wish to come with us, you may, of course. But I cannot see that as a wise choice, though it breaks my heart to say it."

Tears sprang into Annis' eyes, which she tried to keep fixed on Gem. "I do not wish to be parted from you all. I told you as much in the Greatrocks. I tell you again now."

"And it is the last thing in the world I would wish for. But this is not forever, or even for very long—only until we have done our duty there, and can return to you."

Annis barely held back a sob, and turned it to a sniff instead. "But you will take Gem."

"Gem will not be hunted high and low by his family, for he has none."

"What do you mean to do with me, then?"

"Nothing without your agreement," said Loren. "I tried before to make such arrangements without asking you. I will never do that again."

"You know my meaning," said Annis. "Where would I go?"

"With Kal, I think. I will ask him to take you to Ammon. I can scarcely imagine a safer place for you in all the nine lands. And I mean to make my way there in any case, once we leave the Seat. There I will find you again, and together we will set forth upon the road once more."

"Do you promise me this, Loren? You will not abandon me there and go your own way?"

Loren snatched her hands and pulled her down to sit on the deck so that they were facing each other. "I swear it by the sky above and the darkness below. When I sent you on ahead of me in Cabrus, I did not stop searching until I had found you again. When Xain was seized by madness and took you from me, I found you and plucked you from his lair. Hear me now: I will come for you in Ammon as soon as I may. You are my dearest friend, Annis of the family Yerrin."

"You are more than a friend," said Annis, who could no longer keep her tears within. "You are my sis-ter—nearer to me than blood, and twice as dear." And she fell forwards to throw herself into Loren's arms, let-ting her tears spill silently down. Loren kept her own from falling—but only just.

TWENTY-FIVE

THEY ALL SPENT A RESTLESS AND FITFUL NIGHT ON THE
boat. Loren had not slept well when they sailed on the
riverboat along the Dragon's Tail, and she found it no
easier on a ship so large. Almost she thought to go into
the town and find herself an inn for the night. But she
feared discovery by the Shades, and Annis would have
been distraught besides. The girl spent the night in Loren's bed, curled up to her like a pup to its mother, and
seemed to have no trouble with her slumber. So Loren
stayed, waking in fits and starts, and when morning
dawned she was miserable.

She had spoken with Kal the night before, and to her surprise he had agreed easily to the idea of taking Annis with him. "It is a sensible choice, and one I am surprised to hear the two of you make," he said curtly. "Mayhap Jordel saw something of worth in you after all. I cannot promise you the girl will enjoy Ammon, but neither will she starve there. I shall put her to work."

So, on the deck of the *Long Claw*, they bid each other farewell just after dawn. Annis would scarcely let go of her, although she no longer wept. Then she said her good-bye to Chet, which was somewhat awkward for the both of them, and then to Xain, which was somewhat cool, for Annis could not entirely forget the way he had acted in the battle of Wellmont, or after. Gem she saved for last, and Loren half expected some grand confession to spring from the girl's mouth. But she only held him close, and made him promise to come for her when he could. Gem, for his part, seemed mostly confused, and said of course he would be with Loren when they all came to fetch her.

Annis watched them go from the dock, and stood waving until she was out of sight. Probably, Loren guessed, she stayed there long afterwards, until she could no longer see her friends, but only the thick black dot of the ship growing smaller and smaller upon the sea. Some time after, she would no doubt shuffle halfheartedly onto Kal's vessel, there to take passage with him to Dulmun and complete their journey to Ammon.

"Do you think she behaved at all oddly?" said Gem. "It was as though she feared we would never come for her. And twice I thought she meant to say something to me, but both times she closed her mouth again."

Loren rolled her eyes and turned away from him. That was not a conversation she was at all prepared to begin.

She returned to her cabin once they were upon the water, and there rested upon the pallet that Captain Torik had provided for her, trying to recapture some of the sleep she had missed in the night. But if sleep had been hard when the ship was docked at night, it was much harder under sail when the waves tossed them back and forth. After an hour of fruitless trying, there came a knock at her door, and Xain let himself inside.

"There is something we must discuss before we reach the Seat," he said. "I have only just thought of it. It concerns your dagger."

Loren blanched, reaching for its hilt. "Sky above. I did not think of it."

"I thought not. You cannot march into the High King's palace with it. It could spell the very end of the Mystics."

"What must I do, then?" said Loren, fear rising thick in her throat. "There is little between here and there save the open water. Must I cast it into the waves?"

He smirked. "Not quite. I have a friend upon the Seat, someone in whom I have the utmost trust. He will take care of your dagger for you, holding it out of sight and out of mind until you come to reclaim it."

She let loose a great sigh of relief. "That is well. But what if I never do return? You cannot have forgotten that that is a distinct possibility."

"Indeed I have not. In that case, he will sail out into the Bay and cast the dagger into the water. I do not think you will miss it, if it comes to that."

Her smile was weaker than she meant it to be. But just then, she heard pounding steps in the hallway outside, and Chet burst into her room.

"Loren!" he cried. "Come quickly! It is the Seat!"

She stood from the edge of the bed and went up to the deck with him, Xain hobbling along more slowly. Seizing her hand, which no longer felt so strange to her as it once had, Chet took her to the railing near the prow.

There sat the High King's Seat, like the prize jewel in a great crown made all of sapphire. It shone in the midday sun, golden and bright and glistening like a dewdrop. Even from so far, at the edge of vision, it took Loren's breath away. Beside her she saw Chet and Gem's mouths hanging open in awe, and realized with a start that her own mouth gaped wide as well.

The closer they drew to it, the more it dazzled her. Soon she saw golden spires shooting up from the white stone walls that bordered the whole island. A tower that looked to be made of silver stuck up like an arrow from the back of a practice target. Perfectly cylindrical, it caught the sun's rays from every direction and flung them into their eyes, so that they could scarcely bear to look at its splendor. And from every battlement, rampart and tower flew the many banners of the high kingdom, blue and green and red and gold all together, fluttering in the wind like the feathers of some great bird.

Loren looked over at last to find Xain standing there, observing them all with clear enjoyment of their dumbfounded excitement. "Welcome to the High King's Seat, Loren of the family Nelda," he said. "I hardly thought I would ever come here with you. Yet it pleases my heart to see the look it puts upon your face, nonetheless."

"You lived here?" said Loren. "How did you ever go about your life? If I lived upon the Seat, I could do nothing but walk around and look at it all. I have heard tales and stories aplenty, but it is ten times better than any of them."

"It wears on the senses soon enough," he said, his tone a bit darker than before. "I am certain you will soon find yourself as weary of it as I was when I left."

He drew up his hood as they sailed closer. The dock itself was a masterpiece. Loren had seen docks before, but only of wood and never of stone. The ships she saw moored there were more grand even than the *Long Claw*, their masts reaching for the sun.

Torik skillfully guided his ship into the port, and in no time his crew had lashed it to the moorings.

Then they all followed Xain and threw up their hoods, setting off down the pier and into the streets of the Seat.

The city was not paved in gold, as Loren had heard, but with fine white cobblestones that were perfectly fitted and sealed together, and then worn flat by some craft she did not know. Few people were on foot. Many constables rode horses, and royalty or wealthy merchants rode in fine carriages. Some craftsmen drove wagons, but even those were of far finer make than anything she had seen on the streets of Selvan's cities. Every building was of stone, none of wood, and each was an exquisite display of craftsmanship. Even a butcher's shop was no lowly venue; burning braziers hung outside above the door, and their pungent, sweet aroma banished the normal charnel stink.

Erik marched before them with Weath, and the other two Mystics behind, so that most passersby gave them a wide berth. Their steps took them towards the High King's palace at first, but Xain tugged at Erik's sleeve for a quick word.

"We have one burden we must deliver first. Do you know the way to Aurel's smithy?"

"I do not," said Erik.

"Then follow me, and closely."

He turned them to the left, so that they began to move around the palace in a wide circle. The streets were well-ordered, and in no time they stood before a fine-looking shop with a low, red door made of wood.

Above it hung a sign with the mark of a silversmith burned into it. The door stood open, but Xain took them around to the back of the building, where a more modest service entrance awaited.

He rapped sharply on the door, and they had to wait only a moment before it swung open. Behind the door stood a thin little man, his grey hair sticking out in all directions, spindly hands clutching each other in curiosity. When he saw the four redcloaks waiting outside, Loren saw him square his shoulders.

"What is this about?" he said. "What service can I be to the Mystics this day?"

"Not to them, old friend," said Xain, and he threw back his hood. "But to me."

The man looked as though sheer surprise might strike him dead on the spot. He rushed forwards, eyes watering up, and clutched the front of Xain's cloak. "Xain! Xain, is it truly you? I never thought to look upon you with my own two eyes again." Then he recoiled, not in fear, but to look around in sudden suspicion. "But my boy . . . you must know the island is not a safe place for you. Come, come inside, and quickly."

"No time for that, Aurel. I have a burden I must ask you to bear, for a little while at least. It is for the girl here."

"A . . . a burden?" said Aurel, blinking at Loren as though he could not quite see her.

"You must keep it hidden from all eyes, even your own," said Xain. "If all goes well, she shall be back to fetch it presently. If not—if you hear that anything has happened to us, or if you hear nothing at all for a month—you must take it into the middle of the bay and drop it into the waters."

"Of course, my boy, of course." And though the old man's eyes burned with curiosity, he ushered Loren inside. Xain waited on the street for her, raising his hood once more.

"Do you have a box I can put it in?" said Loren, reaching for her belt.

"Yes, my dear, of course. Take your pick," said Aurel, gesturing around. Loren found herself in his workshop, with many tools lying about on benches and tables, as well as many crafts in progress—everything from serving platters to buckles to fine pins with exquisite designs. And against one whole wall was stacked a massive mountain of boxes. Loren chose one and pulled dagger and sheath from her belt to drop them inside. Then, struck by a thought, she reached into her cloak and drew out the packet of magestones. They joined the dagger at the bottom of the box. She would no sooner be discovered with them than with the dagger, after all, and both could spell her death within the High King's halls.

She closed the box again, twisting the little silver latch on the front, and then placed it in Aurel's hands. He blinked at her again, then stared down at the box, hefting the weight.

"I can keep it in my floor easily enough," he said.

"And rest assured, girl, no harm will come to it. I shall not even look inside myself, that I vow."

"Thank you," said Loren, bowing low to him. That seemed to surprise him, and in his haste to return the bow, he nearly dropped the box.

Soon she had rejoined Xain on the street. But before they set off, the wizard drew close to Aurel and spoke quiet words in his ear. But not quiet enough, for Loren overheard much of them.

"I do not think I go to my doom, Aurel. Yet I cannot see all ends. If things should go poorly, I would have you send a message."

"I think I know it, my boy."

"Still, I will tell you. Send word of my love—and my death—to Trill, whatever you must do to find her."

"Of course, Xain. Of course. Only, do not place such a burden on an old man. Return here, and send the message yourself."

"If fate be kind."

Then Xain pushed past her in a rush, face hidden within his cowl again. Loren followed, cautiously, not wishing to upset him any further. Trill was the name of Jordel's sister, and the Mystic had told Loren how she and Xain had fallen in love. Trill was the mother of his son, but she had been married off to another man after their child was born, and Xain had not seen her since.

Now Xain marched like a man possessed, and even the Mystics struggled to keep up with him. Through the streets he passed like a returning prince, and indeed mayhap he was such in his own mind. He stepped in front of carriages and horses without heeding them, and more than one reared at his coming. Everywhere he went, heads turned to watch, though they could not see his face beneath his hood.

Soon the walls of the High King's palace loomed before them, though its splendor was somewhat lost on Loren. They were near the end of their road now, or might be, and the fear of what they might find dimmed the sight of the place. Still, she could not help but notice the high walls trimmed with gold, and the fine white stone that made the black battlements stand out all the more.

A guard stood before the gate, clad in the white and gold armor of the High King herself. She took one look at Xain, and Loren and Chet and Gem beside him in their plain clothes, and raised her spear to cross it over her chest. "Begone, beggars," she said. "There are kitchens aplenty for you, by the High King's charity. That is where you will find your next meal, not here."

Xain's bitter laugh poured out from beneath his brown hood. "Ah, Sera, you old fool. Do not tell me you have forgotten the sight of a friend so quickly." And he threw back his hood to show the guard his face.

Many things happened then, and all of them quickly. The guard nearly froze in her shock, but kept just enough composure to call the alarm. Then many more guards rushed out of the gates, surrounding Loren and the rest of them with sharp spears. They were grabbed firmly, their hands tied behind their backs—even the Mystics—and then they were marched through the gates and into the palace, prisoners at the High King's mercy.

TWENTY-SIX

LOREN WAS DRAGGED THROUGH THE HIGH KING'S palace so quickly that her feet scarcely touched the floor. She could not see the beauty of the high, vaulted ceilings or the mural-covered walls, for her mind was filled with dread of what might lay ahead. The elegance that surrounded them barely registered in her mind, something noticed only by instinct, stowed away to be examined later—if she would have any time later to think of it, and was not put to death at once.

Beside her, Xain seemed frighteningly calm. Indeed, a grim smile played across his lips beneath his gag—for the guards knew he was a firemage, and had taken steps to remove him from his power. Loren thought she might be able to guess at the reason for his high mood; since before they first met, he had been a fugitive from the King's justice, fleeing from city to city and kingdom to kingdom to evade punishment for his crimes. Now at last that flight had come to an end. One way or another, Xain's days of running were over.

They came soon to the doors of the throne room, which lay open. Guards raised their polearms to let the procession through. These wore more splendid armor than the guards at the front gate, their plate gleaming with white enamel and trim bedecked in gold leaf. Their eyes were harder, and Loren could see the strength in their frames. They looked upon her with contempt as she passed.

The throne room was so wondrous that it dragged her mind to the present, as if the place itself were impatient for her to notice its finery. Pillars rose high to form arches along the walls, and the arches rose up until they joined in points that ran all along the center of the roof. From each point sprang golden spikes that ran across the white marble ceiling, like starbursts all in a row. They shrank in size from the entrance to the rear of the room, descending to the far wall so that they formed a sort of arrow, commanding the eye to look at the throne upon its dais.

Upon that throne sat the High King Enalyn. Loren

had never had cause to see the High King, but she had heard many descriptions—and in any case, there was no mistaking her now, for no one else would dare to sit in that high chair. It was made of silver, with gold for the armrests and surrounding the head, and cushioned in plush white cloth. Enalyn sat in a pose of rest, one arm draped over the throne's right side, while her other elbow was propped up so that her chin might rest on her fist. She was a slight woman of no impressive height, but her gaze was keen and piercing. A thin golden circlet rested upon her hair, which had once been as raven-black as Loren's own, but now showed many strands of grey. Rather than any appearance of old age, it only gave her a mighty dignity that radiated through the room.

It was quite a long moment before Loren could tear her eyes away from the High King to see the others in the room. Many guards there were, in the same fine white and gold of the royal guard that she had seen at the throne room door. Then there were the courtiers, clustered in their splendid suits and gowns all along the sides of the hall. She also saw quite a number of Mystics in attendance, their red cloaks marking them as certainly as the badges upon their chests. But where all the Mystics she had seen before wore armor, and tended to look somewhat threadbare, like breeches worn from many months of hard travel, these ones were as clean and well-kept as the courtiers themselves. It was somewhat of a shock to Loren to see them wearing patterned breeches and tunics, and draped in cloaks of fine cloth and fur that she would have laughed to see upon Jordel.

They came to a stop at the foot of the dais. Loren raised her gaze to the High King—and then she noticed the two men standing to either side of her. One wore a red cloak over a suit of armor that looked more ceremonial than functional, and Loren took him at once for the lord chancellor of the Mystics. The other man wore grand, ornate robes of black with silver-threaded trim, and curious designs embroidered with gold and purple. That, and the hateful way he glared at Xain, led her to guess he must be the dean of the Academy.

A sharp kick from a plated boot made Loren's legs give out, and she fell to her knees before the throne. The guard who had met them outside the palace stepped forth, helm under her elbow, and spoke sharply to announce them.

"Your Majesty. I bring before you Xain, of the family Forredar, criminal beyond the King's law, sentenced to death by order of the Mystics."

"I see him, Sera," said the High King. Her tone was neither condescending nor sharp, but Loren thought she heard the hint of a joke inside it. "And who are these others you drag in his wake?"

"We do not know them, Your Majesty, but they came in his company."

Loren looked up to see the High King wave a hand,

and Sera stepped back. "You may speak for yourselves then, travelers. Who are you, and why do you walk in the company of this wizard? Come, you Mystics. Speak up."

Erik looked up doubtfully from where he knelt. When no one seemed likely to shove him back down, he lifted one foot to plant it flat on the floor and then laid his arm across the knee, in the position of a soldier reporting to a battlefield commander. "Your Majesty. I am Erik, knight of the Mystics. You do me great honor—but this girl, in the black cloak, is the one who should speak for us."

Loren's stomach did a somersault at that, and stars danced before her eyes as the High King turned to look at her with one eyebrow arched. Titters and excited murmurs burst from all the courtiers in the room, who whispered to each other behind their hands.

"Indeed?" said the High King, and now her voice betrayed real interest. "I find myself curious why a Mystic would cede the floor to one so young. Unless she is from some noble family, and I do not know it?"

Loren looked sideways, panicked. Xain only raised his eyebrows at her. She shot to her feet and raised her head—then, mortified, she realized where she was and fell back to one knee. The courtiers burst into subdued laughter.

"No noble girl, then, I take it," said High King Enalyn, but her voice was not unkind.

"No, Your Gra—Your Majesty," said Loren quickly. "I am Loren, of the family Nelda, hailing from the Birchwood."

"A forest girl," said Enalyn. "Tell me, Loren. Why do your words hold more weight in this room than a knight of the Mystics?"

Loren reached into her cloak and withdrew the letter from Kal. "Your Majesty, I . . . I bring a letter."

Enalyn looked to Sera, who took the letter from Loren's hand and gave it to one of the royal guard. The man climbed the dais to place it in the lord chancellor's hand. The lord chancellor was a spidery man, with spidery fingers, and Loren did not like the grimace on his face as he pried loose Kal's wax seal. Though he hardly paused before speaking aloud, Loren saw his eyes flit quickly back and forth across the paper, taking in the message before he spoke.

"She bears a letter from Chancellor Kal, of the family Endil. It declares that these travelers bear grave news of utmost importance to all the nine kingdoms, for the ears of the High King and her closest advisors only."

"This is a gesture so haughty as to be almost offensive," said the dean from Enalyn's other side. "Lord Chancellor, can you not keep your own Mystics in better order than this?"

"This was done without my knowledge or consent, of course, Your Majesty," said the lord chancellor, who looked as though he very much wanted to burn the letter in his hands, and mayhap the Mystics at the foot of the dais as well. "Please, allow me to remove this matter to my own chambers, and deal with it there where it need not trouble you."

"The Mystics may be your concern, but Xain is not," said High King Enalyn, her voice just sharp enough to bring the throne room to complete silence. "It was I who issued the order for his arrest—an arrest that your men have failed to carry out all these long months. Now he comes to the throne room of his own accord, bearing a letter from one of your chancellors. I think I shall pay it heed."

She nodded to one of the royal guard, and he moved quickly to clear the throne room. In no time it was done; the only ones who remained were Loren's party, the lord chancellor, the dean, and the royal guard.

"Now, Loren," said Enalyn, and once again Loren's heart skipped a beat at hearing her own name. "Tell me this grave news that threatens all my domain. And for goodness' sake, stand as you tell me, for the top of your head is not nearly so comely as those remarkable green eyes."

Loren swallowed hard, and found for a moment that her legs had failed her utterly. But at last they heard her command, and she forced herself to stand.

"Your Majesty. I have come . . . that is to say, we have learned . . ." She faltered, for the words would not come, no matter how hard she tried to muster them.

Enalyn leaned forwards, clasping her hands in her

lap. "You need not worry at your choice of words," she said gently. "Nor for how they will sound. If it helps, simply say it as plainly as possible. And worry not, for you are not the first to find your tongue tied in this room. Indeed, that was mayhap the greatest purpose of its design."

Loren smiled at that, if weakly, and cleared her throat. "Your Majesty. The Shades have returned, and the Necromancer with them, after many centuries. Even now they muster to make war upon all the nine lands. We found them in the Greatrock Mountains, and they have pursued my friends, and myself, ever since."

The High King's eyes flashed. But at her side, the lord chancellor only scoffed. "She comes here barking the words Kal has taught to her. He has said much the same thing to me, and many times over the years, as has his pet, Jordel. If he wished to trouble us with this nonsense, he could simply have sent a letter and saved us all much trouble."

Against her good judgement, Loren found wrath rising hot in her breast, and not the least at the lord chancellor's use of the word *pet* to describe Jordel, who had been one of the greatest men she had ever known. She spoke almost without thinking, and did nothing to hide her anger. "They *are* real, and they *have* returned. We know, my friends and I, for we have seen them. And Jordel would be here to tell you himself, but he cannot, for he died fighting the Shades, alone save for us, far away in the highest peaks of the Greatrocks. You should consider yourself honored if you ever so much as stood in the same room as such a man."

The room fell silent as death, save for the echo of Loren's own voice rebounding from the walls. The lord chancellor fixed her with a glare, while the dean's mouth sat open in a small *o* of disbelief. But the High King stood from her throne, one hand falling to hold on to it, as if for support. Immediately the lord chancellor and the dean fell to their knees, and Loren dipped her head again.

"Say again, girl. Jordel, of the family Adair, is dead?"

Loren's rage had fled her, and now she found it hard to speak around the lump in her throat. "Yes. He fell in battle, saving our lives at the cost of his own. Our road has been darker ever since. Your Majesty."

Enalyn bowed her head, silent. No one moved, or dared even to breathe too loudly. When the moment passed, she sat again. The lord chancellor rose, as did the dean, although somewhat stiffly.

"Remove Xain's gag," said Enalyn.

"Your Majesty," said the dean quickly. "I urge against that. He is a criminal, and sentenced to death for his crimes. Furthermore, he is an abomination, an eater of magestones. We cannot know that his mind is his own."

Enalyn turned to him, mouth twisted in displeasure. "Look at his gaunt cheeks, his wasted limbs. He is half-dead. Can you, as the dean of the Academy, not protect me and my court from so weak a wizard as this? For if that is the case, I know I would feel more comfortable with a much more powerful wizard holding your position."

The dean glared down at Xain, and there was more than a hint of anxiousness in his look. But he shook his head quickly. "Of course I will, Your Majesty, and it will be my great honor."

"Good," said Enalyn. "Remove it."

A royal guard hastened to obey, and once the cloth was removed, Xain flexed his jaw once or twice until it popped. Loren saw the dean holding his fingers in a claw by his side, lips parted as if ready to strike with magic. But Xain only rose to one knee and looked up at Enalyn—neither with anger, nor with shame. He looked only expectant.

"Did you speak over his grave?" Enalyn asked him.

Loren had not expected that, and by his look neither had Xain. He bowed his head. "No, Your Majesty. None of us could, for the grief of his loss was heavy upon us. But he fell from a bridge that spanned a great chasm, and into the stones of that bridge I inscribed my words."

"Tell me."

Here fell a great man
A clarion trumpet against danger
In darkness where none could see
His name was Jordel

Xain spoke the words as if they were a prayer, and suddenly Loren was back on the bridge by his side. She saw Jordel's mangled body once more, and the cairn they had built him of rocks, and his red cloak, which they had buried him in. She bowed her head, and tears sprang unbidden into her eyes.

Enalyn nodded at Xain when he was finished, a quiet smile on her lips. "That was very like him."

Then she clapped her hands, and it was as if a spell had broken. "Very well," she said. "If you speak the truth, and the Shades are indeed gathering power once more, we must put a stop to it immediately."

"Your Majesty, it would be a mistake to act too quickly upon this," said the lord chancellor. "You would be taking action based on the words of a known traitor and criminal, witnessed only by street urchins and children of whom we have never heard."

"They came escorted by four of your soldiers," said Enalyn.

"Soldiers who will receive appropriate discipline," said the lord chancellor, staring daggers at the Mystics, who studiously avoided his gaze.

"I fear I must confess myself still in mystery," said the dean, eyes narrowed as he looked from Xain to Loren and back again. "Who are these people the girl speaks of?"

"Time enough for a history lesson later," said the lord chancellor. "For now, I recommend that we rid ourselves of these . . . visitors. Your Majesty, with your leave, let us dismiss them and hold an emergency council to determine the best course of action."

"But you cannot mean to simply let Xain go free," said the dean quickly. "He has committed many crimes against the King's law, and must face his punishment."

Enalyn cut him off with a look. "No. At least not yet. If he has returned here of his own free will, then I can at least entertain the possibility that he has atoned for his crimes—or begun to." She turned to Loren and the others. "You will remain here, in the palace. Under guard, I am afraid, for I cannot let Xain roam free any more than I will consign him to a swift and brutal punishment. But you will not face justice until I know what is just, if you take my meaning."

"Your Majesty," said Xain, raising his head. "My son. If I could be permitted—"

But she fixed him with a hard glare, and he subsided. "I have not yet decided what to do with you, Xain. I will not reunite you with your son only to force him to part from you again. That is a cruelty I would visit upon no child, least of all my own kin, however distant."

Xain bowed to her once more, but Loren could see him fuming. The palace guards came forwards, lifted them to their feet, and escorted them towards the throne room door. But just as they turned, Enalyn called out sharply for them to halt.

"Forest girl," she said. "I had heard that a young girl of the family Yerrin was traveling by your side. Was I misinformed?"

Loren found her head spinning at that, for it seemed impossible that the High King should know anything at all about her. But she forced herself to think hard, choosing her words very carefully. "The girl was with us upon our road, but no longer."

Enalyn's head came up slightly, like a dog catching whiff of a scent. "And do you know where she is now?"

"I have some idea where she might be, but not exactly, Your Majesty." That was true enough, she reasoned. She knew Annis was on her way to Ammon, but she knew not where she was on the voyage, and in truth she did not even know where Ammon lay.

The High King nodded, and Loren felt that nod held understanding beyond words. "We will speak more of this. Farewell."

Then the guards' hands were upon her again, and the throne room was soon behind them.

TWENTY-SEVEN

They were whisked through a series of serpentine halls in which Loren was soon lost. Erik and the other Mystics were separated and led in another direction before Loren could say farewell. Soon she found herself before a chamber with a great wooden door. Inside were quarters more lavish than any she had seen in her life: in the middle was a large chamber with plush chairs around the walls, as well as an ornate table surrounded by many smaller chairs for eating. Many doors led off from the main room into bedchambers, each one of which was as large as the common rooms of any inn Loren had ever visited. Gem's eyes nearly popped from his skull at the sight of it all, and Chet was struck dumb. But Xain shrugged as he surveyed it.

"They are modest chambers by the palace's standards," he said. "Still, it is better than the prison cell I thought to find myself in."

Outside their door were posted several guards. There were two palace guards, as well as two Mystics— neither of whom had been among the Mystics they arrived with. One of them carried no weapons, and Loren guessed she was a wizard. Then there was a wizard from the Academy, wearing the same type of robes as the dean had worn, though nowhere near as lavish. Each type of guard looked at the other with as much distrust as they gave to Loren and her friends.

They spent all the rest of that day in the chamber. Gem ran about, ruffling the plush pillows and jumping on the beds until he had chosen one for himself. But Loren, Chet and Xain sat in the main room, silent save for the occasional answer to one of Gem's questions. Loren could not forget that, as fine as the quarters were, they were still prisoners, and they had no guarantee of any future safety. It put a damper on any conversation, and that night they went to sleep in their separate rooms with heavy hearts (though Loren still liked the soft feather mattress a great deal more than the hard ground of the road).

The next morning, servants brought them breakfast in the main chamber. There were eggs and sliced ham, and fine juices that Loren did not recognize the taste of. Gem wolfed his meal down, but she and the others ate more slowly. After all, they had nothing to do after they ate, and so there seemed no reason to hurry.

But in the midst of their meal, they heard an animated discussion just outside the door, and one voice in particular speaking very loudly. Then the door was thrown open, and a young man in fine clothing came barreling through. He took one look at them, and then fixed his eyes upon Xain.

"Xain!" he cried. "You mad, mad, *mad* fool. What in all the nine lands ever possessed you to come back to this forsaken island?"

Then he leaped forwards, dragging Xain from his chair and into a tight bear hug. Xain's eyes widened as though the very life were being squeezed from him. Loren and Chet stared at the man in shock. His clothing was nearly as fine as the High King's own, and was gold and white like hers with the same kind of breeches and a fine shirt. But he also wore a coat, and it was silver, and its threads shone in the early morning light that poured through the windows of the east wall.

"Loren, and Chet," said Xain, when the man had finally released him. "May I introduce, with some reservation, the Lord Prince Eamin."

Then Loren felt her throat seize up, and she shot to her feet just as Chet did the same. She wondered briefly if she should kneel, but before she could act upon it, the Lord Prince had her wrist in his hand and was shaking it as though she were a bag filled with coins that he hoped to loosen.

"The girl and the boy from the Birchwood, or so I have heard," said Eamin, and the smile upon his face was brighter than sunlight. "And you will be Gem, of the family . . . was it Noctis? I have never had a gift for names."

Loren thought Gem's smile might split his cheeks and keep running all the way to his ears. "You have mine perfectly, Lord Prince, and so I would call you a liar."

"Gem!" said Loren, gripping his ear tight. The boy squealed, but the Lord Prince laughed and patted his shoulder. But as he looked at Loren properly for the first time, his smile vanished, to be replaced by a look of wonder.

"You . . . Loren, is it? Come here a moment."

Loren looked at Xain uncertainly, but he seemed just as confused as she was. Slowly she stepped towards the Lord Prince. Without warning he took her shoulder with one hand, and with the other he tilted her chin up to look him full in the face. She smelled a faint whiff of perfume on him, pleasant and not at all overpowering, and on his breath was the scent of mint.

"You are touched with Elf-glamour," he said, voice scarcely above a whisper.

She swallowed hard and looked over to Chet. He

had looked somewhat annoyed as the Lord Prince drew her so close, but now he seemed concerned.

"Your . . . Your Highness?" said Loren, unsure of what else to say.

"I can see it in your eyes," said Eamin in wonder. "You have had concourse with the Elves. Only once before have I seen such a thing, and the tale behind it is well worth the telling. Speak, child. How came you to meet them? What did they say?"

Loren swallowed hard and looked nervously at Xain. She saw in his eyes the same wonder that was in Eamin's—and also a sort of understanding. He had seen it too, she realized. The day after she met the Elves, he had noticed something different in her eyes, though he knew not what he beheld.

Eamin seemed to think he had frightened her, for he released her shoulder and stepped back quickly. "My apologies. Only I have always been intensely curious about the Elves. It made me forget my manners. Forgive me."

Loren shook her head quickly. "There is nothing to forgive, Your Highness."

"You need not tell me the tale of this if you do not wish it," he said, insistent now. "I pressed too hard, and we have only just met."

"Though I, for one, would like to hear such a story," said Xain.

"Leave it be, Xain," said Eamin in a warning tone, though it was couched in a smile. "Tales of the Elves are things magical and precious, and belong to those who have lived them. If the girl does not wish to speak of it, you must not press her."

"As you say, Your Highness," said Xain. But Loren saw the look in his eyes and wondered how long he would keep that promise.

"Others have often told me I may have some relation to the Elves," Gem piped up, apparently tired of having lost the Lord Prince's attention for so long. "I doubt there is much truth to it, but they must be fooled by my exceptional appearance and cunning wit."

Eamin laughed out loud at that. "City children are such a welcome change from the stuffy sort we always get around here. And foresters, too," he said, beaming a quick smile to Loren and Chet. "Really, anyone who has not spent the last few years upon the Seat is preferable to anyone who has."

"Have I been away long enough to fit in that narrow category?" said Xain with a wry grin.

"Xain, my dear, dear friend, you have never been better company than *anyone* in this thrice-damned place." Eamin gave lie to the words by wrapping him in another embrace. Loren half expected to hear a rib crack. "Now, take your seats again. I am livid that I missed your arrival, and so to make up for it, now you must tell me the tale of all your journeys since you left the Seat."

Loren suddenly found her food bland in her mouth,

and her appetite gone. It seemed that all she had done for the past few days was recount the stories of their travels, and she had no wish to do so again. Standing and pushing her chair back, she nodded to Eamin. "Forgive me, Your Highness, but I will take my leave."

He looked up at her with concern. "I hope I have done nothing to offend you."

"Not at all," she said quickly. "Only I lived the tale, and have told it too many times, and have no wish to live through it again."

He nodded, and in his eyes she saw compassion. "Of course. And you need not call me Your Highness—in this room, you need call me nothing more than Eamin."

She bowed again, but could not stop herself from saying, "Thank you, Your Highness."

He smiled, and she left. Chet stood silently to go with her. Gem, however, stayed behind, for his eyes had lit up with glee from the moment he had beheld the Lord Prince.

Loren and Chet went to her room. It had a door set in the back wall, which led out to a wide stone balcony that overlooked a peaceful courtyard. There were chairs in which to sit, but she felt the need to stay on her feet. She went to the railing instead, leaning her elbows upon it and looking at the grounds below. Chet joined her there in silence. A beautiful garden was laid out before them both, and they saw gardeners going about their business among the flowers and the hedges.

"I know we are confined to these quarters," said Chet. "Yet it is hard to feel as though we are being cooped up. Scarcely in my life have I imagined such luxury as this."

But Loren had stopped looking at the garden, and instead she stared away north and east. Beyond the grounds below was the palace's outer wall, and then the city, and then the Great Bay stretching for miles. Somewhere on those waters was Annis. Or mayhap she had landed already in Dulmun, and was on her way to Ammon.

"I wonder how far away she is," Loren said softly. "And in what direction. I hardly spared a thought for her yesterday, but now I find myself missing her far more than I expected."

"She will be safe. I know it."

"You cannot know that for certain."

Chet turned so that he was leaning back against the railing. "But I can. You devised the plan for her safety, and if I have faith in anything in all the nine lands, it is your cleverness."

She gave a wan smile at that, but said no more. They spent a while looking out at the Bay, and then at the courtyard, and when Loren tired at last of standing they went to sit in two of the balcony's chairs. There they rested in the sun and the silence, until the door swung open and Gem came running out to find them. He looked thrilled enough to burst.

"The Lord Prince just left," he said. "Never have I

met such a man as he. Always quick with a joke, yet courteous to the border of fault. And Loren, you will not believe this—when I told him of the swordplay Jordel taught me, he promised to join me in practice. I will practice with the Lord Prince! I could never have dreamed of this when I was a starving little boy scuttling along the rooftops and gutters of Cabrus."

Loren smiled at him, and he fawned like a puppy whose ears had been scratched. He ran to the railing and drank deeply of the scent of flowers wafting up from below. But then Loren saw his gaze drift upwards, just as hers had, until he too was looking out across the Great Bay. He turned to them, seeming somewhat deflated.

"I wish I could tell Annis of this. I miss her."

She felt a pang of sorrow at the look upon his face, and rose from her chair to stand beside him. With one arm around his shoulder, she tried to mask her own worry with an encouraging tone. "I miss her as well. But mayhap we could write her a letter. Not to Annis herself, you understand. But we could write to Kal to tell him of the success of our mission, and include a secret message for her."

Gem perked up at once. "That is a fine idea. I can write it, since I know you have not learned your letters. But where will we find a quill and parchment?"

"Ask the guards at our door," she said. "I think they are under orders to provide us with anything we may require."

"Be quick about it, and remain cheerful," said Chet with a smile. "We will soon see her again, for with the Lord Prince at our backs I am certain this will be sorted out in no time."

TWENTY-EIGHT

THEY SOON DISCOVERED THAT CHET'S OPTIMISM WAS, if not foolish, at least misplaced. Day after day passed, and they received neither word nor summons from the High King. Nor could they leave their quarters, and spacious as those rooms were, Loren felt chafed by them before a week had passed. There were only so many chairs to sit in, so many soft cushions upon which to rest, before she felt she would rather fling herself from the balcony than spend one more day idle within her room. Their pleas to the guards outside their door fell on deaf ears, and even the Lord Prince Eamin grew frustrated. He visited often, and told them that he spoke to the High King every day on their behalf, but to no avail.

"I am on her council," he said, "yet she pays me no more heed than one of the guards standing in the corner. Everyone seems intent on doing nothing more than dragging their feet. Though the dean only learned of the Shades' existence less than a week ago, he acts as if he were the greatest authority in all of Underrealm when it comes to their motives and intentions. When he is not pontificating as to their next probable course of action, he claims that this is all a ruse on Xain's part to distract my mother while he destroys all the nine lands. Meanwhile, the lord chancellor counsels only caution—except that my version of caution would entail investigating the Shades' whereabouts, whereas his version means that we should do nothing."

If the rest of them were anxious for action, Xain was nearly beside himself with impatience. "What of the High King?" he asked, for what seemed to Loren to be the thousandth time. "In which direction does she seem inclined?"

"She withholds her judgement," said Eamin with a sigh. "She is not so shy as the lord chancellor, but neither does she wish to rush into a rash decision."

"There is wise prudence, and then there is indecisiveness," said Chet. "I would call this the latter."

"When your decisions can change the lives of many thousands, you yourself may find much reason for being indecisive," said Eamin. But though he spoke in defense of his mother, Loren could hear the frustration beneath his words. Xain only snorted and stared out the window with a dark expression.

After nine days had passed, the Lord Prince brought them different news altogether. This time he spoke to them in a low voice, leaning across the table with a sidelong glance at the door. "I thought I should tell you that the family Yerrin has been trying desperately to see you—or, I should say, to see Loren in particular."

Loren's throat went dry. Sweat sprang out upon her palms. "What do they want?"

"What do you think?" said Eamin, arching an eyebrow. "They seek the girl Annis. But the High King has forbidden them from obtaining an audience with you. Their representatives grew so insistent that finally she banished them from the palace grounds while you remain here."

"Well, at least that is one worry sorted," said Gem hopefully.

"I would not be so optimistic as to call that the end of it," said Xain.

"Nor I," said Eamin.

"Was it Damaris who was asking after us? Or servants of hers?"

Eamin blinked at her. "I am sorry, I thought you would know—no one has heard from Damaris or her caravan in weeks. Not since the time that you saw her last in the Greatrocks. When you arrived here and told the High King that part of your tale, all the palace chatter about her ceased at once. Either she has fled, knowing the High King would seek justice against her for siding with the Shades, or something else has happened to her that we do not know."

That gave Loren some relief. And at the same time, she found herself wondering after the caravan's fate. She doubted she was so fortunate that she would never hear from Damaris again. But then, she had assumed the merchant was alive. Now that she thought further, it seemed entirely possible that the Shades, or mayhap the Necromancer himself, had taken revenge on Damaris for the disaster in the Greatrocks.

It was a chilling thing to think that Damaris might be dead, and to her surprise she was not entirely certain how she felt about it. Moreover, she did not look forward to telling Annis the news. That would be no matter for a letter; it would have to be done in person, once they left the Seat.

If indeed we ever do leave the Seat, she thought to herself.

It was twelve days since they had arrived at the palace, and evening was working its way towards night. The dying red of sunset filled the sky through the window, and servants had already come to light lanterns throughout the room. The Lord Prince sat with them at their table for supper, and he and Xain were deep in their wine. Loren and Chet had poured themselves each a cup, but Loren found the palace wines too strong for her, and had only sipped gingerly.

Nightfall was the worst time for their mood, for it meant another day had passed without anything happening. Gem was slumped so far down in his chair that he looked like he might fall out of it at any moment. Though the Lord Prince tried to engage Xain in conversation, the wizard stared silently at his plate and hardly moved. Chet tried to smile each time Loren looked at him, but she could see it was forced. She felt, as she had for so many days now, the deep lethargy of their confinement.

There was a sharp sound outside their door. In her distraction, Loren almost did not recognize it, but deep instinct prickled the hairs on the back of her neck. Half a moment later, she placed it: the hiss of drawn steel.

They heard a great crash, and then the screams of people being killed. The door crashed open, and in rushed many figures holding daggers.

Loren shouted and leaped to her feet, and together the rest of them rose from the table. At once she dove for their weapons; the High King had ordered they be returned, but they had sat useless in a corner for the last twelve days. Now Loren snatched up her staff and turned to face their attackers. Chet was only a heartbeat behind her.

The figures struck, two of them coming for Loren with their knives bared. She backed up, forced away from Chet in the fight, and swung her staff wide to keep them at bay. They wore hoods and black masks that kept her from seeing their faces. She could only see their eyes, glittering in the light of the lanterns, and the flash of their daggers as they swung.

Though they had caught her off balance, she swiftly recovered. One of them fell to a heavy blow from her staff. As the other backed off a step, Loren struck the one who had fallen once more across the temple.

Behind her foe, she was scarcely aware of Chet facing another of the attackers. Farther off, the Lord Prince used his chair to fend two of them away from a weakened Xain. Gem battled another with swings of his sword. The boy showed far more grace than Loren had come to expect from him. It seemed his training had paid off at last.

All this she took in at a glance, and then the masked figure came for her. Her staff batted his dagger away, but he kept his grip. A smaller knife appeared in his other hand. This thrust towards Loren's stomach, but she sidestepped—almost too slow. The blade grazed her side, and she winced with the pain. But her attacker had stepped in close and was off balance. Loren brought her fist crashing into his nose. In surprise he dropped his blades, and Loren drove her fist into his gut. As he doubled over, she brought her staff down upon the back of his head with all her might. He fell to the floor and lay still.

Chet and Gem were still fighting. The Lord Prince

had managed to down one of his opponents, and had found a sword to deal with the other, who was being forced slowly backwards. Chet was holding his own, but Gem had his back to the wall. Loren could see the terror in his eyes.

She ran for him. He saw her coming and with a scream swung wildly at his opponent. The man leaped back, arms wide—and Loren drove the butt of her staff into his lower back. He clutched at where she had struck him, until she brought her staff about to knock him senseless.

Wincing at the pain in her side, she turned to Chet.

She was just in time to see his opponent drive a dagger into his chest.

The world seemed to freeze. All she could see was the shocked look in Chet's eye, and the silver hilt of the dagger that protruded from near his heart. The blood that poured from her side, and the glowing pain that came with it, vanished. There was only Chet's face, which even now grew pale before her sight.

Someone was screaming, and with some surprise Loren realized it was her. She tackled Chet's foe from behind, bearing him to the ground. With both hands she gripped his head, then slammed it into the floor twice in quick succession, until the man lay unmoving beneath her.

But above her, Chet was still on his feet, and his eyes had moved past her. She looked back to see the last attacker had disarmed the Lord Prince, and sat atop him trying to press the blade into his throat. Chet rushed past her and threw himself at the attacker, knocking him to the ground. The Lord Prince rose up and took the knife, using it to slit the man's throat.

Chet rolled off and away, falling to his back on the stone floor. He shivered, clutching with both hands at the hilt that stuck straight up from his breast. His teeth were gritted, lips peeled back in a grimace of pain. Loren was kneeling by his side, holding his hands, trying to stop him from pulling the knife out, for surely that would send his lifeblood streaming out of the open wound.

She was shouting, Gem was shouting, both of them screaming for help. Finally, far, far too late, guards came running through the door. They tried to pull Loren away from Chet, but she fought them off. Dimly she was aware of Eamin ordering one of the men away, away to find a healer, but she did not look up to see him go. She was looking at Chet, holding his gaze, willing him to keep his eyes open.

But she failed, and his eyes slid shut, while she screamed at him to open them again.

TWENTY-NINE

THE HEALERS WORKED THEIR CRAFTS UPON CHET through the rest of that night, and through the following day, and still they were there the morning after. All the while, Loren sat by his bedside and held his hand. Again and again Xain told her to try and rest, until at last Gem shouted at him to leave. Someone, probably Eamin, told her that the healers were the High King's own, and the best in all the nine lands. She did not listen. It did not matter. All that mattered was seeing Chet's eyes open again, yet hours turned to days and still they remained shut. Only the rise and fall of his chest, and the ragged breaths that scraped their way from his throat, told her he had not left her forever.

Gem stayed with her, sitting on the other side of the bed, and Xain was there during all the daylight hours. The Lord Prince was there nearly as often, now always escorted by members of the royal guard, and when he came Gem would give up his chair to sit at the foot of the bed, like a dog hovering near an ailing child. Eamin only left for the most vital duties from which he could not excuse himself, and always with deep and regretful apologies. The words fell empty on Loren's ears, but Gem would thank him, and greet him warmly whenever he returned.

On the second day, with Chet's eyes still closed, Eamin told them in muted tones of all that had transpired in the palace since the attack. "I owe you all a life debt now, and that is not the sort of thing I take lightly. We know the attackers were Shades, of course, and so I have been speaking strongly to the High King on your behalf. It is clear now that their threat is altogether too real. If they are confident enough to strike even here, then they must be wiped out before their power grows any greater."

"And is Her Majesty heeding your advice at last?" said Xain.

"Oh, indeed," said the Lord Prince. "She may not show it often in courtly settings, but as it turns out, my mother is actually quite fond of me. I can tell she is leaning towards our way of thinking, and now the dean and the lord chancellor fear to speak against me. When the dean tried, the High King nearly tore his head off."

It all passed like water over Loren, and when the words did register in the back of her mind, they came with a great wave of guilt. Chet had urged her often to turn from this course. He had come here only out of loyalty to her, and mayhap out of love, but not because he believed in their cause. And now he was the one with the gaping wound in his chest, clinging to life with his chances stacked against him.

Finally, on the fourth day, he opened his eyes—but only to shoot up in bed with a cry, fingers grasping at the bandages that covered his chest. Thankfully one of the healers was present. She commanded Gem and Loren to hold Chet's arms down while she gave him dreamwine. This soon calmed Chet, and he drifted back into slumber nestled in the thick pillows of the bed.

Thus came the second stage of his healing, and it was far, far more terrible for Loren than the first. Now Chet would awaken, but only to groan in great pain, and mayhap to weep into his pillows. Always she was ready with the dreamwine, and after a few swallows he would drift back to sleep, senseless. His eyes never seemed to fix upon her, nor did he recognize her voice. He existed in two states: the numb oblivion of sleep, and the unthinking agony of wakefulness. It tore at her very soul, and whenever she was alone she whispered her fervent prayers to the sky that it would end—but then, too, she was aware it might yet end in his death.

And then, on the eighth day, he opened his eyes and looked at her, and he smiled.

"Chet?" she said, taking his hand gently. "Can you hear me?"

"Scarcely," he said, the word coming slurred. "I feel as if my head is stuffed with wool."

"That is the wine," she said, voice cracking as tears came to her eyes. "You are likely as drunk as anyone I have ever seen."

"So I am," he murmured, lips barely moving. "Only I wish I were drunker still, for my chest hurts terribly."

"Do you remember what happened?" she said.

"Yes," he said, his voice grim for a moment. But it soon lightened again. "I am some sort of hero, I suppose."

"Some sort, mayhap," she said, laughing.

The healer came in just then, and when she saw Chet was awake she rushed to his side. She asked him many questions, of his pain and his breath and if there was any feeling in his hands, and so many other things that Loren lost track. In the midst of the questions Chet drifted back off to slumber.

"That is very good," said the healer, and Loren could hear the stark relief in her voice. "It means the worst is over. It will get easier from now on."

"When will he awaken in earnest?" said Loren.

"It will be several days yet. Such things take time. But he will gain more and more strength, and by tomorrow he should be able to talk for a while."

She left then, and Xain entered a moment later, accompanied by Gem, who had been off to relieve himself.

"He awoke?" said Gem. "What did he say?"

"Drunken ramblings," said Loren. "He has had more wine these last few days than I have in my entire life."

Gem clutched Chet's other hand, giddy, and even Xain gripped the foot of the bed, as though relief had made him suddenly weak.

Chet's eyes opened once more that night, and then again the next morning. Loren gave him more of the dreamwine, and fed him some breakfast when he asked for it, at the healer's instructions. But as she was spooning eggs into his mouth, the door of the chamber swung open, and High King Enalyn strode in, surrounded by members of the royal guard.

Gem fell to his knee before her, and Xain lowered himself more slowly. Loren did not move, though she did put the plate down upon the bedside table. The royal guards fixed her with an ugly look, but she stared right back at them in defiance, for nothing in the nine lands would make her move even that far from the bedside.

For her part, Enalyn did not seem bothered. All of her attention was for Chet. She went to his side at once, and lifted the bandages on his chest. He winced slightly, and she quickly replaced them.

"I am sorry," she said. "I only wished to see for myself that you were being well tended to."

"It is no trouble, Your Majesty. Only a mild sting-ing," he said weakly.

Enalyn sat in Gem's chair, which he had left empty, and scooted it closer to the bed. She graced Loren with a brief but warm smile, and then turned back to Chet.

"I have instructed my healers to give you the very best of care. Do you want for anything? Anything at all?"

"No, Your Majesty. They have been most satisfac-tory. The wine they provide, in particular, is very pleas-ing."

Enalyn smiled at that. "I imagine it would be. The wound will heal, but you will bear the scar of it forev-er. I wish that were not so, and yet you should wear it with pride, and with my gratitude. It is the price you paid to save the life of my son, and such a debt is not easily repaid."

"I will, Your Majesty," said Chet. "And it was my honor."

She laid her hand over his. Loren saw his face grow a little paler, and his jaw twitched as he gritted his teeth. The pain was coming back. Quickly she stood and reached for the wine, leaning over to help him drink it.

Enalyn stood from her chair with one more gentle pat of his hand. "Rest now. I will come visit you again when you are healed, to ensure that you have been well tended to."

When Loren had finished giving him his drink, the

High King fixed her with a look. "Now, Loren of the family Nelda, I must ask something of you. I know you do not wish to leave him, and no one could blame you. But my advisors and I require your counsel—and yours as well, Xain."

Loren set her jaw. "Your Majesty . . . I hardly think my words could be any more useful than theirs. I am a simple forest girl."

"I am beginning to think, as the Lord Prince has told me often in the last few days, that there is nothing simple about you," said Enalyn. "And in this case, I am afraid I must insist, for the fate of the nine lands may well rest upon it. We are all of us on the brink of a great and terrible time, and the bravery you have shown thus far might be the only thing that saves us in the end. But I must ask you to be brave again, and lend your wisdom to our plans, for they will need every bit of help to succeed."

She hardly knew how she could refuse such a request, though she still did not wish to go. But she felt Chet's hand close around hers where it rested on the bed, and he spoke gently to her. "Go. I shall be fine, and will eagerly await your return. But for a short time, I think Gem can get me drunk enough on his own."

"And happily will I apply myself to the task," said Gem brightly.

Loren looked to Xain, the only one who had not spoken. He gave her a solemn nod.

"Very well," said Loren. "I serve at your pleasure. Your Majesty."

"Thank you," said Enalyn. "And you may be assured of his safety—I will leave two of my royal guard here to watch him, and they will remain on post for as long as his healing requires."

"Thank you, Your Majesty," said Loren, this time with earnest gratitude. In the fitful snatches of sleep she had managed, her dreams were filled with visions of more Shades breaking into their quarters to finish them all off. With a final squeeze of Chet's hand, she set off and into the halls of the palace, trailing in the High King's footsteps with Xain at her side.

Enalyn led her back to the throne room, and this time Loren was able to take more time to appreciate the palace's finery as she passed it by. But the trip seemed to take no time at all, for the High King's pace was quick with urgency. They passed through the throne room in a rush, though it still seemed to take an age to cross the massive space. Behind the dais was a door, and Enalyn led them through it into a small chamber beyond.

It looked to be some sort of war room. Upon the great table in the center was laid a map of the nine lands, which Loren marveled to behold. She had seen only one map before in her lifetime, and it was a small, crude thing that Bracken had carried with him. This was drawn in exacting detail, with the names of all the great cities inscribed with beautiful penmanship. But her attention soon went from the map to the men who stood above it, for waiting in the room for them were the dean of the Academy and the lord chancellor of the Mystics.

The dean looked angrily at Xain the instant he stepped in through the door, while the lord chancellor cast a dark look upon Loren. Clearly neither man thought they should be there, and yet she could see that they were not eager to speak up about their displeasure. Instead, as Enalyn bade them to stand at the table over the map, the dean and lord chancellor endeavored to stand as far away as they could without actually fleeing the room.

First Enalyn made them tell their tale once more, in brief, and point out where each event had occurred on the map. Though Loren loathed to recount her journey yet again, she found it more bearable this time, for the High King was understanding and let her skip briefly over the darker memories. She seemed peculiarly interested in the battle of Wellmont, and had both Loren and Xain tell their sides of it, though Loren did not know how her account could be helpful.

"I was within the city, Your Majesty," she said, after she had told the tale. "I saw very little."

"And my mind was greatly preoccupied during the battle," said Xain.

"Yet every detail helps," said Enalyn. "Something

happened at Wellmont. Something we do not yet understand, and may not for a while yet. But say on."

Loren wondered what that meant. But she did as she was bidden, until they had spoken of the fall of Northwood, as well as the location of the Shade stronghold in the Greatrock Mountains. But the map clearly showed where the battles had taken place, and so they spent the greater part of their time trying to pinpoint the spot on the map where they thought the Shade stronghold had been, for of course it was not marked.

"It is as I suspected," she murmured. "All their activities are concentrated in the west, and have likely been strengthened by Dorsean troops."

"It seems that way, Your Majesty," said the lord chancellor.

"Your Majesty does not think the battle of Wellmont was the beginning of some petty border war," said Xain. It was not a question.

"No, I do not," said Enalyn. "I think it is a conflict motivated by the Shades, who seek to sow discord among the kings in preparation for an assault on Underrealm. If we are correct, then you have saved the nine lands by bringing me this information."

"What do you mean to do with it, then?" said Xain.

"The High King will put forth her strength, and the Mystics shall do the same," said the lord chancellor. "Together we will quell this uprising, unifying the kingdoms in preparation for the coming war."

"The Academy will send some of its strength as well," added the dean, sounding like a child who did not wish to be left out of a game.

"I am grateful we discovered it this early," said Enalyn. "As well as for the fact that you survived your journey to the Seat, Loren. Good fortune has blessed your travel, though I am certain it does not seem that way looking back on it."

She thought of Jordel, of Albern and Mag and Sten. "Thank you, Your Majesty, but it does not."

"Then there is only the matter of what to do with all of you," said Enalyn. "Certainly I cannot continue to treat you as prisoners, if for no other reason than your actions to save the Lord Prince. But neither can I allow Xain to leave."

Loren balked, but when she looked to Xain he only looked at Enalyn with grim understanding. "Your Majesty? I do not understand. Has he not proven himself?"

"Mayhap," said Enalyn. "Yet you are still a criminal by law, Xain, and I cannot discount the possibility— however remote—that this is all a deception for the purpose of clearing your name. If indeed we uncover a plot by the Shades behind the war in Wellmont, then I will consider your crimes paid for in full, and grant you pardon. You will be returned to full honor, and I will find you a place in my court, or in any court you wish across the nine lands."

"Your Majesty," said the dean. "You cannot mean to pardon his blatant—"

"That is enough," snapped Enalyn, and she stared at him until he subsided before turning back to Xain. "In the meantime, however, you may go wherever you wish inside the palace itself, though if you leave your chambers you will have to be escorted. And while you remain here under my care, you may see your son."

Xain tensed, his spindly knuckles going white where they held the edge of the table. Loren saw tears welling in his eyes, though he blinked furiously to hide them.

"Your Majesty . . . I . . ." His voice broke, and he shook his head as if to clear it.

"No gratitude is necessary, Xain," said Enalyn. "Go now and see him. You have both waited long enough."

He tried once more to speak, but it only came out as a sob. Hastily he turned, swiping at his eyes, and ran from the room as fast as his legs could carry him.

THIRTY

THE PALACE FELL TO BUSY PREPARATIONS AS THE HIGH King's army prepared to march off to war. Eamin could not come and visit Chet so often now, though he still came by at least once a day. Xain spent most of his time with his son, and was reticent to bring him to their quarters where the guards at the door plainly marked him as a prisoner. Loren saw him but once, a small, wide-eyed boy not half Gem's age, who looked at her green eyes in wonder and blushed as he hid his face in his father's pant leg.

Loren stayed with Chet always, even when Gem finally grew bored and went to practice swordplay with Eamin as promised. When he was finally able to sit up in bed, she would help him rise each morning, and aid him in lying down again each night. When at last the healers would let him try to walk, she would take his arm as he hobbled out to the balcony, there to sit with him and watch the sun make its slow way through the sky. Always Gem would come and visit them with news of the palace's goings-on, but the boy had clearly determined that Chet was no longer in any danger, and meant to experience every minute of the excitement.

For Loren, it was enough to simply remain with him.

Then at last, the day before the armies marched forth from the Seat, the healers came to remove his bandages once and for all. When they arrived, the High King came with them. Chet hastened to sit up, and Loren took his arm to help him. He left the bed and tried to kneel, but Enalyn took his shoulder and bade him to remain on his feet. Xain stood to the side, watching alongside Gem.

Slowly, layer by layer, the healers unwound the bandages from his wound. Soon he stood there bare-chested, clad only in his breeches, and Loren could see his embarrassment by the color in his cheeks. On the right side of his chest was the scar, an ugly and twisted mass of flesh, treated as best the healers could, but not quite enough to leave the skin smooth.

"Now you must still treat yourself with care," said

the healer, tilting her greying head as if Chet were a wayward child. "Engage in nothing too strenuous, and you will remain healthy enough."

"Thank you," he said quietly. The healer bowed and backed away.

"It is you who are owed thanks, Chet of the family Lindel," said Enalyn. "You stand before me healed, and yet scarred by a blade that was meant for my son. Only two men in this room can claim that."

She looked at Xain as she said this, and he bowed his head.

"For that I owe you a great deal. Any service I may give, so long as it does not break my vows to serve the nine lands, I will grant you. Ask for land or a lordship, and it shall be yours."

Chet swallowed hard, and his hand gripped Loren's shoulder more tightly. But he shook his head at last, and ducked his head.

"Thank you, Your Majesty," he said quietly. "I have never longed for anything like that. I only wish to go forth and see a bit of the nine lands, and see if I can find a better place to live than my home. And if I fail, then there I mean to return, for the woods are good enough for me."

Enalyn smiled, and she reached forwards to tilt his eyes up to hers. "That is well. But the young heart may seek to wander, while old bones wish to sit at rest. So long as you roam the nine lands, you shall do so with my blessing. And if the day should come when you wish for yourself a home, only say where, and so long as I sit my throne, I shall grant it to you."

Chet bowed to her, with Loren's help and many words of earnest thanks. Enalyn smiled once again, and then left them alone. All the excitement had rendered his knees somewhat weak, so after she helped him don a tunic, Loren helped him hobble out to the balcony where they spent the rest of their day.

As they sat there in the afternoon sunlight, she found herself studying him from the corner of her eyes, and her heart thundered loud in her ears. To see him there, so happy and carefree, overawed by the grace bestowed upon him by the High King, was a far greater thing than she had hoped for just a week ago. And she knew at last, and for certain, what she had long suspected.

They ate an early supper, alone, for Gem was somewhere wandering and Xain was with his son. Then she walked him to his bed, there in case he needed her support. But he did not reach for her, except to grip her fingers with his own.

He sat at the edge of the bed, and she helped him remove his tunic. But when he lay back and reached for his covers, Loren stopped him. With trembling fingers she undid the strings that held her own tunic closed at the top, and then lifted it from her body. When the cloth came away, she saw him looking at her with wide eyes.

"Loren . . ." he murmured.

She shushed him and undid her belt before climbing onto the bed, and then reached to undo the strings of his breeches.

From the palace walls the next day, they watched the armies march forth. All in a row they stood at the ramparts, Loren and Chet and Xain and Gem. Below them in the streets, the Mystics were gathered in rank and file. They wore shirts of mail and carried shields on their backs, and at their hips hung blades of castle-forged steel. Then came the High King's army, not so great as any of the standing armies of the nine kingdoms, but better trained and equipped with the finest of arms and armor. The tramp of their boots shook the ground so that those upon the wall could feel it, a deep shudder that still struck them long after the soldiers had vanished around the first bend in the road.

"The army will grow bigger as it proceeds south and west," said the Lord Prince, who stood with them to watch the march. He had already told them, with some disappointment, that he and the High King herself would be staying upon the Seat, with a token force to guard the island. "More Mystics shall join them from every city, and all of the Selvan army—that portion of it which was not already committed to the war in Wellmont, that is."

When they decided at last to leave the walls and return to the palace, it seemed incredibly empty. Many of the castle's servants were soldiers in times of war, and they had left, so that only enough remained to serve the royalty who stayed behind. Fewer guards patrolled the wall. The very air seemed subdued, waiting expectantly like a sailor's wife at the door.

Later that afternoon, Loren was sitting with Xain in the main room of their chambers. Chet was napping in his bedchamber, for watching the armies march had tired him out. Xain had a cup of wine in one hand, but he drank from it sparingly. Loren had discreetly asked one of the kitchen maids for silphium, and concocted a tea from it. It did not taste quite so bad as she had heard, for which she was grateful, but still she had lessened its bitterness with some honey.

"I think I know the smell of that tea," said Xain, keeping his eyes on the contents of his own cup.

"Mayhap you do," said Loren, and though she felt her cheeks glowing she refused to look at him. Still she could feel him smiling secretly to himself, and the silence that followed stretched just long enough to grow uncomfortable. "What do you plan to do with yourself now, wizard?"

He looked up in surprise. "Now? Why, wait for the armies to return, of course, and for my fate to be decided."

She rolled her eyes. "You know what I mean. The armies will return, and the High King will grant you your pardon. What then?"

Xain pursed his lips and shrugged. "I will tell you

the truth: I had not thought upon it overmuch. Until only recently, the notion of earning my pardon seemed too far-fetched to plan for. But it seems, to me at least, that you and I have done our jobs. And a wizard is of little value without a court to serve, they say. Who knows but that the High King will wish to keep me around for herself. If not, I am certain the Lord Prince would take me. What of yourself, forest girl? Where will Loren of the family Nelda, the Nightblade, journey from here?"

"First to Ammon, of course, to join with Annis again. After that . . . I suppose I am like you, and had not thought that far ahead. The road here occupied quite enough attention while we traveled it."

"But you still mean to continue your journeys?" said Xain.

"Why not? The nine lands are wide, and I have seen precious little of them. I thought for a time to visit Hedgemond, where Jordel hailed from, and see his family if I could. I may still do that. In any case, the world will always have a place for a thief."

"You are no longer a simple thief, if ever you were," he said. "And though your heart seeks to wander now, it may not always feel the same."

His eyes wandered to the door of Chet's bedchamber as he said it. Loren blushed again, and drank of her tea.

THIRTY-ONE

O<small>NE</small> <small>NIGHT, AS</small> L<small>OREN LAY IN</small> C<small>HET'S BED, HER HEAD</small> resting upon his arm, she heard a crash from outside the window. She shot up straight, eyes peering into the darkness. Nothing followed at first, but then she heard voices shouting, and the sound of many running feet.

Quickly she threw on her clothes and ran out upon the balcony, leaving her boots for the moment. Below her in the courtyard she saw guards running, all of them towards the front of the palace. But soon their footsteps faded from hearing, and the night was still again.

She went back inside, her nerves on edge. Too easily, her mind turned to memories of the night the Shades had attacked. She wished she had her dagger, but settled for fetching her staff and placing it on the floor near the bed. But she could not find sleep again that night, and looked up suspiciously at every wayward sound.

The next morning the Lord Prince came to visit them for breakfast. He seemed cheerful as ever, but she thought she saw worry lurking deep in his eyes. After they had eaten, she leaned back in her chair to look at him.

"Did something happen last night? I heard shouting, and guards running in the courtyard."

His smile dampened, though he fought to maintain it. "A small disturbance, and not cause for much concern. A Shade was discovered within the palace grounds. The guards found him, but in the pursuit they killed him before he could be questioned."

A shiver ran down Loren's back. Chet's brow furrowed as he looked back and forth between them.

"Another Shade?" he said. "That seems cause for a little concern, at least."

"Constables tracked down his dwelling within the city," said Eamin. "He stayed alone at an inn near the western gate, and arrived two weeks ago. It seems likely he was a lone informant, sent to spy on our doings and report to his masters. But they will receive no information from him."

He quickly turned the conversation to other matters, and soon had Chet and Gem talking animatedly. But Loren thought only of the Shade for the rest of their meal, and for the rest of the day besides.

"I think I will go into the city today to retrieve my dagger," she told Chet, as they sat together in his room later.

"Why?" he said. "The guard around our room has been doubled, and the palace is on high alert. The Shades would not try to attack us again."

"It will give me some peace," she said. "I have thought of it often, and though I trust Xain's friend Aurel, still as long as the dagger is gone from me I feel as though something is missing."

He slid closer, and slipped a hand about her waist. "Are you sure? Is there any way I can persuade you to stay?"

She slapped his hand and kissed him, and when at last she pulled back he was smiling. "No, there is not, brigand. I will return presently. If you remain awake, then you may do all the persuading you want."

Her black cloak had hung unused on a hook by the door since almost the first day they arrived. Now she went to fetch it, wrapping it around herself before slipping out the door. She and the others had been given free rein to explore the Seat—all but Xain—and so the guards hardly glanced at her as she slipped past them and out into the night.

Guards challenged her at the gate, but she told

them she only wanted to go for a stroll. They let her into the streets, which were now lit by torches against the darkness. Though the sun had set many hours ago, still there were plenty of wanderers, and she soon lost herself in the crowd.

She remembered the route they had taken to reach the silversmith's shop, and soon found herself standing before his large red door. As they had done last time, she slipped around the back to knock on the service entrance. Aurel opened it after just a few knocks, peering out at her from the warm glow of his home.

"You . . . you are Xain's friend," he stammered. "Forgive me, my memory . . ."

"Loren," she said, with an easy smile. "I have come for my things."

He blinked twice, and then whirled and scampered into the workshop. "Of course, of course! Come in, come in. They have been kept safe, of course, for I heard about all those goings-on at the palace. So glad to hear you and Xain were not beheaded after all." He gave a little cackle, and Loren forced a smile.

There was a crack in the floor she had not noticed, and into it the smith drove a metal spike. This he levered up until one of the stones came loose. Beneath was a shallow hole, and in the hole was her box. Aurel fetched it for her and placed it gingerly in her hands.

"There you are, girl. No one knew it was here, and no one knew what was inside—not even me!" He gave another odd little giggle.

"Thank you," said Loren in earnest, for just to hold it was a relief. He turned away discreetly while she fetched her dagger and the packet of magestones from the box. When she was done, she closed it and handed it back to him.

"I am in your debt. If ever I can be of service to you—"

"Do not make me laugh," said Aurel, waving his hand. "Anything for a friend of Xain. Come and visit whenever you wish, or if you ever need goods of silver."

"I shall. And if anyone asks me who is the best silversmith in all the nine lands, I will tell them it is Aurel of the High King's Seat."

He kissed her cheek at that, and she vanished back into the night. Ducking into a back alley, she pulled forth one of the magestones and bit into it. She drew her dagger and held it reversed in her hand.

The dark streets lit like day, and the torches became like tiny pinpricks of light, weak and ineffectual compared to the illumination provided by her own sight. Now she moved with greater confidence, running through the darkest streets as she made her way west.

Once she reached the gate, she looked about for an inn. She soon discovered a problem: there were too many. The Seat was grander and more populated than any place she had seen before, and offered plentiful places for travelers to stay.

She found an old man leaning in the doorway of a shop, tugging at his beard as he watched her pass by.

Loren stopped short, went to him, and gave him her friendliest smile.

"A good evening, friend. I heard tell the constables came through here, searching the room of some dead man. Can you tell me what inn they went to?"

"I heard something that sounded like that," said the old man. "But age is the great poison of memory, they say, and has only one antidote."

Her smile lost some of its warmth, but she dug into the purse at her belt and drew forth a gold weight. "Is this the antidote?"

The old man snatched the coin with a flourish. "It may well be. The very inn behind you, called the Shining Door, is the one you seek." And he walked away, clicking his heels on the stones of the street.

Loren threw back her hood and stepped into the common room of the Shining Door. It was bustling with occupants, and in the commotion no one gave her a second glance. She studied the room, wondering if she would have to pay another gold piece to find out which room the Shade had paid for. But when she took a look upstairs, she found that unnecessary. One door hung loose, slanted on its hinges, and the jamb was splintered where it had been kicked in by the constables.

Looking over her shoulder to ensure she had not been followed, she ducked into the room. No lamps were lit—a welcome advantage, for while the darkness would keep anyone in the hallway from seeing her black cloak, it was no proof against her sight.

She went to the bed, hoping the sheets had not yet been changed. A quick sniff told her that was unlikely. Running her hand along the pillow, she found what she was looking for: a few pale hairs clinging to the fabric. These she picked up before leaving the room and making her way outside.

A moment's search revealed the nearest torch, which she pulled from the wall and carried into an alley far from sight of any major street. She held the blade of her dagger over the flames as Jordel had taught her, until the air above the blade wavered in the warmth. Then she dropped the hairs onto the metal, where they fizzled and vanished in a puff of smoke.

The black designs on her dagger began to twist and shift, coiling around each other as though they were grasping for something. Then they snapped together, all pointing in one direction: east.

Loren grimaced. This was the magic Jordel had taught her, and now it told her several things. First, that there had been more than one Shade, for the one they found in the palace had been killed. The dagger would not reveal a corpse. Second, the other Shade— or mayhap there had been more than two?—was a wizard of some description, for the magic only worked upon them. And third, the other Shade had left the inn. Mayhap they had even left the Seat.

She owed it to herself at least to search, and so with the dagger acting as her compass, she ran through the city. She never faltered or stumbled, for in her eyes the streets were as bright as day. So she made her way tirelessly eastward, running at the loping, easy pace she had learned after years of running between the trees of the Birchwood.

But at last she reached the city's eastern end, and before her loomed the gate that led to the docks thrusting out into the Great Bay. Still the designs on the dagger pointed east.

Mayhap it meant the Shade was on the other side of the gates, on a ship but still on the Seat. Loren doubted it. More likely the Shade had fled when their companion was killed, and was even now far away on the sea—mayhap in Dulmun, mayhap even farther. Wherever they were, they were beyond Loren's reach, for the guards would not open the gate for her now, at night.

Shoulders slumped in defeat, Loren turned and made her way back through the city to the High King's palace, and spent a fitful night thinking of the Shades.

THIRTY-TWO

Some days after that, the Lord Prince Eamin visited them once more. He had taken to wandering listless about the palace, slouching in his stance and dragging his feet. When he and Xain would sit together and drink wine, Loren overheard him confide to the wizard that he was bored out of his skull, and would much rather be on the road with his mother's army than cooped up here like some prize hog. But today when he came to them, there was a bounce in his step and a rare light in his eyes.

"We received the first messenger back from the

army," he told them. "They reached Redbrook some days ago, and now march west for Wellmont."

"They have made good time," said Xain.

"They are fighters, and have sat here on this island for years and years, with no wars to fight," said Eamin. "They were eager. The letter says the Dorsean army has already retreated from Selvan lands, and its generals have sent messages to the High King's army begging for mercy."

"Have they guessed that we know of their scheming with the Shades?" said Xain.

"That is what it sounds like," said Eamin with a shrug. "And more is the pity! The first time we have marched to war, true war, in my lifetime, and it is over before a single battle can be fought."

Loren found herself looking askance at him. She did not see it as any great loss to have avoided a battle between such mighty armies. But then, the Lord Prince was just the sort of man to long for the glory of battle. As he himself said, he had never truly fought in one. It was a curious thought, that she had seen the horror of war when such a great man had not.

"In any case, my mother—Her Majesty—thinks it might be a ruse. So we will accept their surrender, but proceed with caution just the same. The Dorseans will present all their military leaders, who will be put to the question by the constables' most able practitioners for any connection to the Shades. Those who are found guilty will be executed."

"A neat affair," said Xain. "Though there will likely be more work to do afterwards. The Shades undoubtedly have pockets all over the nine kingdoms. None may be a threat in and of itself, but if united by the Necromancer their power could be disastrous. I do not think you need lament our current absence of war, for the fighting will surely—"

His words died on his lips as horns blared across the walls of the palace.

They all sat there frozen for an eyeblink. Then everyone tried to rise at once, making for the door. It flew open and they nearly fell out of it in their haste, but then the guards were there, blocking the way with their weapons.

"The wizard must remain," said one of them. "By the orders of the High King."

"He is allowed to leave with an escort, you twit," said Eamin.

"While there are horns upon the wall, he shall stay," said the guard. "Forgive me, Lord Prince, but I obey Her Majesty."

Eamin looked as though he might argue it, but Xain pushed his shoulder. "Go. I will remain here. Only do not leave me waiting forever!"

Then they were all running down the hall, and soon they reached the courtyard and took the steps up to the wall. Chet was leaning heavily on Loren as they moved, and his breathing came hard, but still he kept pace with the rest of them.

"The horns come from the east!" said Eamin. "Quick!"

He ran along the wall until he reached the eastern battlements, and there slid to a stop with his hands on the stone. He leaned out, looking with squinted eyes across the sea. Loren and Chet joined him a moment later, searching in silence. The bay was shrouded in mist, for it was still early morning, and at first they saw nothing.

Then at last, they burst forth from the mist. Thousands of sails, lining the horizon from north to south. It was a fleet of Dulmun ships, each of them mightier than the *Long Claw* that had brought Loren and her friends to the Seat, and all ready for war. Though the distance was great, Loren could see the soldiers and sailors running back and forth across the decks as they prepared for a landing.

"Give me a moment," she said quietly, and then ducked away from Chet to run for a torch that sat, unlit, in the wall. She pulled it out, then used her flint and tinder to light it before thrusting her dagger into the flames. It had been days since last she used it, and she had no idea if it would still work. But it did, for the designs twisted upon themselves almost immediately, and just as they had before, they all pointed towards the east.

Loren cursed and stomped out the torch before running back to the others. "The Shade the guards found in the night," she said breathlessly. "He was not alone. His companion fled the Seat and went east to Dulmun, there to raise this fleet."

Eamin stared at her in wonder. "How could you know that?"

"Trust only that I know it," said Loren. "This is not some insurrection by Dulmun, but a planned stroke by the Shades."

The air erupted with horns again, making Gem jump. He stomped his foot and shouted at the spires atop the palace. "Yes, we have heard you! You may stop blowing now!"

"Those are not the same horns," said Eamin, looking fearful. "They came from the west."

Wondering what could possibly be going on now, Loren took Chet's arm again and helped him along as they followed the others in a mad run to the west wall. When they reached it they stopped, and Loren felt hope flee her. Before them lay the narrow strait between the High King's Seat and the shores of Selvan. And upon those shores, still pouring out of the Birchwood forest, came a great army of Shades in grey and blue, mounting their boats and making ready for an assault upon the island.

THIRTY-THREE

THEY RAN BACK TO XAIN AS QUICKLY AS THEY COULD. Loren had already started putting the pieces together in her mind, and when they reached the wizard, Eamin said what she had already begun to suspect.

"It was all a ruse," he said, gasping from their run. "The Shades meant for us to think that Wellmont was their doing. They meant for you all to warn the High King, so that she would send out the Mystics and the greater strength of her own army to put a stop to the fighting. They never meant to start a war between Dorsea and Selvan. They always meant to take the Seat."

Xain's eyes were wide, and for the first time since she had known him, Loren thought he looked truly terrified. "They will sack the city. They will kill anyone they can get their hands on."

But Loren herself felt sick, as though she could barely keep down her gorge. "It is our fault. We thought we were warning them, but we were only delivering the very message the Shades wanted us to bring."

Eamin shook his head quickly. "You cannot blame yourselves for that. You could have done no differently than you did. We have been outfoxed, as simple as that."

"Nothing is simple. I have doomed the Seat, and mayhap all the nine kingdoms. All because I thought to assume Jordel's place, and take charge of a war I was never prepared to fight."

"You did just what he would have done, and so you cannot insult yourself without insulting his memory," said Eamin. "So ask yourself now: if Jordel were here, what would he do?"

Loren swallowed, eyes darting around, trying to think. She could only picture the sails coming in upon the horizon, and the shapes of grey and blue pouring from the Birchwood. "He would . . . he would save the High King. That is the only thing we can do. She must survive."

"Just my thought," said Eamin. "Let us see to it."

They went to the door, but once again the guards stopped them. There were three of them, two swordsmen and a wizard, and their faces were hard.

"I am sorry, Lord Prince Eamin," said the one who had spoken before. "I cannot disobey the High King."

Eamin looked over his shoulder as though exasperated. But he fixed Loren with a knowing look. She nodded.

Quick as a blink, Eamin seized the guard's tunic. His forehead came crashing down on the bridge of the man's nose, and the guard crumpled to the floor. Loren leaped past the other for the wizard, whose eyes glowed white as she reached for her magic. But Loren knew she was a firemage, and Jordel had taught her something of how to deal with them. She clapped her hand over the woman's mouth to keep her from speaking, then drove a fist into her gut. The light died in her eyes, and as Loren punched her in the jaw, those eyes rolled backwards. The woman collapsed.

Behind her, Eamin had already knocked the other guard unconscious. "A poor reward for doing their duty," he said. "I shall have to remember to make things right with them, if any of us survive this."

Then they were flying through the halls of the palace, which had erupted into a torrent of confusion. Soldiers, guards, and servants ran every which way, none of them seeming to know which way to go. But everywhere they went Eamin cried, "Warriors, to me! To your Lord Prince and the High King! The rest of you, flee the Seat! To me! To me!"

They heard him, and armed soldiers in plate stopped their scrambling to follow. Soon they had a fair little procession making its way through the palace, until they came to the throne room and found it guarded by men with spears. They leaped forwards to attack, but stopped when the saw the Lord Prince, and raised their weapons.

Eamin kicked open the door and ran in, Loren and the rest at his heels. The High King stood by her throne, and to Loren's amazement a squire was helping her into a suit of plate armor. But she looked at Eamin and the rest of them as though this were any ordinary afternoon upon the island, and raised an eyebrow as if in mild interest.

"Lord Prince Eamin," she said. "Have you any more news about what is happening, or must I continue listening to counselors who have no counsel?"

"Erin!" Xain saw his son standing among the courtiers clustered near the throne and went running for him.

"Papa!" The boy leaped into his father's arms and held him tight.

"I ordered him to be retrieved the moment the horns sounded," said the High King.

"Thank you, Your Majesty," said Xain, his voice shaking.

"Your Majesty, the Shades attack from the shores of Selvan," said Eamin. "They are pouring from the Birchwood in great strength. Even now they board boats to cross the channel, and may already have arrived at the island's western gate."

"Do you think we can hold them?"

"Mayhap we could, but at the same time a fleet comes from the east. They are ships of Dulmun. We thought the Shades had enlisted the help of Dorsea, but that was a deception. They have mustered Dulmun to their banner, and mean to take the Seat to stake their claim to power."

"A clever ruse," said Enalyn. "I might have known the warning came to us too easily."

"Your Majesty," said Loren, throwing herself forwards and dropping to one knee. "No words can express my—"

"Oh, *stand,* girl. You cannot think to blame yourself for this, for you did nothing wrong. Indeed, had you acted any other way, it would have been treason." The last plate was strapped to her arm, and her squire helped her don gloves of interlocking metal scales. "Now it seems we must have a fight, if we wish to leave this island alive."

"Your Majesty," said Loren, rising to her feet. "I do not see how you can fight your way through so many. There might be another way, a means of escape besides—"

"Be silent, girl," said the lord chancellor, staring at her with venom. "Beside the High King stand the greatest warriors Underrealm has ever known, and each of them would give their life for hers if need be. We will fight our way through, you may count on it."

"Where is the dean?" said Enalyn, as though she

had not heard either of them. "I should have thought he would be here by now."

One of the royal guard standing nearby looked about uneasily, and then stepped forwards to speak. "Your Majesty . . . when we went to find him, we found his chamber empty. A student at the Academy said they saw him fleeing west, probably trying to escape the city before the battle."

"Craven to the very end," said Enalyn, shaking her head with a steely glare. "Let that be a lesson to you, girl: never appoint a wizard based upon his political convenience. Are we ready?"

"Your Highness—" said Loren, looking to Eamin, who was donning his own armor with the help of a page.

"Thank you for your counsel, Loren, but these are warriors all," he said. "They will break through, if it can be done at all."

With that, the High King raised her sword. Around her assembled the members of the royal guard, and outside them a sizable force of castle soldiers. Together they pressed forwards to the door of the throne room.

"Stay close to them," said Xain, holding his son tight in his arms. "Look for a chance to help, but do not join the fighting if you have any choice. Wars fought in cities are often the bloodiest."

Loren did not need the warning, for she still remembered Wellmont. But she nodded.

Quickly the procession made its way into the palace's main hall. Still there was no resistance; Loren hoped they might reach the city before they encountered the Shades. Out in the streets, she thought she might be able to find a path to escape if the High King should become surrounded. Here in the palace, with only a single door to march through, it felt as if they were walking into the jaws of death itself.

The palace's front door crashed open, and soldiers in blue and grey charged in with a roar. Over their heads flew black arrows, some landing among the High King's guard while others narrowly missed Loren and her friends. She fell to the ground with a cry, dragging Chet with her. He landed with a grunt, and together they huddled until the rain of arrows ceased.

When they could stand again, they saw Enalyn's force heavily engaged with the Shades who still poured in through the door. At once Loren saw the truth of what the Lord Prince had said: these were fine warriors. Their armor was thick and true, and the blows of their enemies could not pierce it. Their swords were sharp and gleaming, but soon streaked with the red of blood. Enalyn and Eamin were in the press, and every time an enemy drew near they struck quickly to cut them down. But for every Shade they killed, another stepped into place, and still more came through the door. Loren could see no end to their number. And each man of the palace guard who fell was irreplaceable.

"Retreat!" she cried in panic. "There are too many!"

Mayhap someone heard her, or mayhap they saw the truth for themselves. In any case, someone with a battlefield voice called the withdrawal, and they backed away slowly, making the Shades pay in blood for every foot of their advance. Armored hands seized the High King and the Lord Prince and dragged them backwards, out of the fighting and into the open space behind. The royal guard came with them, while the rest of the soldiers formed a rearguard to slow pursuit.

"Quickly!" said Eamin. Blood ran down his face, but Loren could not tell if it was his own. "They will cover our escape. Into the palace!"

They fled, and quickly, but still the clash of steel on steel followed them through the halls.

THIRTY-FOUR

THEY STOPPED IN THE MAIN COURTYARD, THE ROYAL guard still in a protective ring around Enalyn. Loren and the others came to a halt nearby, and with a sharp gesture Enalyn beckoned them forwards.

"There is another entrance we mean to try," she said. "The rear gate is smaller and more easily defended. The Shades might have ignored it, focusing their strength instead on the wider front gate."

"But then again, they might not," said Loren. "Your Majesty, let us find some way to get you to safety other than force of arms, for I do not think that will serve us."

"She is informing you, not asking for your counsel," said the lord chancellor. "It is a courtesy you should be grateful for."

"If we escape to the east, that only means it will be even harder to make for the western docks and escape," Chet said angrily. "Your duty is to save the High King, not die gloriously in battle beside her."

The lord chancellor's face turned ugly, his voice to a low snarl. "I know my duty, boy. I wager I have had it longer than you have been alive."

Enalyn silenced him with a stern look and turned to Loren. "There is a hidden entrance. But it runs from the palace to the eastern docks. Those docks are currently occupied by the Dulmun fleet. Our foes have planned their attack well, and likely they were long in concocting their strategy. These men know their way about a battle. Put your faith in them."

The sound of tramping boots filled the air, and a fresh group of palace soldiers marched into the courtyard to join them. "There are the reinforcements," said the lord chancellor. "Your Majesty, we should be moving."

He led them on, back into another wing of the palace that Loren had never explored. She soon became turned around and lost, and resigned herself to following the armored backs of the soldiers before her. Before long they pushed through another, smaller door, and found themselves in a narrow open space between the back of the palace and the eastern wall.

There was the gate, smaller than the one to the west. Above, guards on the wall loosed arrows at unseen foes on the other side. But they could scarcely peek out from the battlements without having to duck a hail of enemy fire.

"It looks as though there are many of them beyond the gate," Loren called out.

"Let us hope not enough," said the Lord Prince. "Open the gate!"

The shout went up the wall, and guardsmen in the gatehouse leaned to the wheel. With the groaning of chains, the gate swung slowly inwards. Almost at once, Loren saw swords and spear tips pushed through the gap.

Eamin held his sword aloft and gave a battle cry. The palace guards charged into the fray, and the Shades were thrown back from the wall. They turned in a rout, many fleeing into the streets and vanishing into the alleys of the city. But some of their captains managed to rally, and slowly the grey and blue uniforms came together once more. The Lord Prince's charge stalled, and the palace guards were pushed into a circle against the wall. Loren and her friends could not get through the gates, for it was blocked by armored bodies.

"They cannot get through," said Gem. "They will be cut down."

Loren did not answer him, but looked at Chet, and in his eyes she saw the same fear. Dread seized her heart. She had brought the enemy here and doomed the High King, and now she was powerless to save them.

Shadeborn. Shadeborn. Shadeborn.

A chant had begun to build beyond the wall. Loren quailed, for she recognized the word. That was what Rogan had called himself when they met in Dorsea. She craned her neck, and above the fighting she saw him. He had pressed through his troops to stand at their head, blocking the High King's escape into the city.

Shadeborn, shadeborn, shadeborn.

Bolstered by their captain, the Shades were pressing forwards in earnest, and the palace guard were forced back through the gate. She saw the lord chancellor hacking desperately, trying to cut a path through the enemy. With a cry of rage he threw himself forwards, attacking Rogan himself.

His blade caught in the hook of Rogan's axe and was turned aside. Then they danced, the lord chancellor striking with sword and shield both, while Rogan held his axe in both hands, his shield slung across his back. With the haft of it he blocked strike after strike, the lord chancellor pressing forwards. But Loren could see Rogan's smile beneath his helmet; he was toying with the Mystic, drawing him out and into the midst of his army.

A sword came swinging from the left, and the lord chancellor caught it on his shield. But in that moment's distraction, Rogan struck. His axe came down in a punishing blow that the lord chancellor barely avoided. But he was off his balance now, and Rogan pressed him back. Where before they had been matched blow for blow, now Rogan's axe was a blur of speed, striking so quickly that it took all the Mystic's skill to hold him off.

The axe bit deep into the joint at the shoulder, and the lord chancellor dropped his sword as he sank to his knees.

Twice more the axe rose and fell, first severing an arm, and then taking the head at the neck. The lord chancellor's body fell beneath the boots of his enemy, and the Shades roared their approval.

With renewed vigor they pressed forwards now, and Rogan led them in another charge. The palace guards had to retreat through the inner gate. But the guards atop the wall had been slain, and the portcullis remained raised. Loren, Chet, and Gem threw themselves at one of the doors, struggling to push it closed against the mass of bodies. Loren stood at the edge of the door, just a few paces away from the fighting. Her heart thundered as steel flashed and blood soaked the pavement at her feet.

"Loren!" cried Rogan, drawing her gaze. He wore a rictus grin, blood covering his armor. She saw the hilt of a sword sticking from the side of his breastplate where someone had landed a blow, but the Necromancer's dark magic kept him on his feet. "Daughter of the forest. You have done your duty well. Thank you for laying the path of our conquest."

She gritted her teeth and stepped away from the doorway to snatch her bow. In the blink of an eye she drew, and whether it was by Albern's training or some stroke of luck, her shaft sank into Rogan's left eye and out the back of his head. His body went limp as a rag doll, and he fell beneath the press.

The palace guards gave a great cheer, and the Shades wavered. The Lord Prince led a counterattack, and they pushed their foes back through the gates. But the press of bodies was too thick beyond the walls, and it was all they could do to push the gates closed. The royal guards seized the Lord Prince and the High King and dragged them back into the castle, with Loren and her friends hastening to follow.

THIRTY-FIVE

"THAT WAS A WELL-PLACED SHOT," SAID THE LORD Prince. His helmet had been knocked loose in the fighting, and Loren saw a bruise blooming to life on his cheek. "I had heard from Xain that you had no taste for killing."

"He will not die," said Loren grimly. "A dark enchantment protects him, binding him to life."

"Still, it secured our escape, and I thank you," said the High King, who had knelt to wrap a bandage about the knee of one of her royal guards. The woman had taken an arrow.

"You are welcome, Your Majesty," said Loren. But the words were scarcely out before she turned on her heel and ran down the hallway towards the staircase.

"Loren!" said Chet. "Where are you going?"

"Finding us an escape," she said. She took the stairs two at a time. Chet hastened to follow her, but he soon slowed, wincing at the injury in his chest. Though she wanted to scream with impatience, Loren stopped and went down, taking his arm to help him.

"Why go up?" said Chet. "We cannot fly away from here."

"Mayhap, but one never knows. Certainly it seems that the ground floor has no escape."

She threw open a door leading to one of the wide open balconies that ran all around the palace exterior. Below them she could see the fighting at the eastern wall. As she had expected, Rogan stood at the head of his soldiers again. The gaping wound where his eye had been was already stitching itself shut.

Loren looked around in desperation, searching for some other way, some hidden door she had not noticed before. It seemed impossible. She had been a guest here less than a month. How could she find a new route of escape more easily than those who had lived in the palace their whole lives? But she had to try. She ran down the balcony, around a corner of the building, and the sun blinked as it vanished behind the arches for a moment.

Chet nearly ran into her as she stopped in her

tracks. When he saw her looking up, his gaze followed. "What is it?"

She did not answer him. She was looking at the arches. The palace stretched out in five great wings. Along the top was a balcony, just like the one they stood on now, but thirty feet higher. And from the end of each wing sprang an arch, rising gently before dipping back down to meet the towers that stood at each of the five corners in the castle's outer wall.

"Come with me," she said, and ran back into the palace.

When she reached the High King, the royal guard were engaged in a furious argument with the Lord Prince about what to do next. Xain and Gem stood apart. Gem saw them and came running, eyes wide.

"Where were you?" he said. "I thought you had run off and abandoned us."

"You are not so lucky as all that," said Loren. "You must suffer our company a bit longer—quite a while longer, if I have my way."

"What do you—" he began, but she pushed past him to speak with the High King.

"Your Majesty," she said, cutting through the argument between the Lord Prince and the royal guard. "There may be a chance to get you to safety."

They all stopped at that and stared at her. But where Loren had quailed under their gaze in the throne room, now she had no time. She pressed on before they could answer.

"We have no chance of victory by warfare, as any of us can plainly see. All the castle entrances are blocked. This is not a time for blades and armor, but for stealth and secrecy. Shed your arms and follow me, and I can get you beyond the palace walls."

"How?" said the Lord Prince, incredulous.

"The arches. They stretch from the top of each wing to the towers. They are high, but they are wide enough to walk on, and not too steep. But we have to go quickly, for it will be a dangerous crossing, and if they see us they will try to shoot us down."

"That is madness," said one of the royal guard. "It is fifty feet in the air."

Enalyn studied Loren's face for a moment before turning to Eamin. "What is your counsel, Lord Prince?"

He looked at Loren in wonder, and she could see the thought working its way through his mind. "I . . ." he began.

THOOM

They heard a great crash outside, and the roaring of an army.

"They have broken the eastern gate!" said one of the palace guard. "They are within the walls!"

"Enough," said Enalyn. "If they are in the walls already, we have no choice. Up the stairs, and quickly!"

Loren led the way, jumping up the steps like a satyr on a mountainside, with Chet and Gem just behind. The High King followed, while the Lord Prince helped

Xain and his son make the climb. Four of the royal guard came with them, the rest staying behind to guard the ground floor against the invaders.

Up and up the stairs wound in a spiral, and Loren ran past every floor. Only when she reached the top at last did she take the door leading out of the staircase, and quickly turned about to get her bearings. In a moment she found the door leading outside, and took it to another balcony. She went to the railing and looked down at the courtyard far below, where she saw the Shades doing battle with the palace soldiers on the pavement. The sight of it drew her gaze for a moment, but she forced herself to break away.

A few paces farther along the balcony, she found the spot where the arch joined the castle wall, some two paces below the balcony railing. It was not such a far drop, but it made Loren dizzy now; the arch was mayhap two paces wide, and if they stumbled upon landing, it was another fifteen-pace fall to the courtyard below.

"That is not an easy jump," said Chet beside her.

"It is the only way. Would that we had a rope! There is one in my pack, but I left that in our quarters."

The door opened behind them, and the rest of the procession came out onto the balcony. Xain took one look at the height and reeled heavily away from the railing. But Gem stood brightly on tiptoe, leaning far over the edge. "I made far more difficult leaps than this on the rooftops of Cabrus," he remarked.

"Your Majesty, you cannot think to go through with this," said the royal guard. "It is certain death."

"Certain death is the battle that rages in the palace even now," said Loren. "This is a hope, however slim."

"Two paces, is about how slim I would call it," said the Lord Prince.

"Unless someone is willing to suggest an alternative, my decision has been made," said Enalyn. "Now help me out of this armor."

She and Eamin and the royal guard shed their plate as quickly as they could. Loren tried to help, though she knew little of how the pieces strapped together. Before long they stood only in their regular clothing and light shirts of chain, which would not hinder their movement.

"Now, we must go down one at a time," said Loren. "We should send one or two ahead of the High King, to help catch her and steady her landing."

"I will go first," said Chet, and before she could argue, he seized the railing and vaulted over the edge of the balcony.

"*Chet!*" she cried, running to the rail.

He landed hard on the stone of the archway, taking the shock of the landing with his legs and falling forwards. He spread his hands wide and gripped either edge of the stone path, holding himself steady. For a moment he lay there, recovering. Loren could see the pain in his face where his wound had been jostled in the fall.

"Up, boy," called one of the royal guard. "I am coming down, and have no wish to crush you." He was a burly man with a trimmed beard, somewhat advanced in years but still strong. As Chet scrambled to his feet, the guard lifted himself carefully over the railing, then held on to it as he lowered himself as far as he could. When he was at the limit of his reach, he dropped. Because he was facing backwards, he landed badly and fell onto his rear with a grunt, nearly rolling off the edge. But Chet gripped his shoulder to steady him, and he got back to his feet.

"Make haste," said Loren, for she was looking past the arch to the ground far below. The Shades had broken through the soldiers in the courtyard. Even now they were in the palace, ransacking its halls in search of the High King. "Your Majesty, are you ready?"

"Send them first," said Enalyn, gesturing to Xain and his son.

"Your Majesty, I—" Xain began.

"No time to argue," she snapped. "Your son first, and then you."

Xain took his son, Erin, and held him under the arms. "Look at me, son. I am right here. I will come right behind you. Be brave for me." Erin nodded, though his eyes were filled with tears.

Slowly, ever so slowly, Xain lowered him over the edge. Loren helped, leaning over to grip one wrist while Xain held the other, and together they hung as far over as they dared, until the boy's ankles were just a pace above the outstretched arms of Chet and the royal guardsman. Loren nodded to him, and they let go. Erin fell into Chet's arms, where he clung to his chest.

"You next, wizard," said Loren. "I can lower you down, if you like. You cannot weigh more than a sack of potatoes."

Xain glared at her a moment before climbing hastily over the rail. He landed without trouble, and then they lowered the High King. She jumped down quite nimbly, and Chet was there with her guard to steady her landing.

The door to the balcony flew open, slamming into the wall with a crash. Loren looked over her shoulder to see Shades run into the sunlight, sun gleaming from their gore-soaked blades.

"Run!" she cried, waving desperately to Chet and the others. "Get the High King to safety!"

Xain was already walking carefully along the arch with his son, and was a good distance ahead. The royal guard looked up at her with a grim nod and seized the High King, dragging her away. Enalyn fought him desperately, trying to return to the balcony.

"Eamin!" she cried in anguish. "Eamin!"

"Jump," said the Lord Prince, hefting his sword in his hand. "We will do our best to hold them off."

Three royal guard remained with them on the balcony, and one of them spoke gruffly over his shoulder. "No, Lord Prince. You must get to safety. We shall remain here."

"I am afraid they are right, Your Highness," said Loren. "Forgive me."

She nodded to Gem, and together they gripped Eamin's arms and half-threw him over the railing. He went over the edge with a shout, and they held him at the last second before he dropped. Just before he had time to recover and try to climb back up, they let him go, and he fell to the arch. Chet caught him and dragged him back, just as Loren and Gem jumped over together.

Gem had vaulted a bit farther, and landed catlike on the stone. But Loren had misjudged the width of it, and landed too close to the edge. As she fell forwards on her knees, her left hand came down on air instead of stone. She pitched to her left, and for a terrifying moment hung out over empty space, and her body froze in terror.

"No!" cried Chet. He leaped, landing in a slide on his back and gripping her tunic. Desperately he dragged her back, until she rolled over and came to land on top of him, her face less than an inch from his own.

"Keep your mind on the matter at hand, hunter's son," she mumbled, but her voice shook, as well as her hands where they gripped his shirt.

"It is not my mind that wanders, woodsman's daughter," he replied.

"If you two are quite done?" cried Gem, who was already up and running along the arch, and had turned back to see them there.

They scrambled to their feet and ran. Loren risked one glance back only, to see the royal guard holding the railing against the Shades. But there were too many, and one by one they fell. The last one took a blade to the gut, the tip of the sword thrusting out the back of his jerkin. He seized two of his foes and pitched backwards over the railing, and the Shades screamed as their bodies fell to break on the pavement below. Loren turned forwards and ran on.

Hissing filled the air as arrows whizzed by them, but by now they were too far to get a clear shot, and soon the arch dipped back down to block them from view. The slope was gentle enough to keep firm footing, and soon they had reached the top of the tower at the end. There the others waited for them, but other than that the tower was empty. Loren looked off down the walls and saw no one. The Shades had broken into the palace, and all the wall's guards had been slain already.

"They are coming," said the royal guardsman. Loren turned to see that some Shades had braved the jump, and even now came along the stone archway towards them. One more tried to jump as she watched, but he missed his landing and pitched off into empty space.

"They are foolish," said Xain. Loren could see how it pained him, but still his eyes glowed as he summoned his magic.

Flames burst forth, striking the Shade in the lead,

and she screamed as she beat at the fire. Lurching back, she struck the man behind her, and together they fell screaming from the arch. But more were coming down from the rail, and from somewhere they had found a rope. Even now they were tying it about the railing, and then they would be climbing, not jumping.

"Rope!" said Loren. "We need to flee, not fight."

The tower's hatch lay gaping open, and she went down into it to search. There in the corner she found what she was looking for: a long coil of rope, thick and strong and well-woven. She threw the coil over her shoulder and climbed back out into the daylight. Chet helped her tie it around the tower's outer rampart with solid knots. Xain held the archway against the Shades as they advanced, while one by one the others climbed down the tower's outer wall.

"Your turn, wizard," said Loren.

"Go first," he said. "I will be right behind you."

"Do I need to throw you again?"

He growled and turned, climbing down the rope. Loren kept a careful eye on the archway, but the Shades were too far away. As soon as Xain was far enough down, she followed him, and soon they were all fleeing through the streets of the city.

THIRTY-SIX

THE GREATER PART OF THE FIGHTING HAD MOVED within the palace, but there was still much of it in the streets. They had to move cautiously, ducking out of sight whenever a group of Shades came running by. They had climbed down the northwest tower of the palace wall, and did not have far to go to reach the western gate. But the way was slow, and they could not take the main streets, for those were well patrolled.

Loren felt as though she were suffering the fall of Northwood all over again, for all about them they saw the corpses of citizens in the streets. Only this time she was the one escorting others out of the city's destruction, rather than the one being rescued. She made a silent vow to herself: if need be, she would give her life to save the High King's, in token of payment for Mag, Sten, and Albern, who had sacrificed their lives for Loren.

They heard the tramping of boots and pressed themselves against the wall of a shop. Shades ran by, along the street and towards the palace. Loren leaned out to watch after they had gone, ensuring they were out of sight.

"How will we reach the western gate?" said Eamin. "Surely they will have it guarded, especially if they know we have escaped the palace."

"We may be able to break through," said Xain. "I have my magic, and you have your blades."

"Swords we have, but no armor, unlike our enemies. And forgive me for saying so, my friend, but you are nearly at the end of your strength."

Enalyn turned to Loren. "What say you, girl? We have made it this far by your counsel."

"I do not know, Your Majesty," said Loren. "In truth I had not thought that far ahead, for I was not certain we would escape the palace at all."

"How comforting," said Enalyn.

"We scaled one wall," said Chet. "We can scale another. Where can we go where the Shades will not be gathered in strength, where we can make our way into a tower and then down the other side?"

"To the north," said the Lord Prince. "But the

problem is not the city wall. It is the docks. They will all be swarming with Shades, and we cannot escape the island without a boat."

"One bridge at a time, my lord," said Chet. "If we can make it beyond the north wall, then let us go to the north wall."

"I see you share Loren's gift for not thinking far ahead," said Enalyn.

But Loren was looking out beyond the edge of the building, her brow furrowed in concentration. Not far away, a strong wind whipped at the banners that flew from the western wall. "They have not burned the buildings," she said.

Xain looked at her sharply. "What?"

"They have not burned the buildings. In Wellmont, the Dorsean army sought to burn as much as they could. Here, the Shades are sacking the city, but they are not trying to destroy it. Why?"

"Likely they mean to occupy it," said Eamin. "If they can take the Seat for themselves, it will be a demonstration of their power."

"No," said Enalyn, eyes widening. "They cannot risk their fleet. If the flames spread from the city to the docks, their ships will be destroyed. Then they will be trapped here, unable to flee if we should attack them in strength."

"I do not see how that can help us," said Xain. "Unless we mean to burn the city down ourselves, in the hope that it spreads to their ships."

"I think that is precisely what Loren has planned," said Enalyn with a grim smile.

Loren turned to them. "The ship's crews will have remained with their vessels, as well as some soldiers to guard them. If they see the city beginning to burn, they may leave the ships to come and fight the fires. We could slip past them then, to take a ship for ourselves and flee."

Eamin stared at her as if she had gone mad. "You mean to burn our own city?"

"It is lost already," said Enalyn, who had begun to nod. "I think this plan may be a wise one. A strange sort of wisdom, certainly, and yet it may work."

"Can you muster the flames, wizard?" said the royal guard.

Xain's skin was pale, and his arm shivered as it wrapped around his son's shoulders. "I have little strength left. But I will do what I must."

"You may not have to," said Loren, struck by a thought. "Torches will suffice. Find them, and collect more as we move to the western wall. We will set flames wherever we think they may catch. Then, Xain, you can spread the fires with wind."

"That would be easier," he said.

"Let us go, then, and quickly," said Enalyn.

They set off once more, this time faster, for their steps held purpose again. Many fixtures on buildings held torches, and soon each of them had collected a great armful.

When they reached the west wall, they looked to see if any Shades were nearby to spot them. But none were about. One torch sat in a fixture on the wall above them, but rather than remove it, Loren had Xain light it. Then, one by one, she held the other torches in its flames until they caught.

She, Chet, and Gem ran out and among the buildings. Any place they found a shop with wooden shingles, or an inn with a stable full of hay, they flung their torches. Soon smoke rose from several buildings, and before long the smoke turned into flames. They reached for the sky with angry red fingers, and their heat filled the air.

"Now use your magic, Xain," said Loren.

Eyes glowing white, he put forth his power. The air howled and whistled before his hands, and a heavy gale swept in from the sky. It struck the houses and carried the flames south, throwing sparks and flaming brands across all the western side of the city. In no time it seemed that half the island was burning.

Casting her cloak about her, Loren ran to the western gate. As she neared it she slowed, searching warily for anyone who might spot her. But no one was in sight as she sidled up to the gate. The great wooden doors lay broken upon the ground, torn from their hinges by a battering ram, or else by some powerful magic. The portcullis still hung in the air; the attackers must have raised it during their assault.

She peered around the corner of the wall towards

the docks, and her heart sang. There were the Shades who had been left to guard the ships, and they were running towards the city walls. Behind them the ship crews streamed from their vessels, carrying buckets which they dipped into the waters of the bay.

Hastily she withdrew, and ran back to the others. "It worked," she said. "They are running to douse the flames. We should get closer to the gates, and be ready to run the moment we find an opening."

Step by step they followed her forwards, coughing and casting their cloaks across their mouths to stop themselves from breathing in the soot. Xain's son buried his head in his father's shoulder, crying. Loren soon realized she did not have to worry overmuch about being spotted; the smoke that poured through the streets, as well as the scorching heat of the flames, kept the Shades' attention. Sometimes they passed soldiers only a few paces away in the smoke, but attracted no notice.

Soon they emerged coughing, running as quick as they could into the open square before the western gate. But the moment the smoke left their eyes they skidded to a halt on the paving stones.

There stood Rogan, framed by the gate. His axe and shield were battered and stained, and his armor bore many rents from blows he had taken in the fighting. He stood alone, for all his soldiers were in the city to fight the fires. But Loren quaked in her boots, for she knew that he was easily a match for all of them.

"I see I was right," said Rogan. "As soon as I saw the smoke rising from the city, I knew you were making for the boats. A clever tactic."

Her throat was dry. But Chet stepped forwards to stand at her side, and Gem and Eamin with him.

"You may stand aside, if you wish," said the Lord Prince. "I swear we will let you live."

Rogan laughed at that, blood standing out shockingly red against the white of his teeth. "A precious sentiment, princeling. Here is my counter: kneel and present your necks for my axe, and I will make the killing quick."

"Remember the tattoo. You cannot defeat him," Loren said quietly. Then she turned to Xain and the royal guard who stood by the High King. "Get yourselves out of the city, and the High King as well. We will hold him off as long as we can."

"I will not leave my son," said Enalyn.

"You will if you must, Your Majesty," said Loren firmly. "If he will not run from this fight, still you must reach the shores of Selvan in safety."

"What are you whispering there, Nightblade?" said Rogan. "I think you have used your last clever strategy. Come, let us make this quick. There is no need for you to suffer as Jordel did."

Loren turned on him. Her bow was light in her hand, and she ached to use it. "You may not speak his name."

Rogan smiled, and despite all she knew of him, it

looked kind. "You truly loved the Mystic, did you not? The look in your eyes . . . it is almost worship. He should not have died. He should have been on our side. I can only imagine the sort of captain he would have made in our ranks. I am what he could have been—but better, for I will never die."

She nocked the arrow without thinking and loosed. It sped true, but Rogan lifted his shield to block it. Then he was charging forwards, and Eamin met the first blow with his sword.

"Get her away!" cried Loren.

Enalyn began to circle around, making for the gate under the escort of her guard. Xain only stood there, looking at Loren in wordless fury.

"Go," she said. "You remember what happened when you tried your magic on Trisken. You are even more useless here than I am."

He nodded and followed the High King, his son in tow.

Loren turned, another arrow nocked. Gem had edged forwards, his sword held forth, but his hands shook and he looked ready to flee at any moment. Chet was a couple of paces ahead, holding his staff, but he seemed just as lost. They knew, as Loren did, that they stood no chance against Rogan. They could only distract him.

But Eamin was doing a remarkable job of that for the moment. He matched the brute stroke for stroke, and even without a shield his guard was impenetrable.

His armor had been left atop the palace, and he used that to his advantage, dodging around blows rather than trying to meet them head-on, and returning light, quick strikes that Rogan had to move quickly to avoid. He hoped to tire his opponent, who was burdened by his armor, and then move in for the final blow.

As Eamin and Rogan backed away from each other for a moment, Loren drew and fired. The arrow glanced from Rogan's pauldron, knocking it sideways. Chet swung with his staff, and Gem took another step forwards. But Rogan recovered quickly and blocked the staff with his shield, then swung wide, forcing them both back. Eamin lunged and struck again, and his blade found purchase in Rogan's hip. The brute grunted and stepped back, hiding behind his shield.

"I had heard you were a mighty warrior," said Eamin lightly. "But it looks as though your enchantment is your only strength."

"It is strength enough," said Rogan with a smile.

Loren looked past him to the gate. Enalyn and Xain had almost reached it, her guard at her back. Rogan's attention was on the Lord Prince—it was going to work.

But that hope proved false. Rogan whirled on the spot as though he had eyes in the back of his head and came at them in a rush. Eamin ran to follow as the King's guard stepped forwards to block her. But with three swift strokes, Rogan knocked the man's sword aside and planted the axe in the guard's chest. He sank to his knees with a grunt, dropping the sword to grip the axe with both hands.

That gave Eamin a moment's advantage. He plunged his sword into Rogan's back beneath the backplate. Rogan cried out in pain, arching backwards and grasping at the hilt of the sword. It was out of his reach, and Eamin held fast, pushing him away from the High King.

"Go!" cried Loren. She slung her bow on her back and ran forwards, seizing Gem's and Chet's arms and dragging them through the gate. Enalyn was beside them, and Xain, with his son. Just beyond the wall she stopped and turned to look.

Still Eamin held Rogan like a pig on a spit. But Loren could see the glow of dark magic around the Shade captain's neck, and already his flesh stitched itself together around the blade.

Like a snake he turned, ripping the hilt from Eamin's hand. His mailed fist crashed into the Lord Prince's face, then his chest. Loren had a horrifying flash of memory, of the way Jordel's chest had caved in under Trisken's mighty blows. Eamin struggled to hold his feet, but Rogan struck him hard with both fists clenched, and he went flying to land on the ground beside Loren.

"Impotent children," snarled Rogan. "Come here, that I may show you the true power of death."

He took a step forwards—and then stopped to look down. The royal guard still lived, somehow, and had wrapped an arm around one of Rogan's ankles. The head of the axe was still buried in his chest. With what remained of his strength, the guard used his free hand to pull it out with a roar. He flung it away, and it went skidding across the pavement towards Loren's feet.

"Girl!" he cried. "The chain!"

Loren's eyes widened. She ran to the axe and wrapped both hands around its haft.

Rogan, oblivious, tore his plated boot free from the guard's grip. The foot came up, and then down with a horrifying crunch. Again and again he stamped, until the sound of it grew horrible and wet.

His gaze rose to Loren, bloodlust making his eyes nearly glow. She stood facing him, at the edge of the gatehouse, all her strength barely enough to lift the axe. Rogan bared his teeth in a grin, and then threw back his head to laugh out loud.

"What do you mean to do with an axe you can scarcely even wield, girl? You cannot kill me."

"I know," said Loren, and swung with all her might at the chain that held the portcullis.

Rogan barely had time to look up before it came crashing down, crushing him under its weight. Two of the three-foot spikes along its bottom pierced his chest, sinking into the stone below, while he screamed in agony.

Loren dropped the axe and ran, helping Lord Prince Eamin to his feet. Rejoining the others, they fled to the docks where a fleet of boats waited.

THIRTY-SEVEN

THE GATES OF THE PALACE OF GARSEC, SELVAN'S CAPITAL city, swung open before them. Limping and sore, Loren and the others made their way through. Inside stood Anwar, king of Selvan, along with a retinue to receive them. Quickly his healers ran forwards, their white robes swishing about their feet, to tend to Enalyn.

"I am well," she said, waving them off. "See to the Lord Prince and the others."

Anwar came forwards at once, taking a knee before her. "Your Majesty," he said. "I cannot express my relief at seeing you alive and well."

Enalyn reached down and took his hands, drawing him to his feet. "King Anwar. Thank you for your hospitality in our time of need."

"I could do no less," he said earnestly. "I blame myself for this. With so many of our soldiers south in Wellmont, we did not keep watch over the Great Bay, and did not see the attack upon the Seat until too late."

"You could not have known."

Loren watched as the healers saw to the Lord Prince Eamin's injuries. They were bruises only, and would heal with time. He kept trying to push them off, but with the High King's command ringing in their ears, they would not leave him alone.

They had sailed the short distance southwest across the water and to the docks of Garsec, and immediately sent word of the High King's arrival. While they waited for a carriage to be sent, they had stood upon the docks and watched the Seat across the water. The smoke grew thicker and thicker, until the orange glow of the flames could be seen all across the island. The fires they had set consumed nearly everything, until the Shades were forced to flee the island's destruction. Across the strait they sailed, to land on the coast and vanish once more into the Birchwood. Meanwhile the Dulmun fleet set sail for the east, returning to their homeland to plot their next stroke. One whole kingdom had risen in rebellion against the High King that day, and who knew which others held treason in their hearts?

"You are deep in thought, girl."

Loren blinked, and then ducked her head in a half-bow. While she had been distracted, looking out through the palace gates, Enalyn had approached from behind. "I apologize, Your Majesty."

"Do not. I, too, find my mind much occupied. Will you walk with me?"

Loren nodded, and Enalyn led her out through the gate. The palace sat upon a great hill, almost a mountain, in the middle of the city. Outside its walls was a wide open space, from which they could survey the city and all the lands beyond. Enalyn took her north, where far away they could see the green of the Birchwood. There she stopped, and stared at the forest for a while.

Just as Loren was beginning to grow uncomfortable in the silence, the High King spoke. "I owe you a great debt. Many times over, in fact."

Loren shook her head quickly. "I did only the duty that was passed down to me."

"Many do their duty. Sometimes that duty requires much of us, and carrying it out should be seen as a fine thing."

"As you say, Your Majesty."

Enalyn turned to her suddenly, meeting her gaze unflinching, and Loren felt overshadowed despite standing a head taller. "I have need of those with honest and loyal hearts. I have had many such servants, but they are all of a type. Like the lord chancellor, or even my son, they think only of the great battle, the wartime stratagem. We need something else now. The strength of the Shades is not their might of arms, but the plans they hatch when they believe we cannot see them."

"Indeed, it seems we cannot. None of us knew their plans, and thus we played the very game they set out for us."

Enalyn looked into her eyes. "That is what I mean to fix, if you will help me."

Loren balked. "Your Majesty? I do not understand."

"I would have you enter my service, Loren of the family Nelda. My personal service, answerable to me, under the direction and guidance of Chancellor Kal, to whom it seems I should have been listening for some time now."

"You . . . desire my service," said Loren. She could not wrap her mind around the idea. *I am a simple forest girl,* she told herself. *A daughter of the Birchwood.* And yet here she stood, and there was the High King. "Your Majesty . . . I do not know what to say."

"Say you will serve me, of course," said Enalyn, but she softened it with a smile.

Loren fell to her knee at once. "Of course, Your Majesty. You do me great honor. But . . . what am I, exactly?"

"I have told you your task already."

Loren shook her head. "That is not what I mean. I

will be the agent of your will. But what am I? When I act in your name, what will I call myself? Your advisor? Your messenger?"

"Your title? There is a name already, I hear, in the stories people whisper about you. Let that be your title. Let them call you my Nightblade."

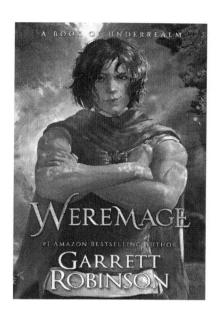

GET THE NEXT BOOK

You've finished *Shadeborn*, the fourth book in the Nightblade Epic.

Your next book is *Weremage*. Get it here:

Underrealm.net/Weremage

CONNECT ONLINE

FACEBOOK

Want to hang out with other fans of the Underrealm books? There's a Facebook group where you can do just that. Join the Nine Lands group on Facebook and share your favorite moments and fan theories from the books. I also post regular behind-the-scenes content, including information about the world you can't find anywhere else. Visit the link to be taken to the Facebook group:

Underrealm.net/nine-lands

YOUTUBE

Catch up with me daily (when I'm not directing a film or having a baby). You can watch my daily YouTube channel where I talk about art, science, life, my books, and the world.
But not cats.
Never cats.

GarrettBRobinson.com/yt

THE BOOKS OF UNDERREALM

THE NIGHTBLADE EPIC
NIGHTBLADE
MYSTIC
DARKFIRE
SHADEBORN
WEREMAGE
YERRIN

THE ACADEMY JOURNALS
THE ALCHEMIST'S TOUCH
THE MINDMAGE'S WRATH
THE FIREMAGE'S VENGEANCE

CHRONOLOGICAL ORDER
NIGHTBLADE
MYSTIC
DARKFIRE
SHADEBORN
THE ALCHEMIST'S TOUCH
THE MINDMAGE'S WRATH
WEREMAGE
THE FIREMAGE'S VENGEANCE
YERRIN

ABOUT THE AUTHOR

Garrett Robinson was born and raised in Los Angeles. The son of an author/painter father and a violinist/singer mother, no one was surprised when he grew up to be an artist.

After blooding himself in the independent film industry, he self-published his first book in 2012 and swiftly followed it with a stream of others, publishing more than two million words by 2014. Within months he topped numerous Amazon bestseller lists. Now he spends his time writing books and directing films.

A passionate fantasy author, his most popular books are the novels of Underrealm, including The Nightblade Epic and The Academy Journals series.

However, he has delved into many other genres. Some works are for adult audiences only, such as *Non Zombie* and *Hit Girls,* but he has also published popular books for younger readers, including The Realm Keepers series and *The Ninjabread Man*, co-authored with Z.C. Bolger.

Garrett lives in Oregon with his wife Meghan, his children Dawn, Luke, and Desmond, and his dog, Chewbacca.

Garrett can be found on:

BLOG: garrettbrobinson.com/blog
EMAIL: garrett@garrettbrobinson.com
TWITTER: twitter.com/garrettauthor
FACEBOOK: facebook.com/garrettbrobinson

EPILOGUE

ROGAN'S BOOTS SHUFFLED UNCERTAINLY THROUGH THE soil of the Birchwood, and his path swayed back and forth. He tried to muster his strength. It would not do for the Shades at his back to see their commander weak and wandering. His hand went to his chest with a grimace. Still the wounds had not fully healed, where the portcullis had punched through plate, flesh, and bone all at once.

His teeth ground together. He did not fear his father's wrath, but only the thought of failing him. Rogan was the favored son. All his life it had been said to him. And now he had failed the man to whom he owed everything.

"Are you disappointed, my son?"

Rogan staggered to a halt, as did the soldiers behind him. His eyes filled with tears at the voice.

"Wait here," he said, keeping his back turned so that they could not see his face. "Do not move until I give the order."

He stalked off into the woods, towards where he had heard the voice. He did not have to search far before he stopped, the tears spilling down his cheeks.

"Father," he whimpered. He sank to his knees, leaves crunching beneath him. "My father. Forgive me."

"Forgive? You committed no sin, child. Stand. This was no fault of yours."

He bowed his head. "I took the task upon myself. Tomorrow should have been a day of rejoicing. We should have sent word to all the nine lands that the High King was dead and the Lord Prince captured."

"I gave you your task, Rogan. The blame lies with me, not with you."

Rogan shook his head fervently, almost maniacally. "No, *no*, Father. You are the greatest among us. No design of yours is at fault. I am your arm, meant to carry out your aims, and I am weak."

He felt the fingers resting on the top of his head, gently stroking his hair. His tears fell harder, and he curled in upon himself at the touch.

"When Trisken fell in the Greatrocks, I was wrathful. I held him accountable, for I thought he had underestimated the girl. But now I have made the same mistake. She was the perfect messenger, but I did not think she could save the High King."

"I should have stopped her," whimpered Rogan. "Forgive me."

"You are forgiven. Her victory will soon be hollow, like wine turned to ash in her throat. The High King has lost this war before it is begun. For I have found the trail of my great foe, and soon my children will bring her to me."

Rogan tensed, eyes glittering, and he looked up with hope. "You have found the Lifemage?"

He was answered only by a smile.

Made in the USA
Middletown, DE
11 April 2018